"AN INTERESTING GAME, MY PET," HE MURMURED. . . .

Laughing softly, he seized her shoulders with hands of steel and pressed her soft curves against the long, hard length of him. Enfolding her in his arms, he fastened his lips on hers in a stupefying kiss that seared her very soul. Too stunned to resist, she leaned weakly against him, pliant in his arms, drugged by the overwhelming response spreading through her. Then, with a stunning deftness, he had the robe from her body. She stared at him, dazed, only vaguely conscious of the burning fire of passion smoldering in the eyes caressing her unbridled charms.

Books by Lucy Phillips Stewart:

BRIDE OF A STRANGER
BRIDE OF CHANCE
BRIDE OF TORQUAY
BURNING FIRES OF PASSION
THE CAPTIVE BRIDE
DESTINY'S BRIDE

BURNING FIRES OF PASSION

Lucy Phillips Stewart

A DELL BOOK

Published by
Dell Publishing Co., Inc.
1 Dag Hammarskjold Plaza
New York, New York 10017

Dell ® TM 681510, Dell Publishing Co., Inc.

ISBN 0-440-10850-0

Printed in the United States of America

First printing—January 1983

BURNING FIRES
OF PASSION

CHAPTER 1

Lord Richard Mitford, captain of His Majesty's frigate *Minotaur*, stood at a window of his father's town house on St. James's Square, looking down at the letter in his hand. Although the morning was a fine one, he was in no mood to appreciate it. It seemed that Lord Melville, First Lord of the Admiralty, desired him to proceed immediately to Plymouth, there to join Rear Admiral George C. Allenwood's Atlantic Squadron. "Damn the timing!" the captain swore, crushing the letter into a ball and hurling it toward the open grate. An angry flush suffused his cheeks. Leaving London at this time had no place in his schemes. Seeing before his mind's eye Jennie Brodie's cornflower-blue eyes and flaxen curls, a look of profound regret crossed his face. There had been a suppressed excitement about her these past weeks that augured well for his plans. For all her look of sweet innocence, she was a carefree miss. There would be others to replace him soon enough. Grimacing at his ill fortune, he cast himself down in the chair at the escritoire and drew forward a sheet of heavy hot-pressed paper. Dipping the pen in the standish, he sat for a moment lost in thought and then began to write, choosing his words with care.

June 16, 1812

Dear Miss Brodie,

I regret to inform you that I will be unable to do myself the honor of waiting upon you this evening as planned. I have just received orders from the Admiralty and must report for Atlantic duty.

Yours, etc., Mitford

Having read the letter through, a sardonic smile curved the corners of his mouth. "And so the affair ends," he mused, striking the hand bell at his elbow.

The aging tar who materialized in the doorway bore little resemblance to anyone's notion of a gentleman's gentleman. It was not surprising. Sawyer was by trade a sailor, hard-bitten and taciturn. The decks of the *Minotaur* comprised his world, and no man among the crew was more proud to serve his captain. "You rang, sir?" he said, rolling forward.

Lord Mitford folded the letter and penned Miss Brodie's address across its front. "You will see that this is sent around," he said, affixing a wafer. "We leave for Plymouth immediately I have discourse with my father."

There would have been a time when Sawyer would have been appalled by the haste involved in packing for so precipitate a departure, but the years at sea with the captain had left their mark. "Aye, sir," he said, without the smallest sign of surprise.

"You will pack a valise with the articles I will require for two nights upon the road. My curricle will be out front in one hour."

"Will Your Lordship be wishful of a reply?" Sawyer asked, glancing at the address scrawled across the missive.

Mitford's brows shot up. "Do you think me incapable of terminating an association with a female?" he demanded, amusement in his tone.

Sawyer had had occasion to observe the female in question and did think it, but he knew better than to admit it. "If you don't mind me saying so, Cap'n," he said, "there's none in any port of call as can hold a candle to Your Lordship, not when it comes to sweet-talking the ladies."

Mitford, in his shirt sleeves, stood. "You flatter me," he said, reaching for his coat.

"No, Cap'n," Sawyer protested, assisting him into the garment. "That's not to say that a well set up frame and a handsome phizz don't count, for they do, but Your Lordship knows the effect regimentals has on women. It so happens I just this morning pressed your best undress uniform, Cap'n. If you will say the word—"

"Content yourself with my appearance," Mitford interrupted, striding toward the door. "I don't aspire to set the countryside by its ears."

In his mind's eye Sawyer had been picturing them bowling along in the curricle behind as sweet a team as ever was put between the shafts. His Lordship would be all spit and polish, with himself sitting proud beside him. Sighing, he gave over the vision and bent to pluck Lord Melville's crumpled letter from the floor. "Me knowing town servants

11

like I do, they'd be sure to read it," he muttered, tucking it into a pocket.

In this utterance he was doing the butler a disservice. To persons of consequence Lashmore was unfailingly polite, but with the exception of the housekeeper, he wasted none of his deference on the staff. Very severely did he give them to understand that any effects touching upon the family lay solely within his own jurisdiction. Thus it was that when the captain arrived downstairs, Lashmore looked worried and, it seemed, more than a trifle nervous.

"Where will I find my father?" Mitford inquired, crossing the hall. "I understand he wished to see me."

"I am to conduct you to the library, Master Richard," Lashmore replied. "His Lordship isn't in the best of health, I'm afraid. It's the gout again."

"As bad as that?" Mitford ejaculated, considerably startled.

Lashmore had been in service to the earl of Afton since before the captain's birth. He therefore felt free to remonstrate. "If I may venture to say so," he began in fatherly tones, "you shouldn't ought to distress His Lordship. It's his age, Master Richard. He becomes regularly blue-deviled when you get yourself into some scrape."

"So I'm to have a peal rung over my head!" Mitford said, smiling affectionately. "Come now, Lashmore, what is it this time? I'm dashed if I know."

"It would ill become me to say," the butler replied, his face assuming an expression of schooled impassivity.

"I'm to be kept sitting about while Papa enjoys my discomfiture," Mitford remarked, breaking into a chuckle. "Bless you, Lashmore, do you think I don't know my father?"

Lashmore did not pretend to misunderstand. "You know you were never able to hide anything from His Lordship, Master Richard," he pointed out, unbending slightly. "It is only that this time you may have gone too far."

"Let us hope not!" Mitford replied more cheerfully than he felt. "Send in a bottle of port. I've a notion I may stand in need of it."

"His Lordship has instructed me to do so," Lashmore said, and bowed, then turned to lead the way down the hall.

It would never have occurred to Mitford to anticipate his father; even so, the interview was to take a turn for which he was unprepared. The earl, his patience at an end, had every intention of putting a period to any further reprehensible conduct on the part of his younger son. It was high time the boy settled down, and while he would never urge him to do anything distasteful, he had every right to expect him to agree to the marriage planned for him.

Afton was now in his sixty-seventh year, and while his body was slightly stooped by age, his hair was only slightly graying at the temples. Despite an appearance of fragility he was capable of a degree of determination to equal that of his offspring, and he had a far more subtle resolution in getting his own way. Mitford had learned at an early age that it did not pay to cross him. "You wished to see me, sir?" he said politely.

Afton ran an experienced eye over buckskin breeches hugging muscular thighs and sighed. The ladies, he knew, found his son irresistible. "Help yourself to the port if you feel in need of sustenance," he said, indicating the decanter of wine with the wave of one white hand.

Mitford poured out a glass and then sat down. "Sir, why should I feel the need of sustenance?" he said.

"Do not misunderstand me, Mitford," Afton replied in his quiet way. "I raise no objection to your amusing yourself with opera dancers or with other women of that class. Young men should enjoy themselves before they settle down."

Mitford looked startled. "Matrimony has not entered into my plans," he said.

"Nevertheless, it is a dangerous game you play," the earl countered blandly. "When you raise the hopes of a girl of Miss Brodie's respectability, you run the risk of forming an alliance that I would find unacceptable. No, your bride must come from your own station in life."

Mitford's brows rose. "I wish you will tell me why," he said, "when you did not see fit to marry until you were well nigh past your thirties, you seem determined to march me up the aisle before I quit my twenties. I confess, sir, that I find your strictures a trifle out-of-date."

The earl smiled. "You do, in fact, find them devilish inopportune," he said.

Mitford flushed. "Doubtless you've a bride in mind," he said, not bothering to mask the indifference in his tone.

That the lady he indeed had in mind, from possessing an uncertain temper and a tongue to match, was not at all a female his son would care to espouse, had not occurred to the earl. "Clara Leyton," he said positively. "A marriage between the two of you would seal the long friendship between our families. You needn't frown, my boy. I am not the least interested in your emotional involvement. Should you choose to bestow your regard away from the nuptial couch, no eyebrows would be raised, provided you were discreet."

A smile twitched at the corners of Mitford's mouth. "You perhaps speak from experience, sir?" he said.

The amusement crept back into Afton's eyes. "You may not take it from that," he said, "that I will longer condone your own transgressions. You will bestow your notice not because I wish it, or to avoid still another scandal, but to provide an heir to carry on our name."

Mitford regarded him in frank amusement. "You forget, sir," he said. "I am not your eldest born. Edward is your heir."

"I am not in my dotage," the earl replied in his most damping tone. "Edward may have distinguished himself in the Peninsula, but it is just conceivable that he could yet suffer a grievous wound. I suggest you face facts, Richard. Should the war with Bonaparte drag on much longer, the odds cannot continue in his favor. It is with this in mind that I ask you to resign your commission and return to civilian life."

"Don't ask it of me, Papa," Mitford begged in a constricted voice. "War with the United States could come at any time. It has been brewing for years, God knows."

The earl took snuff. "I am sorry to disillusion you," he said implacably, "but the Americans are ill prepared to fight. From what I have been given to understand, their War Office is a shambles, and their politicians can find little to do other than to pit one state against another. Even their bankers refuse to fund their military establishment."

"They will find a way to reconcile their differences, sir. They must, if their nation is to survive. For myself, I find their dilemma perfectly understandable. Their uniquely prosperous merchant marine has suffered greatly, both at

15

our hands and at the hands of the French. They will be forced to act."

"It was imperative that we blockade Napoleon's Europe," the earl shot back, frowning.

"But he retaliated by declaring all trade with us illegal," Mitford pointed out in his most palliative tones. "America's seaboard states have built their livelihood on commerce with both our nations."

The earl felt obliged to concede the point. "I will agree that we dealt them a telling blow when we forbade neutral ships access to French ports," he admitted grudgingly.

"We have no right to insist that the Americans clear their cargos with us and pay export duty, any more than we have the right to confiscate their freight," Mitford argued, prepared to stand his ground. "If you want my opinion, sir, our British courts took a lot upon themselves in ruling it legal to seize her ships trading with the French, just as though they were enemy vessels. It isn't America's fault that France reserves to herself the exclusive right to trade with her."

"Your loyalties appear a trifle mixed," the earl remarked, fixing his offspring with a stern, if not belligerent, eye.

"I am only saying that America will not indefinitely continue her policy of peace at any price," Mitford explained. "Between France and us, we are choking her to death. She will fight, sir, and we must not sell her short. She humbled us once before, don't forget."

"There is little likelihood that she could do so a second time. Melville tells me that we have a thousand ships on active duty, including some one hundred and twenty-four ships of the line and one hundred and sixteen frigates."

"We do, sir, but throughout our fleet the majority of our

vessels are sadly in need of a refit. Rotten gun breeches are in danger of giving way on recoil, and gun tackle bolts are more than likely to be loose. Melville has become entirely too complacent."

Few things in life provided the earl with more enjoyment than an argument with his son. "I should think the Admiralty knows what it's about," he remarked, refilling their wineglasses from the decanter at his elbow. "We not only took the battle honors at Copenhagen and the Nile, we thoroughly trounced both France and Spain at Trafalgar. How can you compare such victories as these with America's paltry skirmishes at sea?"

"I am only saying that we should not become overconfident," Mitford said with a grin, hitching his chair away from the warmth of the fire. "The Americans can muster only sixteen fighting ships in all, but it could be disastrous to assume that the one battleship and seven frigates we have on station at Halifax will prove adequate to deal with them. They will have gained invaluable experience from those minor battles you hold in such low esteem."

"I find your opinions extremely illuminating," Afton murmured, blandly surveying Mitford over the rim of his glass. "You have perhaps found a way to excuse our sailors deserting from the navy?"

"We can hardly expect our seamen to view themselves as empire builders or to boast that they rule the waves. They are more immediately concerned with the situation aboard their ships, and rightly so. Living conditions are generally appalling, and the discipline is inhuman. It is scant wonder that they desert to the Americans by the hundreds."

"You have talked yourself into a corner," Afton commented, chuckling. "The war with Napoleon has stretched our manpower very thin. We must recover our deserters. You should be the first to know that our vessels cannot sail with their complement dangerously undermanned."

"The Americans would raise no fuss at our rounding up our own deserters. They do object, and I do not blame them, to our hauling off their sailors when it suits our purpose to do so. We should recognize the fact that we have no jurisdiction over citizens of an independent nation, regardless of their ancestry. For my part, I shouldn't care to sail with foreign nationals among the crew."

"A point well taken," the earl conceded. "You have yet to lay any blame at America's feet. What of President Jefferson's announcement that America considered the entire Gulf Stream as her waters?"

"A bad business, that," Mitford agreed. "The British lion would never bow to the American eagle on that score. Our differences could have been resolved peacefully, had there been fewer hotheads in both camps. But no, there must always be threats, though neither side wants war. It's an absurd situation."

"Most conflicts are," Afton remarked. "I had hoped that the election of President Madison would put a period to the nonsense."

"I shouldn't expect it, sir, if I were you. Not with the War Hawks in his own party spurring him on. His only hope lies in the possibility that we will back down. Perhaps we will. Wellington must have supplies, and with Napoleon's blockade of all parts to us, we must trade with the Americans. Their shipping has trebled, I'm told, since we became involved in Bonaparte's wars."

The earl became intent on the huge emerald glowing on

his finger. "Lashmore tells me a communiqué from Melville arrived in this morning's post," he said quietly.

"Yes, worse luck." Mitford chuckled reassuringly. "Convoy duty, Papa, would you believe it? I will find myself enduring months of boredom on the Bermuda run while other commanders enjoin enemy ships in battle."

The earl exhaled his breath on a sigh, almost overcome with relief. "When do you leave?" he inquired in his matter-of-fact way.

"At once, sir. I sail with Admiral Allenwood's squadron on Friday next. The *Minotaur* is already anchored at Plymouth for a refit. You may be sure my ship is no rotting hulk."

"I presume you go by curricle? You will allow me to send a groom to bring it back to town. I will not embarrass you by cautioning you to look to your safety."

"I should hope not." Mitford grinned. "I'd best be off now, Papa. Time and tide, you know."

"Not so fast, my boy!" the earl commanded, staying his movement to rise by the lifting of one hand. "The exigencies of your calling may occupy your thoughts, but we have yet to resolve our discussion of your marriage."

"You are worrying unnecessarily, I'm sure," Mitford said, leaning forward to take his father's hand gently in his. "Edward will come home from the Peninsula unscathed. He must. I have no wish to step into his shoes. Only consider how *Captain Lord Viscount George* would sound."

Afton refused to be beguiled. "I am no longer young, Richard," he growled, taking refuge in decrepitude. "I should be entitled to bounce a grandson on my knee before I die, the same as other men."

"You will, I've no doubt, live to spoil any number of

Edward's brats. Come now, Papa. It won't fadge, you know."

"We will be on the safe side, sir!" the earl retorted, changing tactics. "Mark my words! You will marry before the year is out!"

"Be reasonable, sir," Mitford demurred, without any real hope of being attended. "There is no lady among my acquaintance whom I should care to wed."

"You must not think me insensible," Afton replied. "You cannot spend all your days at sea. A year should allow you sufficient time to attach your sentiments. If by then no eligible female has taken your eye, Lady Leyton it must be. I trust I make myself clear?"

Mitford looked at him with grim, defiant eyes. "Quite clear," he said, rising. "If that is your final word, sir, I trust I stand excused?"

"There is one thing," Afton replied, smiling benignly. "Don't settle for half a loaf, my boy. Find yourself a cozy armful."

An unwilling chuckle escaped the captain. "Had you had a shred of proper feeling, Papa, you would have sired any number of sons in your image," he said, crossing to the door.

"Ungrateful, aren't you," the earl remarked. "I cannot imagine why you think that."

"Had I had brothers other than just Edward, I would not now be cast in the role of family progenitor," Mitford shot back, and, with his father's laughter ringing in his ears, he went out of the room, quietly closing the door behind him.

While he might think it singular that the earl, whose own youth had included more than a nodding acquaintance with the demimonde, could fail to appreciate the intricacies of a discreetly conducted and (as matters now stood) quite harmless flirtation, he was ready to put it down to a parent's natural inclination to do the right thing by his child. The plague was, he had taken marriage into his head. And what a choice it was! From the single state to spouse was a long step to take; from bachelorhood to husband of Lady Leyton was a longer step still and one he had no intention of taking. Pondering the problem brought Jennie Brodie to his mind and the thought that in this instance the earl had come off with the honors. Only a confirmed nodcock could suppose him less than serious. It was an awkward business.

When Mitford arrived out front, his curricle was waiting for him before the door. A lackey was in the act of lashing his sea chest to its back and a groom was at the wheel horses' heads, but of Sawyer there was no sign. Mitford pulled on his gloves, mounted to the box seat and gathered up the reins. The grays were on the fret, dancing with impatience to be away. "Stand back from their heads!" he commanded the groom just as Sawyer came rushing down the steps.

"Cap'n, wait!" Sawyer cried, consternation written all over his face.

"I said one hour!" Mitford called over his shoulder and swept on around the square.

Sawyer ran to the corner of St. James's Street and jumped aboard the curricle the moment it turned into the avenue. "Horrible!" Mitford murmured, glancing at him. "If this is the best you can do, I would advise you to stay out of the rigging."

"A rolling ship can't hold no candle to this contraption of yours," Sawyer retorted, collapsing upon the seat in some disorder. "Begging Your Lordship's pardon, of course."

21

"Your scruples are very fine, I make no doubt, but I will appreciate it if you will display a modicum of respect before the crew. I can't have you putting ideas into their heads."

Sawyer sighed. "It will seem good to be back aboard, won't it, Cap'n," he said. "If Your Lordship will but put 'em right along, we should reach Plymouth by tomorrow night."

"I am sorry to disappoint you, Sawyer, but I have no intention of springing my team. I shelter two nights in Tavistock. It seems I heard mention of a prizefight somewhere in that neighborhood. Either you remain with me or you find your own way to the *Minotaur*."

"A mill, is it?" Sawyer grinned. "We should put down a wager, my lord. Do you think you could see your way clear to an advance against next month's pay?"

Mitford's lips quivered. "I sincerely trust not!" he said.

CHAPTER 2

The pace at which Mitford drove his horses might have alarmed anyone less prejudiced in his employer's favor, but, as Sawyer had occasion to know, the elegantly gloved hands holding the reins possessed the strength to control any team put between the shafts, however mettlesome. To Mitford's disgust, the farther they progressed into the countryside, the worse the roads became. The worst of the potholes were avoided, and if they did occasionally bounce over some inequality in the surface, at no time were they in danger of overturning.

Arriving at a crossroad, he drew his team to a halt and stared at the shattered remains of the signpost sheared off and lying forgotten in a ditch. The expression of irritation on his handsome countenance became ever more pronounced. "Some young cawker, no doubt," he remarked. "If anything had been needed to prove me right in thinking this excursion a mistake, this has supplied it."

Sawyer had been steadily scrutinizing the road ahead, but at these words his eyes went to the captain's face. "A mistake, my lord?" he repeated blankly.

"It is my belief," Mitford continued, "that we would make better time if we were to get down and walk."

"Walk, my lord?" Sawyer uttered, considerably taken aback.

Mitford turned his head to glance amicably at him. "A little exercise would do you a world of good," he said, giving his horses the office to proceed. "You've grown soft of late."

"If you was to ask me what I think," Sawyer began with the familiarity of a privileged retainer, "I'd say Your Lordship took the wrong turning some four miles back."

Mitford sighed, acknowledging the truth of this pronouncement. "The same thought had occurred to me," he admitted with a touch of the saturnine. "I am sure that only an overriding sense of propriety prevented your saying so at the time."

Sawyer returned no reply to this, for while he had had no more notion than His Lordship of the direction to take, he had the good sense to remain silent. To his very certain memory the captain had never before lost his way when en route to attend a fight. It was seldom enough that one came in their way. With the worst of ill fortune they could miss it.

"This is insupportable," Mitford said at last. "I have seldom encountered a road in worse condition."

"No, my lord," Sawyer agreed, his expression one of unconcerned detachment. As little as he betrayed any alarm did he allow himself to comment on the inadvisability of setting forth upon an outing with no clear understanding of the highway to take.

His air of gloomy disapproval was not lost upon Mitford. "Come down from your high ropes, Sawyer!" he said in the voice of a man goaded beyond endurance. "You know very well I hadn't time to put about inquiries."

Sawyer looked startled and seemed not to know what to say. They had left London ahead of schedule, but he doubted the old earl was at the bottom of it. More than likely His Lordship's latest flirt had a fancy to become Her Ladyship. The captain had been wise to flee.

To his relief the sound of thunder rumbling in the distance claimed the captain's notice. The day had turned leaden and a breeze had sprung up, carrying with it the promise of rain. "Devil take it," Mitford muttered, casting a glance skyward. "We will become drenched."

Sawyer stirred and looked back over his shoulder. "If we was to turn around," he suggested, "there's an inn I saw a mile or so back. Your Lordship could bide there until the storm has passed."

"From the look of it we will be stranded here until morning," Mitford remarked, drawing the curricle across the road. "I hope this inn of yours can supply the amenities, but, judging from the neighborhood, I am much inclined to doubt it."

Sawyer's face reflected his own misgivings, but he had a disposition to match his lean, spare frame and held his tongue, watching with pride as the captain first backed his team and then set them forward along the way they had come. In the rapidly darkening gloom Mitford failed to see a slight figure trudging along by the side of the road and nearly ran him down. He was a slender youth in a loose-fitting jacket and with a cloth bundle clutched in one grimy hand. It became abundantly clear to Mitford that he

25

had chanced upon a delinquent child. "Run away from school, have you?" he said, drawing the curricle to a halt.

A pair of frightened blue eyes stared up into his gray ones. "There is an illness in my family, and I have been summoned home," the youth said, ready to take to his heels at the least provocation.

Mitford could not help but chuckle. "If that is true," he said, "why are you wandering about the countryside with a bundle for your clothing?"

The boy fished a somewhat grubby missive from a pocket of his coat. "It is from my father, and extremely urgent," he said, holding out the letter. "My valise had become misplaced, you see, and I hadn't the time to replace it."

"Perhaps you aren't a runaway," Mitford remarked, a slight smile lifting the corners of his mouth. "In any event, you seem to have arrived, silly-nilly, at the end of your rope. One thing is sure—you are in need of shelter on such a night as this."

The youth made a rather jerky bow. "I am, but I must not inconvenience you, Mr.—?"

"Captain Lord Mitford," His Lordship supplied. "Inconvenient or not, I can't leave you stranded here. Up you come, but first kindly put away that revoltingly filthy piece of paper."

The youth flushed and restored the letter to his pocket. "I have sufficient funds with me to cover any charge I might incur," he said, scrambling to the seat of the curricle. "All I require is refuge for one night."

Mitford realized that it was a very slight child indeed, only a boy, in fact. His hands were thrust deep within his trouser pockets and a flush suffused his cheeks, but there was a determined set to his chin. Only the slightest trembling about the mouth betrayed his perturbation.

They soon came abreast of the inn. Thinking from its ill-kept appearance that the hostelry was an unlikely place for any traveler to spend the night, Mitford turned into the courtyard and came to a standstill before the door. Hitching up his reins, he jumped lightly down from the box seat and strode inside, closely followed by his newly discovered charge.

He found himself in a small, poorly lit chamber with a fireplace along one wall and with several doors opening out of the chamber, one of them affording a glimpse of an enclosed staircase leading to the floor above. A swinging lamp, a trestle table with several chairs drawn up to it and a settle before the fire comprised the furnishings. Mitford glanced around, by no means enchanted by the prospect.

"You will furnish us with two bedchambers," he said to the proprietor. "You will, I believe, find quarters for my valet."

No gentleman of the Quality had ever before set foot on the premises. The landlord came forward, startled, bowing and wringing his hands. "Two bedchambers, Your Worship?" he repeated, nonplussed and uncertain of the proper mode of address.

"*Your Lordship* will do nicely," Mitford corrected in some amusement.

"But I only have one bedchamber," his unfortunate host gasped.

Mitford remained calm. "Then one must suffice," he said. "Pray convey our estimable young gentleman's . . . bundle to our chamber. You will find my own baggage out front."

27

A gasp brought his head around. The youth had grown very pale. "I beg you will not expect me to share your room," he murmured, casting down his eyes. "I will pass the night on the settle before the fire."

Mitford raised his brows. "My good fool," he said with a touch of contempt in his voice, "your fears are quite groundless, believe me. My taste runs to the well-rounded female form."

There seemed little left for the youth to do but blush. Which he did. Profusely.

"Oblige me by removing that travesty of a cravat," Mitford continued severely. "I have rarely seen a sight that depressed me more. And it would not go amiss if you were to comb your hair," he added, eyeing tumbled curls that were as raven as his own. "What is your name, by the way?"

There came a pause. "It is Charles," the youth said finally, with an obvious disregard for the truth.

"No one would credit it, I assure you. It sounds entirely too adult. I shall call you Charlie."

A nervous giggle, hastily choked, greeted this. "Have you a Christian name, my lord?" the youth asked, eager to stand on equal footing.

"I am known as Richard to my family and friends," Mitford shot back crushingly. "You, I might add, do not fall into either category."

"You don't look much like a Richard," the youth commented, not in the least chastised.

"I don't?" Mitford uttered, startled.

"No, I shall need to make up a name for you. Willie, I think."

"Willie!" Mitford ejaculated, shuddering. "Rid yourself

28

of the notion that I will permit it! Very well, brat. Richard it shall be."

In the face of this capitulation young Charlie could not suppress a laugh. "I will gladly comb my hair," he said, "but I'm not much good with a cravat. Do you think that you—"

"No!" Mitford snapped, nodding toward the floor above.

"Oh, very well," Charlie muttered, going with lagging step. "What will you bespeak for dinner, Richard? I'm particularly fond of ham."

"You will, I think, eat what is put before you. The Lord only knows what that will be. Run along now and freshen up. And don't leave the wash basin in a mess," he called after his newly acquired charge vanishing up the stairs.

Space for a bedchamber had been carved from the attics. A large four-poster bed placed in the center of the room took advantage of the head room, while a chest bearing a basin and a brass can of hot water had been shoved back under the eaves. Charlie crossed the threshold and stood gazing about, his thoughts in chaos. Captain Mitford bore the appearance of a Corinthian of whom any father must be proud. Tall and powerfully built, he carried himself with the easy grace of a gentleman long addicted to the more strenuous forms of athletic sports. And although it was evident that a master hand was responsible for the cut of his coat, he adopted none of the extravagances of fashion. An admirable figure surely, but could he be trusted? It was a situation fraught with danger, and Charlie did not know what to do. For the present, it seemed, there was very little he could do. Seeing no help for it, he undid the tie holding his bundle together and added his crumpled cravat to its contents. Having washed his hands and face and combed his hair, he carefully wiped all vestiges of his toilet from the basin and hung the towel on a nail to dry.

"Very commendable," Mitford's voice spoke from the doorway, causing him to start in fright. "It only remains for you to remove that repellent bundle from my sight, and we will do quite nicely."

"What are you doing here?" Charlie demanded, thrusting the offending parcel under the bed.

"Did you expect me to sit down to dinner in all my dirt?" Mitford inquired, shrugging out of his coat. "Be a good boy and help me off with my boots."

"Why should you wish to remove them?" Charlie demurred, glancing around as if desperate to escape.

"We may be at the end of hell and gone, but I still dress for dinner," Mitford replied, sitting down upon the bed. "Now, come over here and assist me. Not like that, you ninny! Turn your back and bend over. When I shove, you pull."

An instant later Charlie felt a foot push against his buttock, tugged, and was sent sprawling forward on his face, one shining Hessian clutched in his hands.

"Horrible!" drawled His Lordship's lazy voice. "Are you under the impression that I mean to maim you?"

"No, but the thing is, I have never helped remove a boot before," Charlie admitted, scrambling to his feet.

"That," said His Lordship, "is obvious. This time brace yourself."

This advice complied with, the other Hessian was off in a trice. "Much better," Mitford approved, his hand going to the buttons of his trousers. "Now what's the matter?"

"I'll—see you downstairs," Charlie gasped and vanished through the door, leaving His Lordship staring.

30

The captain's decision to stop at the inn had been extremely providential, but that they should be forced to share a chamber was nothing if not catastrophic. Charlie, wandering about the courtyard out front, had no idea what course she should follow. For Charlie was a female, and facing a dilemma. Between having her whereabouts discovered and taking her chances with the captain, feminine intuition must prevail. His Lordship's scruples might not be so very nice, but by his own admission, beardless boys held no fascination for him.

Mitford, leisurely descending the stairs an hour later, would have been startled had he guessed what she thought of him. He had donned full evening dress and was quite the handsomest creature she had ever seen. The ladies must flutter around him like moths around a candle, she mused, gazing at broad shoulders molding a coat of blue satin and at silken hose displaying shapely calves. Just as no amount of tailoring could conceal a splendid physique, neither could an air of studied nonchalance mask an intellect as quick as it was keen. Charlie had no notion why she thought so, but she could not help but feel that he could read her mind when he chose.

He would require an explanation, she knew, and she had no feasible fabrication to trot out for his inspection. One thing was certain: It would be wisest to reveal as little of her history as possible. Relieved to find that he did not seem inclined to question her before dinner, she followed in his wake to the trestle table, careful to take the seat on his left. If she found anything to remark in the sight of an officer in His Majesty's Navy dining on bacon and eggs, there was nothing in her face of what she might be thinking. To begin with, she was greatly in his debt for a place to lay her head,

31

albeit a risky one; but, more to the point, she had a distinct wish to avoid troubled waters.

For his part, Mitford found himself strangely drawn to the slender youth. The lad had a lively wit and a store of knowledge sufficiently wide to encompass any number of subjects. Far from being bored, he had to admit that he was highly entertained. By the time the meal drew to a close, he realized that he had somehow acquired an odd liking for the boy.

Leaning back in his chair, he regarded Charlie from beneath his eyelids. "What would you say to a first-class mill?" he said, idly twirling his wineglass between thumb and finger. "My curricle will hold the two of us, if you care to go."

She seemed to ponder her reply. "It would give me much pleasure," she said, "but I seem to recall the mention of a servant. You will need his services, I'm sure."

A quizzical look came into his eyes. "There is a seat up back for him," he said, sipping his wine and scrutinizing her closely over the rim of his glass. "Could it be that you have no stomach for rough-and-tumble pastimes?"

She found herself at a momentary loss. Though she was taken by surprise, her gaze did not falter. Best to say as little as possible, she decided, stretching out a hand for the decanter.

On the instant his hand closed about her wrist. "You have had enough, little man," he said. "You haven't the head for it."

She sat perfectly still, gazing at his fingers, and knew he had discovered the smallness of the bone structure in her arm. Desperately she sought to compose a quite natural agitation. An age seemed to pass before he released her an sat back in his chair, his eyes on her face in a way that was hard to read. With hard-fought calm she returned his regard and waited, sensibly making no reply.

"I take it your home is somewhere in these parts?" he said absently, breaking a silence that threatened to become prolonged.

"Why, no, it is in southwest Devon," she replied, thinking the locale remote enough.

She was in error. "Then you may count yourself fortunate," he said, pushing back his chair and turning in it to face her. "Our host has provided me with directions to Tavistock."

"To Tavistock?" she murmured, completely at sea.

"Near Plymouth."

"Oh!" she said, feeling foolish. "Plymouth!"

"Must you repeat everything I say?" he demanded, exasperated. "I am offering you—or should I say I am endeavoring to offer you—transport, at least as far as I go. The prizefight, remember."

If the truth be told, she knew precisely what the result would be and searched her mind for a way to put him off. She would find herself in a locale where she had no desire to be, in all probability attending a fisticuffs and without the money to retrace her steps. She pushed back her chair and rose. "It has been a pleasant dinner, Richard," she said politely, "but I must make an early start in the morning and will bid you good night."

"The hour is young," he remarked, fishing his snuff box from a pocket. "Don't be difficult, Charlie. Sit down."

It took all the resolution at her command not to turn and flee, but she conquered the impulse and resumed her seat, her eyes anywhere but on his face.

Mitford sighed. "I have told you that you are perfectly safe with me," he said. "How old are you, I wonder."

"I am twenty-two," she said, adding three years to the total for whatever advantages might later accrue.

"May I inquire which school has been enjoying your patronage?" he said, his tone urbane.

"Eton," she replied, without the slightest hesitation.

"You denied being a schoolboy to the landlord, as I recall," he remarked, taking snuff.

She shot him a quick glance from under her lashes. "I've been sent down for—for smuggling a girl into my quarters."

"A short time ago you had been summoned home due to an illness in your family," he reminded her relentlessly.

She gulped. "Yes, and so I have," she assured him as earnestly as she might. "The two things just happened to coincide. Is not that unusual?"

"It is," he agreed somewhat dryly.

"Yes, that is what I thought," she said, thinking fast. "But, then, my mama has been ill off and on for—well, for simply ages. So it's really not so very odd."

"Of course it wouldn't be. May I ask after the health of your father?"

"Oh! Papa!" she said, her tongue tying itself in knots. "Papa's fine. He travels, you know. Ladies' shoes."

"How fortunate it was that he happened to be at home. Otherwise he would not have been about to pen a letter to you requesting your return."

"Yes, wasn't it," was all she could find to say.

Mitford refilled his wineglass and carefully set the decanter down. "Either your family is the strangest in my memory," he said, "or you are the most precious little liar ever to cross my path."

This was definitely a check. She drew a deep breath and ventured, "I think perhaps I should tell you the truth."

"If it is not beyond the realm of the possible, yes, you just might."

"I'm not on my way home, you know."

"You have no need to tell me that."

"Well, but you see, I couldn't be. I'm an orphan." She paused, assessing his reaction. Unable to decipher the enigmatic expression on his face, she continued. "I haven't been residing in an orphanage, I assure you. Papa's lawyers saw to that. I've been living with my tutor."

Mitford swirled the wine in his glass, apparently intent upon the ruby liquid sparkling in the candlelight. "Of course there would be a tutor," he murmured softly. "How fortunate for you."

"He is old and crotchety and thinks I should be forever at my books. Don't you feel there should be more to life than that, Richard?"

"When one attains a certain age, yes. So you have run away from your tutor. What now, halfling?"

What now indeed, she wondered, embroidering her tale. "I have a cousin who will gladly take me in. She—he is recently become a widower and has no son of his own."

The captain put down his glass and touched his napkin to his lips. "Did you not promise me a moment since that you would tell the truth?" he said, his eyes alight with laughter. "Are you running from the law?"

She regarded him with a smoldering eye. "Only civility compels me to reply," she said stiffly. "No, I am not!"

"Don't bristle," he said. "I really hadn't supposed you were. But we drift from the point. Do you or do you not go with me en route to—I believe you said your cousin's?"

She stared at him in dismay, already regretting their chance acquaintance. Suppose he was not what he seemed? Anyone could lay claim to a title and rank—the thought brought an unpleasant possibility into her mind and a frown to her brow. Had she fled one form of debauchery, only to run afoul of another? She felt her heart begin to thud alarmingly and drew a deep breath, calming herself. She was sure of only one thing: She was being foolish. She would be in worse straits if she traveled about alone. She would strike a bargain and wait upon events. "Would you force me to attend the prizefight?" she asked bluntly.

"Oh, I think not," he replied, a faint smile curving his lips. "When you have more of my acquaintance, my dear boy, you will know I seldom put myself to the trouble of forcing anything."

She nodded and again rose. "Then I will bear you company, sir, and gladly. At what hour do we leave?"

"When it suits our fancy," he said, pouring out more wine. "Good night, Charlie."

"Good night, Richard," she replied, crossing to the stairs.

A thought occurred to him. "Hold!" he called. "Do you snore?"

"Snore!" she exclaimed, pausing. "Certainly not!"

"See that you don't," he said, turning away and thereby missing the red rushing into her cheeks.

His words brought their appalling sleeping arrangement back to her mind. The pleasures of the evening had banished it from her thoughts. Her first impulse was to admit all and suffer the consequences, but a vision of Lord Ashmore rose up to haunt her, bringing discretion into perspective. She would rather die, she thought, imagining marriage to His Lordship. Gross and depraved, he had not

36

one attribute to recommend him. Her guardian must be mad. Between the two of them, the captain must emerge as a paragon of virtue.

Having made up her mind to accept the challenge laid down by fate, she bent her thoughts to the problem of keeping her sex a secret, no easy task. His Lordship was entirely too perspicacious. Once or twice during dinner she had feared that he saw through her disguise. It was entirely too observant, that lazy gaze of his.

The sight of the large bed waiting in their chamber very nearly put a period to her courage. The desire to flee returned. She curbed it. Wasting no time lest he walk in unannounced, she removed her coat and shoes, wrapped herself in a blanket and lay down upon the bed, hugging the edge of the mattress farthest from the door. Too weary to stay awake and too sensible to try, she composed herself for slumber, self-possessed to the last.

CHAPTER 3

Awakening early the following morning, she was first disoriented and then mortified when memory came flooding back. Her head turned on the pillow almost of its own accord. There was no blinking it. The captain lay by her side, sleeping soundly. She supposed he had taken care not to disturb her upon retiring, a consideration for which she was devoutly grateful. As it was, facing him was a task almost beyond her powers. How could she possibly do so, she wondered, almost afraid to breathe. In the middle of these reflections he stirred, sending her pulses racing.

"Must you jiggle the bed?" he muttered, groaning.

Her sense of the ridiculous stood her in good stead. Putting in checkmate a high and mighty Captain Lord Mitford laid low by wine was a temptation she found herself unable to resist. "You should not drink," she murmured, slipping from the bed. "You haven't the head for it."

He opened one bloodshot eye, glared and closed it again. "Don't press your luck," he growled, wincing.

"Does your head ache so very much?" she said, clutching the quilt more tightly about herself lest it should fall from about her slender form.

"Vilely!" he admitted, shuddering.

"What you need is food," she remarked, retrieving her shoes and jacket. "Shall I have your breakfast sent up, or will you come downstairs?"

He regarded her balefully. "I take back what I said about liking you!" he told her, sitting up and swinging his legs over the side of the bed. "I don't!"

"My, but we are up on the wrong side of the bed this morning, aren't we?" she teased, glancing at him. It was a mistake. The ruffle of his nightshirt brushing against his chin underscored the intimacy of the scene.

"Do you always sleep rolled up in a blanket?" he demanded, making matters worse. "You reminded me of a mummy."

"No, but it seemed——" She paused, biting her tongue.

"——the prudent thing to do," he finished for her. "I would be obliged to learn what I have done to warrant your mistrust."

In fear that he might perceive the swell of feminine breasts beneath her shirt, she turned her back to don her coat. "You have been kindness itself," she said, glancing at him over her shoulder.

He became aware of her state of dress and stared. "You slept fully clothed?" he demanded, incredulous.

"Do you mind?" she said, bending over to snatch her bundle from beneath the bed. When she straightened up again her color seemed a trifle high, but it could have been caused by the stooping posture.

"I should hope that you are not quite intending to travel with me in wrinkled clothing," he observed, reaching for his robe. "Take off your breeches. The landlord's wife will sponge and press them."

She appeared to ponder. "I make no doubt that she would only succeed in ruining them," she said, shaking her head decisively. "Thank you, no."

"Now that I come to look at you more particularly," he remarked, eyeing her in distaste, "I have never seen a shirt more in need of laundering. You look positively grubby."

She had been inching closer to the door while he spoke. "I'm an urchin," she said, pleased to have the final word. "Urchins never wash."

He opened his mouth to retort, found himself gazing at empty space and closed it again. Amusement and irritation warred within his breast. Amusement won. Chuckling, he crossed the room to pour cold water into the basin and douse his head in it, easing his aching brow.

Charlie, meanwhile, arrived at the floor below, crossed the common room and stuck her head around the kitchen door. "Where will I find the captain's man?" she asked of a tall, rawboned woman standing with her back to the door. "His Lordship will wish his team put to."

The landlord's wife glanced up from the task of basting a fowl turning on the spit of an open fire. "Out front," she said brusquely, gesturing with a wooden spoon. "He's been out there brushin' since first light. You'd best put a stop to it before he has the hide right off them horses."

Charlie accepted with equanimity the suggestion that she

issue orders to the captain's servant. "I will," she said, "but first I must order breakfast. Bacon and eggs, I think."

"You'll eat what's handy!" the good dame corrected, indicating a thick slice of bread and cheese lying on the table. "Now get along with you. I'll not have you comin' in here tellin' me what to do!"

A mischievous twinkle came into Charlie's eyes. "Is His Lordship thus to break his fast?" she said, picking up her portion of the meager fare.

"Don't be cheeky!" Madam snapped. "Just take your food and be off. I've got work to do."

Charlie went with alacrity. It was now considerably past nine o'clock, but although the rain had ceased, the sky was still leaden and the air chilly. Sawyer, who was walking the impeccably groomed horses up and down, received the news that the captain was taking up a youth as passenger with perfect equanimity if no understanding. "You'd best not chatter," he advised her, not without a touch of severity in his tone. "The cap'n don't hold with pushy upstarts."

Her eyes twinkled. "I shouldn't think many would come his way on the quarterdeck of his ship," she observed, her bread and cheese suspended in midair halfway to her mouth.

"There was young Rob," Sawyer pointed out. "Not that he was the gabby sort, for he weren't. Leastways he had more sense than to annoy His Lordship."

"Is he the cabin boy?" she said, her voice unsteady with bottled-up mirth.

"Was," Sawyer explained. "His mum took sick, so he went off home. Won't be back, I shouldn't wonder, seeing as how his enlistment's up."

"How old is he?" she asked idly.

He looked frowningly at her. "No older nor you, I shouldn't think. But don't go getting ideas into your head. The cap'n wouldn't sail with an inexperienced boy aboard."

Since such a thought had not occurred to her, she found his attitude offensive. "You seem to feel that you speak for His Lordship," she said coldly.

"It's only what he will say," he returned just as stiffly.

"You may safely leave his business in his hands," she flashed back. "I trust I have done nothing to incur his displeasure."

Her trust was soon seen to have been misplaced. Mitford, emerging from the inn, took in the situation at a glance. "You will cease your bickering, at least within my hearing," he said languidly, but with decision. "My head aches like the devil."

"Have you had your breakfast?" she inquired, rising to brush the crumbs from her breeches. "One shouldn't travel on an empty stomach."

He turned on his heel and strode to the curricle. "If you desire to go with me, you will contrive not to prate about food," he said, mounting to the box seat. "And for the future, let me tell you, I will thank you not to interfere in my concerns."

"I will try to remember not to," she agreed, picking up her bundle. "What shall I do with this?"

"Give it to Sawyer," he replied, reaching down a hand. "And that reminds me. We will need to purchase a portmanteau for you if any respectable inn is to grant us shelter."

She placed her hand in his and climbed to the seat beside him. "I haven't enough money with me to expend it on luggage," she said, her color a trifle high.

43

"It's a small matter," he said, gathering up the reins.

"No, I will pay my way," she insisted, though she had no idea of the cost of a valise. She only knew she would never again be beholden to any man.

There had been a grain of truth in the little of her history she had let fall. She was an orphan, but with no remembrance of her mother and little more of the laughing giant who had been her father. At first she had been too young to understand. It was only later that she knew in some vague way that the man who called himself her guardian really didn't want the responsibility of a child. Since she had been removed from her father's house to the cottage of a tenant, to be reared by the farmer's wife, she could scarcely think otherwise. His one true act of stewardship had been in arranging for her to receive her schooling through the good offices of the vicar. Thereafter she had spent the better part of her days at the parsonage, eagerly absorbing all the good priest had to teach her and poring over the contents of his small but select collection of books. By the time she entered on her sixteenth year her store of knowledge far outstripped that considered necessary, or even desirable, for young ladies of her station.

Since her acquaintance was limited to the few families seen at the parish church on Sunday, she knew nothing of the social world and could only suppose that the trend of her nature was toward solitude. Perhaps surprisingly, such a childhood of enforced seclusion had strengthened rather than diminished a natural belief in her ability to fend for herself. She was seldom disconsolate and, not expecting the tenor of her days to alter, made the best of things.

The first hint of change came in a brief scrawl from her guardian alerting her of his impending arrival. She had had

44

the good fortune, he wrote, of attracting the notice of a most distinguished suitor, Sir Randolph Ashmore. He trusted she would direct her energies toward only those preparations deemed necessary for a bride-to-be, keeping in mind the extremities of her pecuniary state.

She had been stricken, and tears had been shed, for Sir Randolph owned a property in the neighborhood and was well known. Gossip told of the life he led. It was far from exemplary. Even she, sequestered with her books, had heard whispers of London orgies and of serving girls defiled and turned out into the streets. Of his previous wives, two had succumbed to the rigors of constant breeding, while the third had met an untimely end as yet unexplained. Debauched and jaded, he was now casting about for an innocent maid to feed his carnal appetites.

For any female in her position the prospect was bleak indeed and seemed to offer no choice between a marriage of degradation and the uncertainties of striking out on her own. Not for an instant did she entertain the thought of becoming fourth wife to a lecher. Unfortunately convention decreed that single ladies of marriageable age did not live alone. Neither did they fly in the general way of doing things by roaming about the countryside unattended even by a maid. The accepted mode for young gentlemen, however, was considerably less strict. A tour of the Continent mandated an escort, but otherwise they were free to come and go very much as they pleased.

If thought is father to the action, then desperation is mother to its fulfillment. Before another day was out she had visited the village shop, for the ostensible purpose of aiding a needy tenant, and had purchased a suit of boy's clothing. With an adroitness born of practice she smuggled the parcel into her bedchamber, assembled the toilet articles she would need and tied them up in a shawl unearthed from the depths of a cupboard. That evening she crept from the house under cover of darkness, sped on her way by the intelligence (conveyed by the vicar) that her guardian, having written the priest of his plans, was due to arrive on the morrow and would be accompanied by Lord Ashmore.

It was no use thinking of a conveyance. The wheels of the one wagon in the barn were prone to squeak with a shrillness certain to awaken the farmer and his wife, who were asleep within the cottage. There was nothing for it but to sally forth on foot. From being an indefatigable walker, she arrived at the village just in time to board the cross-country stage. By the time Captain Mitford crossed her path, she had come to view her temerity with extreme foreboding, the reason, no doubt, for her indefensible acquiescence to his autocratic whims.

"You are strangely quiet this morning," he remarked, interrupting her reverie.

"Oh!" she murmured, marshaling her thoughts. "Sawyer said you cannot abide boys who chatter."

He turned his head to gaze down into her upturned face. "It is my belief," he said, "that you have never in your life followed anyone's advice. I can't think how I came to befriend you."

"The pastor of our parish church was used to say that we are repaid a hundredfold for the good we do. Perhaps you stood in need of the Lord's blessing."

"So it's a religious youth," he remarked, surprised. "Would you mind telling me, in the spirit of brotherly love, of course, where you obtained the letter you displayed for

46

the landlord's edification? And don't give me any folderol about receiving it from your father!"

"Of course I didn't. How could I? He's been dead any time these fifteen years. I wrote it myself."

"Would it be expecting too much to ask you why?"

"I didn't wish my guardian to discover my whereabouts," she replied with perfect honesty. "You see," she explained, thinking fast, "my father had no other children, so when he died he left me a very considerable competence. My guardian has been importuning me to sign some papers that he claims will allow him to increase the size of my inheritance. Personally I think he only wants to get his hands on my money."

There came a pause. "Suffice it to say he would find it difficult," he said dryly.

"I'm glad you agree," she returned handsomely.

"Do not diminish your credibility more than you have done," he advised her. "Daughters are left a competence to provide an adequate means for their support. You must know that sons inherit an independence free of control since they are assumed to be sufficiently versed to handle their affairs."

"Well, you know what I meant," she said, coloring. "It's just that I get my terms mixed."

Glancing at her, he said severely, "The landlord was accurate in his assessment. You haven't a groat to your name. Furthermore, since I have known you, you have run the gamut from a tutor, to lawyers, to a guardian."

She chuckled suddenly. "It does seem rather a surplus," she said, her eyes brimful with laughter. "Must you frown?"

"Take that silly grin off your face!" he commanded, not in the least amused. "You resemble the village idiot. I have

47

been unable to decide whether your propensity to lie is a cultivated thing or whether you come by it naturally."

"Well!" she said, unabashed. "I must say you are a fine one to talk!"

"I am rather inclined to think there may be a guardian," he continued, ignoring her remark. "There usually is. Perhaps I should restore you to his tender mercy."

She turned rather white. "You wouldn't!" she breathed. "You don't understand! He would force me into a marriage I would find abhorrent!"

"So that's it!" he mused, a good deal of sympathy in his voice. "I am under a like cloud myself. Knowing my father, I should think my own bachelor days are numbered. Is the chit who is to be foisted off on you so very unattractive?"

She glanced at him but did not trust herself to speak.

"Well, cheer up, halfling," he said, having arrived at a decision. "I shan't be your nemesis. The mill will take your mind off your troubles."

Since any argument against attending the fight that she could bring to mind would only result in a further interrogation, she nodded and remarked that the diversion would be welcome. "To tell the truth," she added, "a prizefight has never before come in my way. You will need to explain what is transpiring. You will know, will you not?"

"I believe my knowledge will prove adequate to the challenge," he replied, a good deal surprised. "I wonder at your guardian. Your own training should have included the manly art of boxing."

Sawyer, clinging to his perch up back, interjected suddenly, "There ain't any kind of fighting the cap'n can't tell you about. How do you think he come by a captaincy at his age? He's near the youngest commander in the navy, and not because his father's an earl, neither. Why, I could tell you tales—"

"But you won't, I trust," Mitford interrupted, seemingly not at all annoyed by the unwanted outburst.

Charlie, intrigued, turned her head to stare at Sawyer. "Does he *fight with swords*?" she asked, her eyes round.

"Aye, and with pistols and cannon, too," Sawyer replied, enlarging on his theme. "It was off Martinique His Lordship saved my life. A French brig—"

"That will do!" Mitford interposed forcefully, a look of embarrassment crossing his face.

Charlie wondered at his reticence and decided that he was uniquely free of conceit, a singularity in itself in view of the many distinctions that must be accorded him as the commander of a man-of-war. Regretfully she had yet to learn when to let well enough alone. "Do let Sawyer tell me," she begged. "Knowing you will be such a thing to boast of."

"I dare say," he said, "that when you know to refrain from discoursing on a topic I find distasteful, you may do tolerably well."

"I hope you are not offended," she murmured, rather perturbed. "I meant no harm."

"No, I am not offended," he replied. "You are behaving very much as I supposed you would."

It was a snub and had the effect of causing her to subside. They were now bowling along a pleasing stretch of road, but she had no eye for it from wondering what she was to do. The captain had put himself to the trouble of assisting her, and although in the circumstance of this putting a good deal of distance between herself and Sir Randolph it must be considered a plus, still she had yet to formulate a plan for the time she would part from him. Having never been

49

farther from home than Gillingham, she knew nothing of Plymouth or, she could not help but reflect, of the dangers lurking there. Before many more miles were covered she became extremely apprehensive of her future.

She had very little money in her pocket, and she supposed the costs already incurred would make an end of the little she did have. Still she could not regret her flight. She need only bend her mind to the problem of supporting herself and all would be well. It must, so long as she clung to the safety of boy's clothing and avoided contact with her fellows. Her problem, though it was difficult, was not insurmountable. There were several occupations which, she deemed, by reason of her training and aptitude, were open to her. Lacking the proper credentials, the post of tutor was soon seen to be impossible to attain, as was that of a secretary or librarian. By the time it came down to a choice between delivery boy or lackey, she was feeling very moped indeed. No amount of sensible thought could convince her that one form of lowly employment was in any way superior to another.

She was roused to her surroundings by the rattle of the curricle's wheels on cobblestones. They had turned in under the archway to the courtyard of The Checquers at Shortacombe, some nine miles north of Tavistock. The captain threaded his way between the vehicles drawn up before the inn and came to a standstill before the door.

"We appear to have arrived with time to spare," he remarked, motioning an ostler to the wheel horses' heads. "Are you hungry, Charlie?"

"To own the truth, I'm not," she said, her mind very much on her troubles. "I'd as lief drive on, if it's all the same to you."

"That's what I like in you, I think," he said, springing to the ground. "Always willing to fall in with my plans. Down you come, brat. I shan't leave you alone out here to commit some devilry."

She muttered something under her breath that sounded to the captain much like an oath and went into the inn ahead of him, nearly colliding with a gentleman on his way out. "Here, now!" the stranger exclaimed. "What are you about? Why, Richard!" he added, catching sight of Mitford. "My compliments, but I didn't expect to run across you here. Where the devil have you been? I'll lay you a monkey you have learned of the prizefight."

"I should rather think I have," Mitford said, and smiled. "As to where I have been, my dear Charles, you would never credit it, believe me."

"Try me," Charles murmured, his eyes on Charlie effacing herself in the background.

"It's a long story," Mitford demurred politely, his attention taken up in removing his gloves.

Charles made a slight gesture indicating Charlie. "Our new cabin boy?" he said.

To her astonishment Mitford threw back his head and gave a shout of laughter. "Charlie on a man-of-war?" He chuckled. "You have scant acquaintance with my halfling. The crew would soon be run amuck."

"Who is he? Some young relative of yours?"

Mitford motioned Charlie forward. "Charlie, meet Charles," he said. "My lieutenant commander, child. Lieutenant Lord Charles Brompton."

"How do you do, sir," she said, uncertain whether to shake hands or bow.

51

"What's your last name, boy?" the lieutenant demanded, casting a suspicious look at her.

"Fitzhugh," she replied, forgetting to lie.

A puzzled frown creased his brow. "Fitzhugh," he mused, cudgeling his brain. "It has a familiar ring."

"It is a common enough name," she murmured, attempting to cover her slip.

"Not that common," he persisted.

"I think," Mitford said, bored, "that we will be better employed in ordering luncheon."

The lieutenant turned to retrace his steps. "Try the plaice," he recommended, leading the way to the coffee room. "Believe it or not, the cook in this place has a way with seafood."

The waiter, when summoned, regretted that the fish was gone, but yes, he could provide cold meat and fruit. He would fetch it without delay. Charlie retired to the settle before the fire while the covers were being laid, and Mitford, chagrined at not having learned Charlie's last name himself, stood with his back to the fire discussing the latest developments in the troubles with America until the landlord came into the room bearing their luncheon on a tray. He would, it seemed, serve them himself.

"I took the liberty of uncorking a bottle of my best brandy, Lord Captain, sir," he said, respectful if a trifle inaccurate. "I hope its being from France won't spoil it for Your Lordship's palate. It's not smuggled, my lord. It was laid down in my cellar before the war."

"About the only attribute I have been able to discover in the French is their ability to produce fine wines," Mitford said with a smile, motioning Charlie to the table. "Rest assured we will enjoy it. How about you, Charles? Will you join us?"

"I believe not, thank you," Brompton said, taking a seat a little way back from the table.

"Why so diffident?" Mitford inquired, carving the ham. "You are as a rule a notable trencherman."

"Damn it, Richard," Brompton said, "are you going to drag the boy along to the mill with us? There is something in particular I want to ask you."

"Don't be an ass!" Mitford snapped. "Charlie's no bother. Leave him be. You can ask me later."

"You've never been a cub leader, that I recall," the lieutenant remarked, pouring himself a glass of wine and tossing it off in one gulp.

"It is not so very marvelous," Mitford explained. "Charlie stood in need of transport, and I supplied it."

"Transport to where?"

"I have no idea."

Lieutenant Brompton goggled. "You're bamming me," he accused, his gaze swinging to Charlie's face.

"My cousin resides in Plymouth," she explained.

"His widowed cousin," Mitford amended.

"I'm an orphan, you see," she continued, ignoring the interruption.

"Sent down from Eton for smuggling a girl into his quarters," Mitford interjected, an unholy gleam coming into his eyes. "Mixed up in it somewhere is a mama who is ill and a papa who sells ladies' shoes, not to mention a guardian bent on marrying him off to a chit he can't abide. Oh, yes, I almost forgot. He is most prodigiously wealthy."

"No, by God, Richard, this won't do," Brompton protested, incredulous. "I never heard the like. It's all a pack of lies."

"But of course, dear boy," Mitford agreed. "Charlie wouldn't recognize the truth if it rose up and smote him in the face. It's a part of his charm."

Brompton looked skeptical. "Something about this is devilish queer," he said. "Are you sure the Bow Street runners aren't after him?"

"He says not. Strangely enough, in this instance I feel inclined to believe him. However, that is neither here nor there. We part company shortly. In the meantime we've a prizefight to attend."

Brompton grinned and stood. "We've more than a mill to look forward to," he said. "Ensign Morley had it from the admiral's bosun that the old man is planning quite a party. To be plain with you, he hit upon the notion of bringing a bevy of lovelies down from London to gladden our last night ashore. For myself, I rather fancy a blonde."

"Or a brunette, or a redhead, if the truth be known."

"What of you, Richard? When I left town rumor had it that you'd cast adrift your latest barque of frailty."

Mitford shrugged. "I will better be able to answer your question when I have seen the ladies," he said.

"They are bound to be beauties. Trust the admiral to see to that. He enjoys a tumble with a cutie the same as lesser men."

Mitford frowned. "That is a crude way of putting it," he said succinctly.

Brompton looked at him in a puzzled way. "It is the way the admiral would put it," he said.

"But not, I trust, within the hearing of a child," Mitford replied, his face rigid with disapproval. "You had best run along out front, Charlie. I will be with you when I have paid our shot. And don't go wandering off. I have no intention of waiting about for you."

She went, feeling oddly dejected. It was apparent from the lieutenant's attitude that he found something to remark in her friendship with the captain. In his own words he found it devilish queer, which was tantamount to how the world would view it. She had trusted the captain from the moment of setting eyes on him, and not even when pitchforked into the closest intimacy with him had she found her confidence to be misplaced. But try as she would she could not look upon her situation as an enviable one. By masquerading as a boy she had put herself in the melancholy position of being unable to unmask.

CHAPTER 4

Mitford had no qualms about ordering Lieutenant Brompton to take Sawyer with him in his curricle. Charlie would need to have the fight explained, and they would go on very much better without Sawyer's loquacious and highly contradictory remarks. Finding this unanswerable, Brompton made haste to entrust a bottle of the landlord's brandy to Sawyer's care, a charge he took seriously enough to ensure its safety by cradling it in his arms. As for Charlie, past fears, flight and anonymity were at once as nothing. The captain would protect her a few more hours. Beyond that she refused to think.

She allowed several minutes to pass before she spoke. "I want to thank you for the care you have bestowed on me," she said then, embarking upon the speech she felt compelled to utter. "I have not before known a friendship quite like yours. It wasn't that I was ever lonely—I had my books, you see—but I had no one to share my thoughts, no, or even to scold."

"If all I have done is scold, I marvel at my restraint," he remarked, his eyes on the road ahead. "You deserve much worse."

She flashed him a quick glance from under her lashes. "I am sorry to have put you in an awkward position before your friend. It cannot be pleasant to be obliged to defend one's reasons—"

"To do what!" he demanded ominously.

"To explain one's actions," she corrected.

"How dare you!" he ejaculated furiously. "If you imagine that I will permit you to suggest—"

"I am trying to say that you needn't worry about discussing your lights of love within my hearing. I know all about kept women, and orgies, and—well, what Mrs. Cogswell calls scandalous behavior. She lives in the cottage next door, you know. I am persuaded she suffers from some disorder of the system, for she is forever taking Professor Lanny's Little Liver Pills. I fancy that may account for her odious disposition. Whenever the subject comes up, you see, she goes on forever about the ungodliness of loose women and quotes the Scriptures until one is heartily sick of it. Personally I am strongly of the opinion that men—that we—have all the best of it. At least we aren't called upon to atone for a life of sin."

"A life of sin!" he echoed, stunned by the spate of words. "Good God! This Mrs. Cogswell of yours deserves a thrashing. You are much too young to know of such things."

"Not at all," she responded, preparing to add the crowning touch. "You must surely see that I am now warned against having mistresses or indulging in drunken revels in the company of women who are no better than they should be."

"Don't be ridiculous," he said, a muscle twitching at the corner of his mouth. "A pretty figure you will cut once you've passed the downy-cheeked stage."

"That's an unjust thing for you to say," she remarked, smug in the belief that she had put a period to any suspicions of her sex that he might have acquired. "You have no doubt had an amusing time of it as a bachelor."

"So it's to be shuffled off on my shoulders," he said and chuckled, vastly entertained. "You must think I live a life of sin."

"I daresay you feel the ball is worth the cannon," she offered in a palliative tone. "Sailors usually do. Even I know that."

"God grant me patience!" he said with a grin. "Next you will accuse me of littering the countryside with any number of base-born brats."

"Now that," she objected, "is coming it very much too strong. I never intimated anything of the kind. Have you?"

"Not to my knowledge," he said with a perfectly straight face.

"No, I can see that you wouldn't have. You must spend the greater part of your time at sea, so you could not—" She checked herself, flustered, and added, "I can't imagine how we got off on this!"

"You brought up the subject," he reminded her, the amusement in his eyes becoming replaced by a look of interrogation. "You appear to have been too much in the company of women. Your conversation is full of very feminine ideas, let me tell you."

She was spared the necessity of a reply by his checking his horses to turn off onto a country lane. The traffic immediately became very much more heavy, to her ever-lasting relief. Mitford's attention was so taken up in threading his way among the various equipages thronging the road that the remainder of the drive was accomplished in silence. By the time an open field with a stage set up in it and with every conceivable kind of conveyance drawn up around it had been reached, her ill-judged utterances had been forgotten.

"Why is everyone booing?" she inquired, anxiously scrutinizing the crowd. "Will there be trouble?"

"The challenger's colors have just been tied to the ropes," he replied, edging the curricle into a place beside the ring. "It is not that anyone holds Legguns in disdain. It's just that Meacham is the better man. Ah, here he comes now. The tall chap in the tan greatcoat."

To Charlie, watching the combatants disrobe, they both appeared formidable. Never had she dreamed that men could possess such bulging muscles or look so tough. Feeling somewhat embarrassed by the sight of the naked male thorax, she dropped her eyes and listened only halfheartedly to the captain's explanation of rounds, and seconds, and bottle holders. The noisy approval of the spectators brought her gaze back to the ring. "What are they doing?" she asked, watching the contestants cautiously circling with their hands clenched into fists.

"Sparring," he said. "Each is searching for a weakness in the other."

"They don't appear to me to have any."

"Watch Legguns's left. He drops it after every feint by Meacham. If he isn't careful he won't last the first round."

In point of fact a right to the jaw at full arm's length felled him less than two minutes into the fight. Charlie watched his seconds drag him to his corner, unaware that the mill was over until the crowd sent up a cheer. Though the gentlemen present might signal their enjoyment of the fight, she could see no sense in it.

Mitford scanned the crowd but failed to discover Lieutenant Brompton's face among them. With no reason to linger, he gathered up his reins. "What did you think?" he said, setting his team in motion to join the stream of traffic heading for the exit.

"I think it excessively silly that grown men should have put themselves to the trouble of attending."

"They will now be able to speak knowledgeably of having seen the great Meacham in action. Don't judge them too harshly, child. They lack the felicity of your acquaintance."

"If you feel that way about me, why did you bring me?"

"I had thought that masculine companionship would do you a world of good. I trust you will not insult my intelligence by pretending that you found the fight other than repugnant."

Not knowing what to reply to this, she lapsed into a silence that lasted for several miles. The pace of their progress soon obtruded on her thoughts. They must be covering nine miles in an hour, she determined, and wondered at the need for speed. The answer to this became apparent when they swept through Tavistock without a check and proceeded on their way toward Plymouth. The admiral's party was at the root of it. She had no wish for the journey to end and certainly no wish to be put down alone after dark. By the time the outskirts of Plymouth came in view, however, she had become reconciled to the prospect and had determined to seek sanctuary with the pastor of some church.

Something in her quandary must have communicated itself to Mitford. "You are wrong about one thing," he said, once they were driving through the outskirts of the town. "It is not my intention to cut you adrift tonight. Tomorrow we will see what we can do."

She saw that he was watching her and realized that he had been doing so for some time. "You seem to be plunging deeper and deeper into a morass of my making," she remarked, leaning forward to view the substantial-looking houses lining the avenue down which they were passing. "Necessity forces me to accept your offer, but I should warn you that I haven't the money to repay you."

"No one asked you to," he said absently, his attention taken up in dealing with the traffic clogging the streets.

Awed by her first glimpse of city life, she sat drinking it all in. Never had she dreamed so many people would throng the pathways or so many carriages come and go along the thoroughfares. There was so much to see she felt bewildered by it all and could only wonder that the captain seemed to know which turnings to take. Just when she had come to believe that he had lost his way, he reined in his team before a large hotel and drew to a stop before the door. "You will go immediately to your room and remain there," he said, hitching up his reins. "Should I find you in the corridors tonight, I will tan your hide, make no mistake about it."

She would have liked to make some scathing reply, but when none came to mind, she descended to the ground without comment. To one accustomed to the simplicity of a country cottage, the splendors of The Royal Arms could not fail to impress beyond anything that could be imagined. The doorman, the polished brass escutcheons, the heavy paneled doors—all combined to make her agog with excitement. Not even the ignominy of being pushed up the front steps ahead of the captain could diminish the sparkle in her eyes.

The facade, outstanding though it was, proved only a prelude to the comforts to be found inside. Charlie, waiting beside the captain at the registration desk, gazed around, enthralled. The rugs, the furnishings, the cut-crystal chandeliers, were in the best of taste, she knew, though she had had no past experience with luxurious surroundings. A number of gentlemen seen in the salon were in civilian dress, but the majority of the visitors wore naval uniforms. Since no ladies were in evidence, she could only conclude that the hotel preferred a clientele of men. She would have liked to remain with the captain, but he vetoed the suggestion, saying he would have her dinner sent to her room on a tray. There was nothing she could do but thank him and follow in the wake of a chambermaid to a bedchamber on the floor above.

The hotel manager, busy with preparations for the evening's festivities, could not tell Mitford whether Lieutenant Lord Brompton was as yet among the officers crowding his establishment. So many gentlemen had seen fit to descend upon him without notice that he scarcely knew whether he was by his head or his heels, but, yes, if His Lordship would but be patient, hot water would be sent to his room. With nothing left to do, Mitford strolled into the coffee room, Charlie very much on his mind.

He had reason to know that the boy was of an extremely

confiding disposition; he was, in fact, friendly to a fault. He seldom saw a stranger, was perfectly willing to converse with any person at all and showed an alarming tendency to bestow his trust indiscriminately. Left to his own devices, there was no telling what mischief might befall him. Clearly he must be sent home, but first he must be persuaded to reveal its location. Its true location, Mitford thought wryly.

Three ships of the line, of seventy-four guns each, lay at anchor in the harbor, along with four frigates, the *Minotaur* among them, a number of brigantines, several tenders loaded to their gunwales with provisions and the very latest in rocket ships designed to deliver the terrifying Congreve rockets. All were under the command of Rear Admiral George C. Allenwood. The admiral had risen through the ranks solely on merit. Aboard ship he could be a crusty old martinet, but ashore he became an easygoing profligate as willing to hoist a bottle with his men as to lift a doxy's skirts. His parties had attained a certain notoriety throughout the fleet, and few if any of those fortunate enough to be included failed to attend one of his diversions.

At any other time Mitford would have been caught up in the revelry the same as the others were, but on this occasion he found himself indifferent and puzzled as to why. The women provided for their pleasure, though on the shady side of thirty, were not without their charms. At least it had seemed so, at first. It was only after the wine flowed freely that their laughter became shrill and their conversation coarse. The captain imbibed as deeply as any man in the room, but still the gaiety seemed only tawdry and the jokes somehow obscene. To please the admiral he forced himself to evince an interest in a female who went by the improbable name of Ceres, the flight of fancy of some long-forgotten paramour. In a way it was understandable. There was an earthy quality about her that she went to considerable lengths to emphasize. So much so, in fact, that her bosom seemed in perpetual danger of escaping from the flimsy, low-cut bodice straining to confine it.

It was not surprising that the sounds of revelry should penetrate upstairs. They could, in all truth, be heard throughout much of the surrounding town. Charlie, sitting at the open window of her room, stared blindly out upon the deserted street below. It had been, she felt, the most miserable evening of her life. Uncertain just what was transpiring downstairs, she nevertheless knew that some female claimed the captain's eye. It was unfair, she thought, forgetting the indefensible impropriety of her own position. She knew only that she could not go to bed until he came upstairs. And so she sat and waited, forsaken and cold, and alone.

It was long past midnight when a noisy disturbance in the corridor outside her door smote her waiting ears. Curious and strong-willed, her conscience hadn't a prayer. Richard had forbade her to go out into the halls. He had not mentioned peeping. The captain, his mind fogged with drink and staggering past her threshold with his equally drunken doxy draped over a shoulder, had no inkling that she watched, white and stricken. He wove his uncertain way on down the hall and went into his room, slamming the door behind him.

"I'll be damned if you aren't the most eager slut I've ever come across," he remarked, unceremoniously dumping Ceres upon the bed. "It should be quite a night."

She scrambled to her knees and smirked. "Perhaps you

needn't undress," she said, watching him shrug out of his coat and hurl it across the room. "Perhaps it won't do you any good. We haven't talked terms. The admiral would give me twenty quid."

"I'll give you twenty-five," he snapped, sitting down to remove his boot. "Now shut up and earn your pay."

"Well," she murmured, a speculative gleam coming into her eyes. "You did tear my gown. The admiral said—"

"Not another sou!" he shot back, standing up to strip off his breeches. "Come to think of it, I'm not at all sure that you're worth twenty-five."

She ran her eyes down his lean frame and giggled. "Right now I'm worth what I choose to charge," she said, lounging back at ease. "You'd best have a care, Captain, dear. You've a lot to lose, and I just might make you keep it."

In two strides he was beside the bed, glaring down at her. "I will say this just once, so you had better attend me. Playing hard to get ill becomes a woman of your stamp. You know why you are here, so we will have no missish ways."

"You needn't talk like that," she said with a pout, certain of her power. "I like to pretend that the man cares for me. A little romance—"

"Don't blaspheme!" he snapped. "There is nothing holy about this. Come to think of it, you'd best leave. I'm not at all sure that I can stand the sight of you."

Her lips sneered. "I might as well," she jeered. "You have collapsed like a pricked balloon."

He felt the blood rush into his face and clenched his hands at his sides. "Out!" he growled, controlling himself with strong effort.

She should have been warned by the expression on his

face. Foolish beyond reason, she shook her head. "Oh, no, you don't!" she said. "I shan't take one step from this room until I get my pay."

Before she could prevent it, he had seized her wrist and yanked her from the bed. Pausing only to extract the money from a bag of coins he had tossed on the chest, he hustled her through the door. "If I set eyes on you again I'll throttle you!" he said through gritted teeth, dragging her down the hall.

"You're hurting me!" she cried, clawing and scratching at him in an attempt to break free. "If you don't let go of me, I'll scream!"

"Scream away," he growled, flinging her gold sovereigns down the stairs. "Grovel for them, you bitch!"

"My money!" she yelped, rushing down the steps. "If any of it is lost—"

Intent upon retrieving her ill-gotten gains, she missed her footing and tumbled headlong to the floor below. From the stream of oaths issuing from her throat, he knew she was not hurt. I must have taken leave of my senses, he thought, watching her scrabbling for the coins.

The disturbance had reached Lieutenant Brompton's ears in his room next to the captain's. Erupting through his door, he came running down the hall. "Good God, Richard!" he gasped, peering down the stairs. "You could have killed the slut!"

"Don't waste your sympathy," Mitford snapped. "I should have wrung her neck."

"I've never seen you like this before," Brompton remarked, staring. "What's come over you?"

"It's too damned cheap, Charles. It puts us on the level

with a seaman purchasing his pleasure in some back alley. We're just paying more, that's all."

"I will admit it is something beyond the common," Brompton agreed. "Tell me, Richard. Have you ever found any woman worth troubling over? Even a mistress?"

Mitford's lips curled. "Least of all a mistress," he said, shrugging.

"I thought not," Brompton remarked, looking solemn. "Since I've known you, you've been after some wench or other, but you haven't seemed to care for any of them. Why do you bother if you don't contemplate marriage?"

"There is no great harm in a mistress," Mitford replied, turning on his heel to stride back to his chamber. "At least you know they're clean."

It was not to be wondered that the turmoil in the hall should bring the admiral upon the scene. The door to his room was flung open and he stood upon the threshold, gorgeously arrayed in a brocade dressing gown of vivid orange and puce. "Lieutenant Brompton!" he roared in tones usually reserved for the quarterdeck.

It had a sobering effect upon the lieutenant. "Yes, sir! Admiral, sir!" he barked, snapping to attention.

"Who the devil is making all that noise?"

"I believe it is the one called Ceres, sir!"

"Mitford throw her down the stairs?"

"I believe she fell, sir!" the lieutenant replied, acutely aware of the picture he must be cutting with his shirttail flapping against bare flanks.

"Stop her caterwauling, Lieutenant!" the admiral snapped. "That's an order!"

"Yes, sir!" the lieutenant gasped, his world turning upside down.

"And Brompton, for God's sake, put on your breeches," the admiral said, grinning, putting it right again.

Back along the hall Charlie crouched behind her door and felt her own world to be reeling. Never had she dreamed the captain capable of such behavior. She shuddered, picturing him with the black-haired strumpet. She must get away, she thought. She must flee before he discovered her own rounded curves. Her head bent forward on her knees, she sat for a seemingly endless length of time, determining what she should do. She must wait until the hotel was quiet, she knew, before venturing forth. A note left behind telling him that she was returning home should take care of the captain. And then when she was safely away she would seek sanctuary in a church and wait upon the dawn.

At first all went as planned. Wrapping her belongings in the shawl, she tiptoed to the door and eased it open a crack. No one was about. Pausing a moment to gather her courage, she crept out into the hall and down the stairs. The night clerk eyed her suspiciously but could find no reason to deny her pen and paper. Quickly dashing off her letter to the captain, she gave it into the clerk's keeping, with instructions to deliver it on the morrow.

Quitting the hotel, she set off down the street with no sense at all of her direction. In the dim light of a waning moon she hurried past shops crowding the pathways and houses set back from the streets, but nowhere could she discern any building even remotely resembling a place of worship. On and on she scurried, the tang of salt air in her nostrils, but, in her extremity, unaware that she neared the waterfront. Every shadow brought her heart into her throat, and every sound fanned the terror threatening to engulf her. At last she became exhausted, so tired she felt that she could not take another step, yet still she pressed on because she must. A murky mist rose from the stones beneath her feet, and the impenetrable darkness closed in around her, terrorizing her to her very soul. Intent upon her plight, the sound of muffled footsteps failed to obtrude into her consciousness until it was too late. She hadn't a chance. A belaying pin descended on her head, and she sagged backward into a pair of waiting arms, the blackness coming up to claim her.

CHAPTER 5

As a rule Mitford was an early riser, but on the following day he was still dead to the world when Sawyer came into his room close upon noon and cast a glance around. His Lordship's coat was discovered in a corner, and his shirt and breeches trailed in disarray from the seat of a chair to the floor. As for the usually spotless Hessian boots, Sawyer could not look upon them without a shudder. "I heard all about it," he advised the captain's unconscious form. "The whole town's agog with it. Can't say as I blame them, if half of what they say is true."

The sound of his voice penetrated Mitford's wine-befuddled brain. He woke and directed a pained glance at his henchman. "Must you shout?" he groaned. "What time is it?"

"Time you was up, if we're to make the tide. You needn't worry, my lord. It's safe enough. That floozie you threw down the stairs is gone, though why Your Lordship should see fit to waste your manhood on such as that, I couldn't say."

"The devil fly away with you," Mitford muttered. "Hand me my breeches, and then go for hot water."

"Since when did I forget to bring it?" Sawyer demanded, putting forward a chair. "Just sit yourself down here, my lord, while I shave you. Your hand's bound to be unsteady."

"Bacchus, why must thou embrace me?" Mitford murmured, sitting up.

"Beg pardon, Cap'n?"

"Nothing," he sighed, getting to his feet.

An hour later he entered the reception hall to find the desk clerk on the watch for him. "Excuse me, my lord, but this was left for you," he said, passing across a paper twisted into a screw. "The young gentleman was most anxious that you receive it."

Mitford turned his back upon the clerk's palpably avid face and smoothed the wrinkled sheet. A quick glance at the signature confirmed his worst fears. Charlie had written:

> There is no way I can express my appreciation for all you have done for me. Do not distress yourself over my future, please. I am going home. Good-bye, my lord, and may God sail by your side.

"When was this left in your care?" he inquired, turning to face the clerk.

"At three o'clock this morning," the clerk stammered, discomfited by the odd expression on the captain's face. "I took particular note of the time, my lord. As a rule, our guests are not up and about so early."

"Where, in your estimation, could the young gentleman have found to go at that hour of the night?"

"The stage-coach office, my lord. No other place would be open. Will Your Lordship wish someone sent around to make inquiries?"

"Damn the brat!" said His Lordship.

Clapping his cocked hat fore and aft on his head, he made his way out of the hotel, a walking testimony to Sawyer's devotion. Not one crease marred the perfection of his undress uniform. His frock coat of plain navy blue cloth with its stand-and-fall collar was buttoned across his chest with eight highly polished brass buttons. Three equally shining buttons adorned each cuff, as did three more decorating the pockets. Epaulets were attached to the shoulders, and a sword was carried in a black leather sword belt at his waist. A spotless white cravat showed at his throat, and white breeches terminated in Hessian boots that had been polished with a blacking mixed with champagne.

Declining the doorman's offer to call up a chair, he strolled off in the direction of the waterfront, his head clearing in the cool salt air. As was usual on a day when the fleet was due to sail, furious activity ensued throughout the ships anchored in the harbor. Officers stood at attention beside the gangways waiting to salute their captains aboard, while the crews were drawn up in ranks, their eyes staring straight ahead. Small boats plied to and fro between ship and shore, ferrying the commanders to their vessels, and up and down the line the shrill of the boatswain's pipe could be heard. A booming salute fired in honor of the admiral's flagship reverberated across the water just as Mitford arrived at the docks.

With all the bustle it was an animated scene. Just

offshore, sea birds wheeled and dipped over the waves, their cries mingling with the cheers of the populace gathered along the quayside to enjoy the spectacle. Mitford picked his way among the bales and casks crowding the wharf and stepped numbly down into his gig to join the seamen waiting to row him to the *Minotaur*.

Aboard ship out in the bay Lieutenant Brompton ran an experienced eye over the assembled crew. "Mr. Cranston!" he said quietly.

"Sir!" Chief Warrant Officer Cranston gasped, snapping to attention.

"I understood you to say we had a cabin boy aboard."

"He is below, sir. He isn't—feeling well."

"I see," Lieutenant Brompton murmured, his gaze on the captain's fast-approaching gig. "Pipe the commander aboard, mister."

To the twittering of the bosun's pipe, Captain Mitford climbed on deck and received the salute of the assembled crew. "Good afternoon, gentlemen," he said. "Have our orders been brought aboard?"

"They are in your quarters, sir," Lieutenant Brompton replied.

"Up anchor and make sail, Lieutenant. You will then report to me."

Waiting only until all hands ran to their stations, he went below to his large, low-beamed cabin and strode across to the desk that was secured against the forward bulkhead. His hand paused in reaching for the official document bearing the great seal of the Admiralty. I may as well know the worst, he thought, spreading out the single sheet. President Madison had, on June first, delivered a war message to the Congress of the United States. Until it was known what action had been taken, all ships of the British fleet would exercise extreme care when approaching any vessel flying the American flag. HMS *Minotaur* was to shape course for American waters, there to hold herself in readiness to engage enemy ships in battle, should war have been declared.

It would be a ticklish business, Mitford knew. Customarily warships were at liberty to conceal their nationality by flying the flag of another nation while assessing the strength of an opposing vessel. The practice had the advantage of allowing a strategic retreat when confronted by a superior foe but would put the British at a disadvantage until it was known whether hostilities did in fact exist.

He was to put his thoughts in very much the same words when he told Lieutenant Brompton the news. "The Americans haven't much in the way of a fleet, but their big frigates are longer than ours and can carry forty-four guns. The ship best able to maneuver will come off the winner. I intend it will be the *Minotaur*. We will drill the men until they are a better-ordered, better-disciplined crew than that to be found on any American vessel."

"They are a good lot, sir, and spoiling for a fight. They will do anything you ask."

"They will soon find out just what I expect of them. Muster them aft on the quarterdeck. I will be up shortly. Oh, and Charles, tell the cabin boy to pass around a double tot of grog with the evening meal."

"Cranston reports that he's below, and ill. I suspect that a press gang brought him aboard."

Mitford scowled. "God grant he's not the cub of some influential family," he said. "Send him to me on the double."

75

Charlie had heard the sounds of their sailing, but dimly. Dragged back to full consciousness by the shrilling pipes and booming cannon, she had quickly discovered that the slightest movement on her part sent pain stabbing through her head. Coils of rope and kegs of black powder swam in and out of her vision, and she knew herself to be in the hold of some ship. Upon wondering how she came to be there, her thoughts flew back to her flight in the dark of night, but beyond that her memory refused to function. She could hear the creaking of masts indicating that the vessel was under sail, and the slap of water against the hull, but she could see nothing beyond the glow cast by a single lantern.

"Here ye be, laddie," a seaman said suddenly, stepping into the light. " 'Tis sure and the cap'n wants to see ye."

Charlie shrank back. "Where am I?" she managed to utter, trembling with fear.

"Ye're aboard the *Minotaur*, and 'tis right lucky ye be. The cap'n don't hold with mastheadin' the crew. On most ships ye'd find yer back cut to ribbons for missin' a call to parade. If ye'll take my advice, laddie, ye'll look lively when beat to station."

She started, sheer terror staring from her eyes. "Don't whip me, please," she gasped, flinching back.

" 'Tis the drumbeat callin' ye to duty that I'm talkin' of," he said, grinning. "Ye've a lot to learn, like to jump when the cap'n whistles."

"What does he want?" she asked, struggling upright.

"If I could tell ye that, I'd be him," he replied, motioning her forward. "Come along with ye, 'fore ye get us both in trouble."

She swayed, feeling dizzy, and doubted that her legs

76

would support her. For some reason she could not understand, she had the oddest premonition that the captain
would turn out to be Lord Mitford. Having taken the notion
into her head, her spirits rose. She wondered why he had
shanghaied her aboard his ship, but it didn't matter. She had
been imagining much worse.

The seaman led the way upward through several decks,
accompanied by the curious stares of any members of the
crew they happened to come across. Just when she thought
the trek must go on forever, they arrived at a short
companionway. "In there," her guide said with a grunt,
pointing to a door at its end. "Ye'd best knock."

To her utter relief the man who looked up from the charts
spread out across his desk was indeed Lord Mitford, but by
no stretch of the imagination could she think that he was
glad to see her. Quite the contrary. He stared and said,
"What the devil are you doing here?"

It was too much. She had a splitting headache and had a
short time before awakened to a terror such as she had not
known existed. She was angered, and puzzled, too. "Why
have you done this?" she demanded. "Do you think to do
me harm? Is that why you have forced me aboard your ship?
Well, sir, if you think that—that you and I—" Her voice
trailed off, and she dropped her eyes before the sudden
blaze of fury leaping into his.

He rose and walked around his desk. She thought he
stalked. "By wandering alone near the waterfront, you
made yourself the target of a press gang, you little fool.
Why did you run away? Do you think me a despoiler of
young boys? By God, I should order twenty lashes with the
cat! You'd sing a different tune, I'll warrant."

"You are a fine one to talk!" she shot back, the battle

fairly enjoined. "From the sound issuing from the dining room last evening, I would say you supped with the class of woman you are accustomed to. As for that black-haired strumpet—"

"So you were in the halls," he remarked, glaring. "I hated the whole affair. Why couldn't you have asked me how I felt?"

"I owe you no explanation," she replied, her nose in the air.

"You have made a rare mess of things," he informed her, his expression grim. "What am I to do with you?"

Since this last remark was more on the order of speaking a thought aloud, she avoided his eyes and waited, docile for once.

"You are far too frail to be housed with the crew," he said ruminatingly. "They usually bait the cabin boy, and you'd never stand up to it. As far as that goes, I doubt that you are strong enough to perform other than the lightest work aboard a man-of-war."

"I could fetch and carry," she suggested tentatively.

"What?" he demanded. "Powder and ball? Don't be an ass. You'd be sure to drop it. I will keep you here until I find a use for you. Go tell Sawyer to bring a hammock, and for God's sake have him wash your clothing. You stink to high heaven."

She stared at him, speechless, the extent of her predicament borne in upon her at last. There was no place on a ship where she could hide, no nook or cranny where she could escape the fruits of her own folly. There was only one thing for it. She must admit the truth and throw herself on his mercy.

"No, please," she begged, taking a deep breath. "You don't understand. I'm—I'm not a—a boy."

The last thing she expected to greet her disclosure was the deadly silence that followed it. She stood with her head bowed, her eyes on his gleaming Hessian boots, and waited for his wrath. "I should have known," he said finally, but so quietly that she would have preferred to hear him shout. "At times I think I did, but some remark would put me off and I would change my mind. God in heaven, what a coil!"

"It needn't be," she protested, her voice trembling slightly. She firmed it. "Just put it about that I was en route from a masquerade party when the press gang mistook me for a boy."

"We will not reveal your sex!" he said forcefully. "You may not know it, but the best of seamen are a superstitious lot. A ship with a female aboard quickly becomes a star-crossed vessel. Since I will need every jack man of them at his best, I shan't risk it. And while we are on the subject of the crew, you will restrict your activity aboard this ship. You may stroll on deck, but only in the afternoon when I will be with you. In the mornings the men will be there, and most of them will be mother naked. Under no circumstances will you become friendly with any of them. They might see through your disguise and become aroused beyond control. That is putting it bluntly, but better that than having some poor devil beaten half to death for fighting over you. Do I make myself clear?"

She nodded, shattered by his frankness. He couldn't know how desperate she had been to escape the clutches of Lord Ashmore. No man could possibly comprehend the lengths to which a woman was prepared to go to keep her body inviolate.

79

"Since Sawyer and Charles have a previous acquaintance with you, they must be told the truth," he continued. "Everyone else will be given to understand that you are a young relative of mine who was pressed into service by mistake. I will work out the details later. For now, since you have a tendency toward consumption, your doctor ordered bed rest. That will explain why you spend most of your time in my cabin."

"But what will I do all day?"

"It is enough that I must arrange your safety. I cannot be expected to entertain you as well."

"What will Sawyer and Lieutenant Brompton think? We will need to concoct some tale for them."

"It is a long voyage, and the nights become cold. They will think that I am damned fortunate to have a woman in my bed. I don't know who you are or where you come from, but only a strumpet would act as you have done."

She choked on her tears and sought in her mind for the words to correct the horribly erroneous opinion he had formed of her. "You don't understand," she pleaded. "I have a very good reason for acting as I did. I cannot explain, but I am sure you would never consider taking advantage of me."

"Is that what you think I intend doing?" he said, amused. "I shan't force you, my dear. You are usually more than willing, unless I miss my guess."

"Oh!" she stormed. "Of all the contemptible—oh! I hate you, do you hear me!"

"Our bathroom is just through that door," he said, ignoring the outburst. "I will send Sawyer to fill the tub with hot water and to gather up your clothing. It really does need laundering. He will have his orders, so unless you wish him to undress you, you will be wrapped in a sheet by the time he arrives."

"Oh! If I were a man—"

"If you were a man, my dear, this conversation would not be taking place," he remarked, crossing to the door. "The crew is mustered aft on the quarterdeck, waiting for my orders. You will do well enough for now. I shan't be long."

When he had gone, she sank down upon the bed. She had at the moment no interest in learning how a large four-poster bed draped in velvet came to be aboard a British man-of-war. Her problem was more immediate. Putting her head in her hands, she sat lost in thought, trying to determine what to do. Wrath, reproach, even oaths she could have pardoned. The provocation was great; she herself longed to relive the reprehensible events of the past days. But his attitude toward her was beyond everything. He was disinterested, both in her assertions of innocence and in her plight. His air of self-consequence, his assumption that she was his for the taking, filled her with repugnance. She longed to box his ears. To one accustomed to courtesy, the lack of it was almost impossible to accept. There was nowhere she could turn, no one to whom she could flee for succor. Aboard a British man-of-war the captain's word was law. Short of throwing herself overboard, a solution which she did not for a moment entertain, there was no escape for her.

She was brought back to the present by Sawyer unceremoniously entering the cabin, a pail of steaming water in each hand. "Cap'n's orders," he muttered, very red of face.

"I don't care what he ordered!" she snapped, unable to bear the indignity of it. "You can just take your water and go away!"

81

"Look at it this way, miss," Sawyer reasoned, his gaze carefully on a spot somewhere beyond her shoulder. "You aren't going nowhere, so you may as well be clean."

She was not used to a lackey making free in her quarters, and it did not improve her temper. She watched him go into the bathroom and heard the sound of water splashing in the tub. Incensed by the offensive treatment, she remarked fiercely to the room at large, "The crew of this boat is entirely too free with advice."

"It's not a boat," Sawyer corrected, reappearing. "You'd best get it straight. It's a ship."

She drew herself up to the extent of her not inconsiderable height. "I do not care what you call it, and I will warn you that I have had enough," she said. "You may tell your precious captain that he is to find other quarters for me!"

"You don't mean that, miss," Sawyer protested, coloring hotly. "In the first place he wouldn't do it, and in the second place you won't see the likes of this cabin anywhere in the fleet. Cap'n had the bathroom put in himself, and the bed come from Afton House in London town. It was his mum's, so he's right partial to it."

Since he seemed to find nothing incongruous in the captain's reprehensible plans for his mother's bed, it was no use discussing it with him. She saw nothing for it at the moment but to give in. "If I promise to leave my clothing outside in the companionway, will you leave? I won't trick you."

"You'd best not, seeing as how I have my orders," he replied, as anxious to be gone as she was to have him go.

She had a very fair notion of the results, should the captain discover her in the tub. She felt entirely unequal to the coming struggle but reasoned that she stood a better chance if clothed. A thought occurred to her. The captain must possess a firearm of some kind. She gazed around the room, her eyes coming to rest upon the desk. Darting across to it, she pulled open a drawer, a smile coming upon her face. Sighing in relief, she gingerly picked up the pistol it contained.

Speed was of the essence, she knew. Rushing across to the bathroom, she hurried through her bath. On second thought she soaped her hair, quickly rinsed it and wrapped it in a towel. Eschewing the bed for the chair behind the captain's desk, she tucked the firearm out of sight beneath the folds of the sheet and calmly awaited his return.

He seemed to be taking an unconscionable time about it, she thought. The alarm she felt almost seemed in danger of taking possession of her senses. By reminding herself of the gun, her composure returned. Her hands ceased their shaking, and she became convinced that she would emerge unscathed.

Gradually she became aware that the ship had begun to heave, and the sky had turned leaden. She began to feel squeamish and glanced longingly at the bed. "Never!" she murmured above the howl of a rising wind. The captain's voice shouting orders and the sound of running footsteps brought her to her feet, certain that they were destined to end up at the bottom of the sea. The floor seemed to drop from beneath her feet and the ship seemed to shudder as it slid down into a trough and then rose again to the crest of another wave. The sickening motion at last sent her flying to the bed, the towel clapped to her mouth. White and shaken, she lay perfectly still and strove to divorce herself from the storm.

She was unaware that the captain had entered the cabin

until he spoke. "Sick, are you?" he said, stripping off his sodden coat. "Well, take heart. It's little more than a breeze."

"Kindly have the goodness not to talk to me," she muttered, shuddering.

Glancing at her averted face, he continued, in an effort to take her mind off her troubles. "We have just cleared a line of partially submerged rocks that marks the end of the English Channel and the beginning of the Atlantic Ocean. The sea is always rough here, and vicious storms are frequent. We are fortunate this voyage. It could have been quite a blow."

"Please!" she breathed. "If you possess a shred of humanity, you will cease to prattle."

A moment later he gently touched her shoulder. "Drink this," he said, holding a glass to her lips.

She opened her eyes again and groaned. "I couldn't," she gasped. "Just go away and let me die in peace."

"You'll live," he remarked, tipping the brandy down her throat. "That's a good girl."

She choked and sputtered and sat bolt upright. "I always knew there was something evil about you," she snapped, clutching the sheet beneath her chin.

He grinned and sat down to remove his boots. "You no doubt speak from the pinnacle of your own piety," he said with a chuckle, his eyes on the pistol lying on the floor. "Should you decide to shoot me, you will need to know that it throws a trifle high."

To her horror she saw that she had dropped the gun. "It's your fault that I felt in need of it," she said, eyeing him with trepidation. "If you will but listen, I would like to talk to you."

"You have a lot to learn about me, should you imagine that I spend my time with females in talk," he remarked, standing to remove his soaking breeches. "I'm far from monkish."

"Don't!" she implored, closing her eyes against the sight of him. "Please don't disrobe in front of me!"

"Do you expect me to dress in the bathroom?" he said derisively. "I'll swear you know better than that!"

It wasn't easy, maintaining one's poise before a man, not while sitting naked in his bed, with one's eyes closed, and wrapped in his sheet. Somehow she managed it. "We could work out a schedule," she suggested with the courage born of desperation. "I would stay out of your way at whatever times you say. Then I could dress after you have left. I shouldn't mind waiting."

Laughing softly, he went around the room gathering up dry clothing. By the time he had dressed, she had burrowed beneath the covers, completely hidden from his view. She plays the part of sweet innocence very well, he thought. One could almost suppose her virgin. She was young for her profession, but who was he to look good fortune in the face. The last thing he had expected on this voyage was a comely whore to ease his aching loins. He almost reached out to draw back the covers from about her huddled form, but he stayed his hand. The time wasn't yet. It was a slight storm by Atlantic standards, but any blow merited the captain at the helm. Smiling to himself in anticipation of the coming night, he went again on deck to nurse his ship through the rampant sea. That it was odd that a doxy would elect to conceal her wares by dressing as a boy did not occur to him.

Lieutenant Brompton crossed the quarterdeck to stand by

his side. "It spells trouble, Richard," he said quietly, a worried expression in his eyes.

"It will blow itself out by evening," Mitford replied, deliberately ignoring the meaning implicit in the lieutenant's words.

"I hope we may find that it has," Brompton murmured cryptically, his gaze on the roiling waves.

CHAPTER 6

Charlie, meanwhile, wasted none of her precious time indulging in tears. If she were to forestall the captain, she would need a plan. The wine he had given her had settled her queasy stomach. Could he be induced to be more kindly still? Upon reflection she knew it would not serve. He might see to her comfort, but he could not be depended upon to forgo his pleasure.

With a shuddering sigh she tossed back the covers and slid from the bed. If Sawyer could be persuaded to return her clothing, she would be less than alluring fully clothed. With no idea when he would return, she began a hasty search of the cabin for some garment to replace the sheet. A locker attached to the bulkhead housed the captain's wardrobe. For the most part it consisted of naval uniforms, which was no great surprise. She found nothing at all that would not reveal more than it would conceal. The drawers of a chest proved every bit as unproductive. Neatly stacked piles of underclothing and spotless starched cravats brought a blush to her cheeks and despair to her heart. There must be something she could wear, she thought, rushing across the cabin to delve into his sea chest. It contained, in addition to a dress sword with a hilt fashioned of chased gold, a pair of shoes with silver buckles and a casket brimful with jeweled and lacquered medals, several volumes dealing with the lore of the sea and a copy of the Admiralty's *Regulations Governing Naval Operations*. Disappointed, she sank back on her heels and gazed about the room.

A pair of house slippers tucked under the bed caught her eye. "Of course!" she gasped, starting to her feet. "His dressing gown!" Darting across to the bathroom, she flung open the door and discovered the gown hanging on a peg. As was all the captain's clothing, it was of the finest silk in an unobtrusive brown, and tailored to perfection. By wrapping it nearly double around her body and securing the sash with a knot at her waist, she was able to cover herself modestly from her chin to the floor.

She had scarcely time to turn back the cuffs from over her hands when a tap sounded on the door and Sawyer entered bearing her tea on a tray. "What are you about, wearing the cap'n's robe?" he demanded, stopping dead in his tracks.

"He said I might," she replied, the lie falling glibly from her tongue. "At least until you return my clothing."

" 'Tain't dry," he said, crossing to set the tray upon the desk. "When the wind dies down, I'll hang it on the taffrail. Will you be wanting anything else for now?"

"I want my hammock, please. And Sawyer, bring a length of rope and two extra blankets. The captain gave me permission to section off a corner of the room."

Sawyer seemed to find nothing odd in the request. His

Lordship had his own ways of gentling a female, strange though they seemed at times. It never occurred to him that she would think to oppose the captain's will. No one aboard the *Minotaur* did. The men were healthy and content, thanks to a wholesome diet and fair treatment. His Lordship had a temper, to be sure, and the crew were afraid of him at times, but he found ways to punish other than beating a man until the deck ran red. A ration of rum would be cut or a leave ashore denied, but the master's mates were never ordered to swing their loaded canes. In Sawyer's memory no hapless soul had been lashed to the masthead or keelhauled beneath the captain's ship. Since they had never before sailed with a shanghaied female aboard, however, he had no experience of a frightened girl and so no cause to be suspicious.

Charlie watched him go, then sank into a chair, her nerves frayed. The idea of creating a private haven within the confines of the cabin had just popped into her head. Conceived on the spur of the moment, it nevertheless offered the only ray of hope she had. Would the captain tear down the wall she would build and drag her forth? She could only feel apprehensive. Unable to sit still, she jumped to her feet and began to pace about.

Fortunately for her waning poise, she hadn't long to wait. Sawyer rapped and (an encouraging sign for her) waited until she bade him enter. "I brought a hammer and some nails, miss," he offered, obviously eager to please. "If you're wishful, I'll fix things any way you say."

"If you will string a line across that corner," she replied, indicating the one farthest from the bed, "I will be most grateful."

Sawyer hung the hammock and secured the rope with

nails driven into the quarterdeck beams. He was in the act of draping the quilts over the line to form a wall when the captain walked into the cabin. His astonished gaze moved from the makeshift partition to Charlie and on to Sawyer's beet-red face. "What is the meaning of this?" he demanded, a muscle twitching in his cheek.

Sawyer found himself unable to meet his captain's steely eyes and shuffled his feet in acute dismay. "It's for miss, sir," he managed to stammer. " 'Twill give her a mite of privacy."

"Almost you surprise me," Mitford remarked, lifting a blanket to glance at the hammock strung behind it. "When you can find the time from your other labors, perhaps you will bring my tea."

Sawyer was skating on very thin ice and knew it. "I didn't mean to interfere, Cap'n," he said, a note of entreaty in his voice.

"You have no need to tell me who put you up to it," Mitford replied, his scowl deepening. "I trust you will carry out my order in your own good time."

Sawyer bobbed his head and skittered from the room, sped on his way by remorse at having put His Lordship in an awkward situation.

He needn't have worried. Mitford himself was less than concerned. He turned his attention to Charlie and said, amusement in his tone, "The walls of Jericho? Did you think it would do you any good? They came tumbling down, you may recall."

"You would not be so cruel," she whispered, edging a cautious step away from him. "Surely you won't deny me such a little thing."

He chuckled and sat down at his desk. "For the present,

90

no," he said, leaning back at ease and crossing his arms behind his head. "I'm curious to see what you will think of next. You should have been an actress, my dear. Your performance up to now has seldom been equaled on any stage. Not that I mind," he added, struck by a sudden thought. "I had no notion that girlish reticence could so whet my appetite."

Inured to his remarks by now, she bit her lip, unable to decide whether he was teasing. There had been a budding friendship between them when he had thought of her as a boy. How could he change so abruptly merely at the disclosure of her sex? Perhaps he looked upon a woman as a commodity, to be used, then cast aside. Did she have cause to fear him? She did not know when the thought crept into her mind. Acutely aware of the half-mocking, half-considering look in the eyes surveying her so particularly, she felt trapped and wary. Only the creaking of the ship could be heard in the quiet of the room. It seemed to her that every nerve in her body was on edge. Fear at last rising within her, she grew pale, and the final remnants of her courage deserted her. Unable to meet his contemplative stare, she darted behind her wall of quilts and retreated into the corner to cower, trembling, lest he come to seek her out.

She felt exhausted and confused and only dimly heard him bid Sawyer enter in answer to a rap upon the door. She had no way of knowing that a small smile curved his lips as he watched Sawyer arrange their evening meal upon a table. It was as well that she didn't. "When you are finished, you will remove the evidence of your handiwork," he said quietly. "And don't forget the hammock. We won't be in need of it."

Charlie, overhearing, flushed and dashed out from behind

her makeshift wall. "Are you completely devoid of sensibility?" she demanded, angrily facing him. "I did not seek your company. Must you take away what meager privacy I have left?"

"It clutters up the cabin," he explained, his eyes sparkling. "Be a good girl and stay out of Sawyer's way. I am sure that, having erected your cubbyhole without my orders, he is most eager to correct his error."

"Aye, Cap'n," Sawyer muttered, fairly jerking the blankets from the rope. "But I'll need to fetch a prise to remove the nails."

"Remove them tomorrow," Mitford grinned, his eyes on Charlie's face. "Come and sit down, my dear. I find that I am hungry."

"I'm not your dear," she shot back, frustrated. "And you can just eat alone!"

"As you wish," he said and shrugged, taking a seat. "I should warn you, however, that nothing further will be forthcoming until morning."

Her eyes went longingly to the food. Knowing it foolish to go without her meal, she grudgingly took her place and spread her napkin in her lap. "I won't give you the pleasure of thinking me worsted," she said, picking up her knife and fork.

One quick glance at the captain was sufficient to send Sawyer scurrying about his business. Gathering the quilts and hammock in his arms, he beat a hasty retreat to the door. "Will that be all, Cap'n?" he asked, his eyes going from Charlie's bowed head to Mitford's face. At the brief nod of dismissal, he gasped a half-strangled good night and fled, leaving an uncomfortable silence behind him.

It was left to the captain to break it. "There was no need

92

for you to treat him ungraciously," he remarked. "You know as well as I that it was you who placed him in an untenable position."

She refused to raise her eyes. "You seem unconcerned about my own plight," she said, taking a sip of scalding tea.

"Ah, but yours is of your own making," he replied, his gaze seeking out the curves barely discernible beneath the fabric of his dressing gown. "You look charming in my robe, my dear, but a lady's charms were meant to be displayed."

"I imagine you fancy yourself a connoisseur," she shot back vindictively. "I am well aware that you, being a man, can scarcely be expected to appreciate the trap in which I find myself. In all truth it is little better than the one from which I fled. Well, sir, I am made of sterner stuff than some little ninnyhammer freshly emerged from the schoolroom. I shan't be terrorized by you into obeying your every whim."

"I am wholly uninterested in any latter claims on your part of schoolrooms and—but you have yet to assert that you had a nanny, haven't you? You will no doubt get around to it. God knows you have sedulously laid claim to just about everything else usually associated with the fashionable world."

Having no desire to trust to providence that his thoughts would not turn in the direction of her background, she was unable to refute this. Prudently abandoning the topic, she cast back to her original train of thought. "I accept—I could hardly deny it—that my masquerade has led you to suppose that any avowal of innocence on my part must be considered as false. Such is not the case. I beg of you—"

"Since the only entreaties I have thus far received from

93

you have been very much one-sided, I stand ready to collect your dues. Nothing in this world is free, my dear."

"What a wretched sop to offer your conscience!" she shot back trenchantly.

"My conscience doesn't need a sop. One would almost suppose that I suffered some malformation or possessed an ugly face. I'm not a repulsive fellow, you know."

"For some reason or other you seem to have formed an elevated opinion of yourself," she glared, perfectly willing to exhaust his passions in battle. "I cannot imagine why you should elect to squander so much masculine perfection on the likes of me."

Her ploy fell far short of the mark. "I'm damned if I know why, but you arouse me," he replied, chuckling. "It is much against my will and totally beyond my control."

"Oh!" she gasped, appalled. "Of all the insufferable—"

"Why the sudden propensity to talk, my dear?" he inquired, reading her mind with perfect ease. "Do you think to inflame me with such tactics? I need no kindling. Your face was fashioned by an angel and your body molded by a saint."

Outwardly she appeared calm, but the certainty of his intent threatened to bridge her last defenses. Tenaciously holding fast to the last waning vestige of control, she forced herself to convey a bite of ham to her mouth. Though it was quite tasty, she found that she could not swallow it. Raising her napkin to her lips, she surreptitiously transmitted it to the cloth, then unknowingly wadded the fabric into a ball.

"Enough of this," he said suddenly, and rose. "Come here, Charlie."

"No!" she retaliated, shaking her head. "Don't delude yourself into imagining that I will permit you to touch me."

"Still playing hard to get?" he asked. "Of all the strumpets that I have known, you carry off the palm. I will give you just thirty seconds to get out of that robe and into that bed."

"I have no intention of doing anything of the kind," she said, still contumacious. "You must be all about in your head."

"I am not a patient man, my dear," he informed her, the deadly calm in his voice more frightening than any show of temper could have been. "Aboard my ship you will be advised to do precisely as I say."

She should have felt daunted. She didn't. She couldn't afford the luxury. "Jump when you whistle, you mean," she commented. "Well, *Captain*, your crew may tremble at the mere lifting of your brow, but I will point out to you that I am under no compunction to obey you!"

To her chagrin, he threw back his head and laughed. "Perhaps you meant conscription," he said, chuckling.

"On the whole," she said with considerable acerbity, "I should think the better of you if you weren't so—so—"

"Intriguing?" he suggested, the devil in his smiling eyes.

"How enthralled with yourself you must be," she remarked with maddening affability. "No doubt your ego is at fault. When you recover from this latest hysterical seizure of yours, perhaps you will talk sense. Now I come to think of it, sailors are generally known to be a licentious lot, and although I don't set much store by pronouncements from the Admiralty, I do feel that it would not be unreasonable to expect you to remember that commanders in His Majesty's Navy are by tradition held to be not only officers but gentlemen."

She was quite unprepared for the blaze of fury that leaped

95

into his eyes. "I'll soon teach you a few traditions you won't easily forget," he bit off savagely.

Her mind went numb with shock, the full realization of her helplessness borne forcefully home to her at last. She was at his mercy utterly, without hope of reprieve. No man among the crew would dare to intervene. Shaking her head slowly, she watched him advance upon her menacingly and shrank back, the terror staring from her eyes. "No!" she breathed, her legs trembling so that she could barely stand.

He was on her in two strides. "An interesting game, my pet," he murmured, "but all such sport must end."

Laughing softly, he seized her shoulders with hands of steel and crammed her soft curves against the long, hard length of him. Enfolding her in his arms, he fastened his lips on hers in a stupefying kiss that went on and on, searing her to her very soul. She was too stunned to resist and slumped weakly against him, pliant in his arm~~~~

the answering resp~~~~

~~~~g his grasp of Charlie. "How far off is she,

~~~~five miles, Cap'n, and closing fast."

~~~~rd crushed Charlie in his arms for one last, quick

"Don't take one step from this cabin," he growled, releasing her. "Lock the door, and don't unlock it for anyone but me."

He was gone on the words, leaving her staring, tears stinging her eyelids. *Don't open it for anyone but him!* she thought hysterically. Sinking to the floor in a sobbing heap, she clutched her arms about her body and rocked back and forth, crying as if her heart would break. Only gradually she calmed. Wearily coming to her feet, she snatched his robe from the floor and once again swathed her nakedness in its voluminous folds, mortified to the very core.

CHAPTER 7

Mitford mounted the steps to the quarterdeck, plagued by the memory of Charlie soft and pliant in his arms. Her tender curves swam into his mind in a vision of gently cupping breasts and silken thighs. It was certain that she was of a different mold from others of her profession. She had all the guileless innocence of an untouched virgin. Before long he would take her, he knew, if not with gentle persuasion, then by force.

A chill breeze stirred against his cheeks as he trained his glass on the sails of a vessel coming down to windward on their starboard side. With him on the quarterdeck were Lieutenant Brompton, Sailing Master Joseph Allen, and his two aides, Midshipmen Robert Gulley and John William Alexander. Stationed in the fo'c'sle were the bosun, Mr. West, and Midshipman Robert Counts. All eyes were on the sleek craft slicing through the waves, her jib and staysails soaring smartly to the peak. "Lieutenant Brompton! Beat to quarters, if you please," Mitford said quietly. "Clear the decks for action."

"Aye, aye, sir," the lieutenant said and saluted, snapping to the order.

A moment later the ship's drummer tumbled on deck, and the staccato rat-tat-tat beat sent its quick summons down the hatchways to every space of the *Minotaur*. Purposefully and silently the hands rushed to their stations. Mitford nodded with approval as his sharpshooters checked their muskets and the swivel guns mounted in the tops, while others of the crew rove preventer lifts and slung the lower yards with chain.

"Secure against fire, Mr. Allen," he barked, then watched as the men made haste to slosh water where red-hot shot might rain and scattered wet sand over the decks. Up aloft nimble sailors emptied buckets of water hoisted from below over the sails to ward off fire kindled by any wayward spark, and fire hoses were run out along the decks.

Mitford's order of "Marines, to the tops and gangways!" sent the marksmen to position, eager to pick off key men of the opposing force stationed on the enemy's decks and aloft, while others of their number stationed themselves at the stubby carronades on quarterdeck and fo'c'sle.

Down below on the gun deck, Lieutenant Spear commanded the first division of guns, Lieutenant Carstairs the second; and Acting Lieutenant Keith had charge of those that were located in the stern of the ship. Cartouche boxes, leather cases filled with powder tubes, along with fitted gun locks, thirty-two-pound shot and grape were hauled up from the magazines and stacked ready to the gunners' hands. Lashings were cast off, the ports opened, preventer tackle and breechings were cleared away and the tampion plugs whipped out of the muzzles. Next the leaden aprons were cast off, while crowbars and handspikes, sponges and wads were got ready. When the guns were loaded well and cleared away for action, wet canvas was rolled along the lowest deck of the ship, sopping blankets were hung around each hatchway and the magazines were secured against fire with screens.

The ship's main hatches at last fastened down, Mitford ordered the midshipmen to their stations, well satisfied with the performance of the crew. For all the furious activity, only a few minutes had elapsed since the masthead lookout's call of danger had first echoed across the waters.

Mitford turned his undivided attention to the vessel looming ever larger in the waning light. "Gentlemen, war has been declared," he said, his glass on the scraps of cloth fluttering from her mizzenmast. "It's the American sloop *Wasp*, flying her battle flags. She cannot match us for speed even under foretopsail, jib and foretopmast staysail. She may elect to run for it."

"God grant the wind holds strong," Lieutenant Brompton remarked. "It will prevent her from lowering her boats to row away under cover of darkness."

"I hope you may be right," Mitford replied, glancing at the quartermaster standing at the wheel. "Keep her close to the wind, Mr. Croft, and steer a course north-nor'east."

"Aye, aye, sir," Croft sang out, giving the wheel a deft turn. "North-nor'east it is, sir."

"Captain Jones is a plucky devil," Mitford commented, a grin spreading across his face. "He thinks to pass to windward of us, rake us with a broadside and then lay across our bows to rake us anew. Stand by to yaw, Mr. Croft."

"Aye, sir," the quartermaster gasped, ready to put the helm down hard. "Sir, do you mean to run across her stern?"

"I mean to end the *Wasp*'s career in any way I can," Mitford replied, staring across the narrowing strip of water at the American vessel. "We'd be of little use in this war if we fail to defeat the enemy. The *Wasp* carries only twenty guns. She hopes for a lucky shot before we can bring our guns to bear. Buck up, Mr. Croft. We're in little danger."

"I'm not worried, sir," Croft stoutly maintained, his eyes glued to the compass.

"I wish to God I weren't," Mitford muttered under his breath as he strode to the quarterdeck railing. Snatching up his hand trumpet, he called to the men staring up at him, "Stand by to receive a raking from aft. Ready on the starboard battery. And good hunting, gentlemen."

A breathless hush fell upon the *Minotaur*, with only the rush of the bow wave to disturb the quiet. Below down the main hatch on the gun deck, black muzzles of the great eighteen pounders poked their snouts through fourteen ports on either side, their crews waiting to discharge a close, concerted fire.

Mitford narrowed his eyes against the rays of the setting sun, all his being strained toward anticipating the opposing vessel. "It seems she now means to avoid exchanging broadsides with us, cross our wake and rake us from astern," he said grimly. "Steady as she goes, Mr. Croft. Stand ready to luff."

The two vessels were by now separated by a scant fifty yards of water, but not by so much as the batting of an eye did any man on the quarterdeck display his perturbation. Mitford's voice barking orders shattered the tension, startling everyone within earshot. "Luff her, Mr. Croft! Starboard battery, fire when your guns bear!"

Croft instantly put the helm down, swinging the *Minotaur* into the wind. Too late the *Wasp* fathomed the maneuver. She yawed to come about, intending to set a course at right angles before the *Minotaur*, the better to rake her bow. It was a movement well taken, but her mainmast came abreast of the *Minotaur*'s mizzen and the latter's guns roared, sending shot crashing through the *Wasp*'s quarterdeck and into the sea beyond, wounding the quartermaster and leaving a shattered wheel in its wake.

"Hard to larboard, Mr. Crofts!" Mitford snapped. "After quarterdeck carronade, fire at will!"

The deafening reverberation of the shot echoed across the water, mingling with the roar of answering fire from a staggered *Wasp* swinging slowly up into the wind and totally out of control to starboard. As for the *Minotaur*, a shot had plowed through the second main deck gun, shattering the breechings and wounding the crew, while up above other shot wreaked havoc with the rails and bulwarks, sending sharp wood splinters flying around the decks with the speed of musket fire and dropping men where they stood. Choking smoke swirled along the decks, shrouding both vessels. When the smoke cleared, the stretch of water separating the two ships had widened considerably, making it impossible for either of them to bring their guns to bear.

The brief battle obviously at an end, Mitford turned his back on the American vessel. "Put the helm up," he ordered the quartermaster, then stood waiting until the *Minotaur* began a sluggish turn away from the stern of the drifting *Wasp*. Mitford frowned. "Have we a problem, Mr. Croft?" he said.

"The rudder is slow to respond, sir. It must have sustained a hit."

"Lieutenant Brompton, discover the extent of the damage and set the men to repairing it. Drive them hard, if need be. We must be well away before Jones succeeds in replacing his wheel. Otherwise we could become a sitting duck."

Chief Warrant Officer Cranston had slumped down on the spar-deck booms and was staring at the officers on the quarterdeck above when their voices drifted down to him. How can they remain so calm, he wondered, still trembling with terror in the aftermath of his first taste of battle. Though his hands shook, he managed to extricate his watch from a pocket. As near as he could ascertain, only two minutes had elapsed from the time the first gun had fired on board the *Minotaur* until the moment the captain had ordered the helm put up.

"Mr. Cranston!" Mitford's voice barked, bringing him to his feet. "Clear away the debris from the decks and direct your carpenters to repair the rails and bulwarks, if you please. Where is Lieutenant Cook?"

"Forward hoisting the jib, sir."

"Send him to me on the double."

Lieutenant Cook was a gentleman of experience and great good sense who needed few orders from his captain to know what was expected of him. By the time Mr. Cranston relayed Mitford's request to him, the splintered jib pole had been removed and its replacement was being lashed in place. With a few last minute instructions to the men, he struggled to the quarterdeck along planking made slippery with the blood of the wounded, his arrival coinciding with that of Lieutenant Brompton returning to report that the rudder was beyond permanent repair.

"We must return to Plymouth, gentlemen," Mitford said. "I shouldn't think that more than a few days would be required to replace the rudder. Lower the boats and run out the ropes, Lieutenant Cook. We will be able to assist the oarsmen with sail, but it will be up to them to keep us on course. Kedge if need be, but hold us steady. Fortunately the wind is light."

And so the long night began. At times the breeze died down altogether and the men toiling at the oars were forced to haul the *Minotaur* along by sheer muscle power; at other times the wind sprang up strong enough to move the ship ahead of the boats and the crew was forced to trim sail.

Down in the dark space of the orlop, which formed the quarters for the junior officers, where the ship's surgeon toiled over the wounded with knives and probes and saws, no one knew what was transpiring above or had the desire to speculate. Least of all did Charlie. From shortly after Sawyer had returned her clothing until the present, she had been by the doctor's side, performing any task he asked of her while forcing down the gorge rising in her throat. The sounds of the crew clearing the decks for action had been perfectly audible in the captain's cabin, and the resultant suspense had left her more than a trifle anxious. Sawyer had had little time to bestow on her. He would advise her to dress, just in case. Defeat and capture? Why borrow trouble. She would do much better to find something to occupy her mind.

It had proven to be sage advice. The calm authority prevailing in the surgery convinced her that all would be well, and she was able to assist the doctor with a fairly steady hand. Flinching at the sound, she stuffed a gag into a screaming man's mouth and held a basin of clear water ready to the surgeon's hand, only thankful that no additional wounded had been brought below. When the last of them had been administered to and she was free to return to the captain's cabin, it was about half past two in the night watch. Pausing only to wash her face and hands, she sprawled across the bed, her body too weary to control her mind and her mind too numb for worry.

Throughout the endless hours until dawn Mitford paced the quarterdeck, anxious lest the lookout's call of "Sail, ho!" float down from aloft with the coming of first light. Though lanterns had been doused and conversation forbidden for fear that the sound would carry for miles across the water, there was no reason to suppose that the determined Captain Jones would fail to discern their intent. It was only in the time involved in replacing his wheel that he could come up wanting.

With the first glow of light in the eastern sky, Mitford put his glass to his eye and swept the horizon all around. "Our luck holds," he said quietly to Lieutenant Brompton standing by his side. "Jones will know we are stationed out of Plymouth. Either he is unable to make chase or he has assumed that we are making for the dry dock at Southampton. Even at this snail's pace we should reach port within the next thirty-six hours. I shouldn't think we will come across another American ship. They have too few to risk losing them unnecessarily on patrols so close to our shores. I suspect the *Wasp* was en route home from France when she hailed another vessel and learned that war had been declared."

"You wily old sea dog," Lieutenant Brompton said with a grin. "Any sensible man would assume we are bound for Southampton."

"My dear Charles, the unexpected often proves the advantageous course to follow," Mitford remarked, his thoughts veering unaccountably to Charlie's tender curves.

The lieutenant cast a worried look at his face. "I feel certain that you are the only man aboard who has not found an opportunity to rest," he said. "Go below, Richard. I will send for you if the need arises."

Nothing loath, Mitford went. As he was making his way toward the short flight of steps leading to his companionway, the ship's surgeon called to him and came hurrying forward. "Sir, that young nephew of yours is a likely lad," he said, beaming. "I don't know what I would have done without him after my mate was injured. I thought you would like to know."

Mitford stared at him, thunderstruck. "Are you saying that he assisted you in the surgery?" he demanded, his face grim.

"Aye, he did, sir, and right stout he was about it. Most youngsters his age would never have stood up to it. Most of the time I can scarcely stomach it myself."

Mitford clamped a firm rein on his temper, returned a civil reply and strode to his cabin, thoroughly intending to give Charlie a dressing down. Slamming the door behind him with unnecessary force, he cast his hat upon a chair and ran a furious eye over the cabin. Discovering her curled in sleep with her hands tucked beneath her chin, the thought crossed his mind that she looked like a child, and extremely vulnerable. The lines of fatigue still creasing her brow touched a chord, banishing the anger from his heart. Pausing only to remove his boots and shrug out of his coat, he rolled her over to the back side of the bed and stretched out beside her, asleep almost the instant his head touched the pillow.

The sun rode high at noon when Charlie first roused and then woke on a long sigh. Disoriented for a moment, it required only an instant's reflection to realize whose arm was flung intimately about her waist. She stirred and sought to slip from the unwelcome restraint, but at the first slight movement he uttered something unintelligible and tightened his hold about her. She could feel the warm length of him curled against her back and lay perfectly still, feigning slumber.

All to no avail. His chuckle sounded in her ear, and he moved his head to plant a light kiss on her throat, which, as her face was turned away from him, was the only place available to him. "Good morning, pet," he had the audacity to murmur. "What a pleasant way to start the day."

Charlie turned her head and stared at him, speechless, her eyes wide and filled with foreboding. She tried to smile archly to mask her intent. She had a part to play and only hoped she would not boggle it. "La, sir," she said airily enough, "would you take me fully clothed?"

The smile was wiped from his face. "What the devil," he ejaculated, drawing back and thereby loosing his hold on her.

It was the opening she had prayed for. Flying from the bed, she darted across the cabin and took refuge behind his desk. To her utter relief he made no move to rise; instead he folded his arms behind his head and crossed his feet at the ankles. "You will listen to me!" she said, grasping the back of the chair until the knuckles of both hands showed white.

A hateful smile curved his lips. "I will do just about

108

anything you ask," he said. "I will even argue with you if it will earn me your good opinion."

"You flatter yourself!" she shot back. "Nothing could do that!"

He chuckled. "Do you mean to pick a quarrel with me?" he said. "I trust not."

"You are the oddest creature!" she exclaimed. "You cannot expect to convince me that you have developed a tender feeling for me!"

He got to his feet. "You want me to pretend affection," he remarked, advancing on her. "Very well, my dear. If it pleases you, I will utter all the customary phrases."

"Don't you come any nearer!" she exclaimed, a note of hysteria creeping into her voice. "If you do, I'll—I'll fling myself overboard."

The desperation in her voice gave him pause. "Have you been so repulsed by my kisses that you would go to any lengths to avoid them?" he said.

"It appears I would," she replied, sitting down hard in a chair. "I had never been kissed before, you see. Disbelieve me if you must. I no longer care."

He studied her keenly, the light dawning in his eyes. "This puts rather a different complexion on my thinking," he said, taking a seat facing her. "What in God's name have you been about, cavorting through the countryside like the veriest hoyden?"

She could not forgo to gloat. "Then you realize I'm not a strumpet?" she said somewhat mockingly.

"I will have the entire story, if you please," he said, frowning. "We will start with your name."

She was silent for a moment, considering the implacable expression in his eyes. The moment to reveal her identity had arrived, she knew. Lowering her gaze to the floor, she said softly, "It is Anne Fitzhugh. You may have heard of my father, Lord Thomas Fitzhugh."

"The devil you say!" he ejaculated, dumbfounded.

"You needn't sound so surprised," she said, stung. "I hid my identity because I could think of no other way to avoid marriage with Sir Randolph Ashmore. Yes, you may well stare. That was the fate my guardian had in store for me."

"No guardian worth his salt would give a respectable female to Ashmore," he objected, incredulous.

"Mine would," she replied, disputing him.

"Who is he?" he demanded grimly.

"Lord Adam Wroxly, but I am sure my papa would have named someone more responsible had he lived. But he died quite young and could not have anticipated that Lord Wroxly would become so completely self-serving with advancing age. Not that he was ever other than indifferent," she hastened to add.

"You are beyond belief," he said with conviction. "Why didn't you turn to some relative for succor?"

"I have no relatives," she replied, a challenging gleam coming into her eyes. "And besides, I did not expect to become entangled with—anyone."

"Out of the frying pan into the fire, are you?" he said coldly.

She was silent for a moment, aware that his eyes had not wavered from her face. Taking a deep breath, she said, "I know you think me silly, but"—she colored painfully—"I am not usually so unwise. It did not occur to me that—that I might jeopardize my reputation. I thought that no one need ever know." She paused, waiting for some comment from him. When it became apparent he intended saying nothing, she continued. "I thought—no, I—I didn't think. I see that now."

A swift smile lit his eyes. "What, dare you admit to some slight flaw?" he said.

"It is no use to talk to me like that!" she exclaimed, firing up. "I'm not important enough to be gossiped about."

"Of course you would think that," he shot back, no longer amused. "For all you believe yourself capable of looking to your welfare, you are a babe in the woods. If word of this escapade becomes known, no one will think you are above reproach."

"But there is no way it can become known," she protested, looking startled.

He gave a derisive laugh. "Don't you realize that everyone aboard this ship knows you have been alone with me for days? What if one of them recognizes you in skirt?"

"I look very different, I assure you."

"With short hair?" he questioned grimly. "Whatever possessed you to cut it?"

"I have always worn it short. The woman who reared me—"

"Who was she?" he demanded, interrupting her.

"One of Papa's tenants, if you must know," she replied trenchantly. "She found it easier to keep when short. I more or less—fell into the habit."

"It's all of a piece," he muttered, springing to his feet. "I will be forced to keep you under lock and key until it has grown to its proper length."

"How I choose to wear my hair is none of your business," she said, a challenging gleam in her eye.

Turning on his heel, he began to pace about the room. "Since you will shortly become Lady Mitford, it is very much my business," he informed her tartly from over his shoulder.

She gasped and grasped the arms of her chair, unable to believe her ears. "He must be mad!" she murmured to herself, but unknowingly speaking her thoughts aloud.

He gave no indication of having heard. "I flatter myself that you will find the idea of marriage with me somewhat less abhorrent than marriage with Ashmore," he said impatiently.

She could only stare, bereft of speech.

He raised his brows. "Have you nothing to say?" he said.

Her hands fluttered helplessly. "Yes! No!" she stammered, blinking at him. "Yes, I mean I have something to say. No, I won't marry you."

"Oh, yes, you will!" he contradicted her highhandedly. "You have shared my bed and board, however unwillingly. Society shan't label me a rogue!"

"No one could possibly know I sh—shared—"

"Ah, but I would. You must have a poor opinion of me."

She rose and crossed to the observation window that stretched across the rear wall of the cabin. "I am flattered, my lord, but you must have a poor opinion of me if you think that I would accept your offer," she said, showing him her back.

A muscle twitched in his cheek. "We dock at Plymouth sometime early this evening," he said. "Tomorrow morning we will go ashore and search out a priest."

She turned her head to glance at him. "That isn't necessary," she said. "You aren't in love with me."

"Of course I'm not in love with you," he flung at her. "What has that to say to anything?"

"A good deal!" she retorted with a fine show of spirit. "I

didn't dream it would come to this. I thought I need only evade the clutches of Sir Randolph and I could travel back home, with only my clergyman the wiser. I know that it was a foolish thing to do, but I was desperate."

He came up to her and stood scowling down at her. "Of all the cork-brained, ill-judged escapades," he said crushingly, "I have never heard of any to equal yours."

"To own the truth," she admitted frankly, "nor have I. Do credit me with enough sense not to precipitate a scandal. And don't tell me that one can only be averted by my marrying you."

"I don't intend cutting you adrift. A pretty figure I should cut! If there is any virtue in you at all, you will cease to raise objections. They won't serve, so forget them."

Her brain was nothing if not fertile. I will pretend to fall in with his plans, she thought, and then, when I am safely ashore, I will vanish among the press of pedestrians thronging the streets of Plymouth. Accordingly she said, "I will marry you; but not, let me tell you, in any clandestine fashion. We will have a proper wedding—if your father approves, that is."

"It's no use clutching at straws," he said and chuckled, amused suddenly. "My father ordered me to form an attachment to some eligible female before the year is out. It may as well be you."

CHAPTER 8

She had expected to spend a restful night, the *Minotaur* having dropped anchor at Plymouth, but though the ship had ceased its rolling and was, in fact, almost motionless, she found difficulty in composing herself for slumber. Mitford's handsome countenance continually obtruded in her thoughts. Never mind her own extremely reprehensible conduct; his had been anything rather than that of a paragon. He was full of self-consequence, she thought, and though he accused her of impropriety, an accusation which she had to admit was not precisely unjust, still nothing had occurred that should lead him to suppose that they must enter into a marriage contract. His whole concept of honor bordered on the ludicrous. She began, eventually, to consider her future, but in the middle of an involved procedure designed to lull him into assuming her amenable, she fell asleep.

She partook of tea and toast next morning, her mind

having rebelled at thoughts of a more substantial meal. When Sawyer returned to clear away the remains of the light repast, he informed her, not without the trace of a tremor in his voice, that the cap'n awaited her arrival on the quarterdeck. She'd best not tarry. His Lordship was in a naggy temper.

From the circumstance of knowing that she had displaced him from his bed, and fancying that he had passed a restless night in a hammock strung in some unlikely place, this last remark did little to soothe her frayed nerves. Eyeing Sawyer thoughtfully, she wondered if he could be induced to claim Mitford's attention while she slipped away. Probably not, she decided. He appeared frightened, a development that gave her pause. But even supposing she could somehow secure his cooperation, could she quit the ship unchallenged? With no notion of the customs obtaining aboard a warship, she could only reason that it would at best be risky. It did not take her long to conclude that she could not expect to disembark unnoticed with so many of the crew about. There was nothing for it but to put on a brave face and brazen it out. Taking a deep breath to steady herself, she went out into the companionway and up the short flight of steps to the main deck.

Mitford was standing with his back to her, but even so she knew an angry flush suffused his cheeks. It was evident in the very stiffness of his stance and in the way he was gazing straight ahead. Her heart beating so it felt as if it would burst, she swallowed convulsively and climbed to the quarterdeck.

"There is an inn nearby on the waterfront," he said shortly, turning his head to fix her with a level stare. "You will wait there while I purchase a gown for you."

A slight quiver ran down her spine as she glanced at him. Hampering skirts were the last thing she wanted when she fled. It would be easier to evade him in boy's trousers. "I am content as I am," she said persuasively. "I shouldn't like to put you to the expense."

He gave a slight gesture of dismissal. "No priest would wed a grown man to a fledgling youth," he informed her scornfully. "You have no cause to worry. The dress will fit. I am perfectly capable of estimating your size."

Yes, you no doubt are, she thought snidely while eyeing him covertly, breathless lest he divine her plans. "As you wish," she murmured, her gaze falling from his.

"You will walk close beside me," he said abruptly. "It is none too savory a neighborhood. Keep your eyes cast down and do not speak. I have no desire to be set upon by the first white slaver who recognizes the feminine timbre of your voice."

The pink rushed into her cheeks as she nodded mutely and turned to follow him across the deck. Sawyer stood waiting to offer her a hand, but, at a frown from Mitford, stepped back, leaving her to climb down unassisted to the ship's gig. She could not help but think that the sailors cast covert glances their way as they pushed off and rowed toward shore, but Mitford seemed wholly engrossed in the approaching wharf and oblivious to them.

Thinking that they could not fail to pique the curiosity of every passerby, she trudged beside Mitford toward the inn, followed a few steps behind by a glowering Sawyer, who continually looked around suspiciously for would-be thieves and cutthroats.

At a late hour of the night it would be foolhardy to walk the waterfront streets of any port, but in the bright light of day the area appeared more squalid than sinister. The inn was situated midway down a narrow side street in which half a dozen skimpily clad urchins were playing a game resembling skittles. Mitford picked his way among them and crossed the threshold without a backward glance.

Though the taproom was already crowded, the landlord came bustling forward the instant they entered his establishment. His Lordship was no doubt master of the frigate hove to in the harbor? He beamed, eyeing Mitford's uniform in some surprise. How could he serve them? But of a certainty he could provide a chamber. If his lordship would but enjoy a mug of ale or perchance a glass of wine, he would see to it that the room was set to rights and a fire lit in the grate. Mitford nodded to Sawyer and proceeded, with Charlie in his wake, to a table in the corner, while Sawyer followed their host upstairs to inspect the accommodation.

They attracted no little attention, and many were the curious glances sent their way by the waterfront hangers-on lounging around the room. Mitford seemed not to notice, but Charlie soon became only too aware of low whispers and hastily averted eyes. Though she would have preferred the bracing effects of a glass of wine, she said nothing when Mitford ordered tea. She didn't dare. His lips were clamped together, and a muscle twitched in his cheek. In fear lest she say something to irritate him further, she folded her hands in her lap and tried not to draw his ire.

With a start she realized that he had spoken. "That is a very feminine gesture, let me tell you," he repeated softly, his eyes dropping to her fingers. "It is not wise to titillate these men."

Charlie glanced around surreptitiously and concluded that he could just be right. One or two who appeared to be common seamen were frankly staring. Propping her elbows on the table, she hunched her shoulders in a very fair imitation of a surly and recalcitrant youth. Mitford leaned back in his chair, his lowered eyelids veiling the appreciative gleam in his eye, and fished his snuffbox from a pocket. "You are a never-ending source of amazement," he remarked, taking a pinch between thumb and finger.

She would have liked to utter some clever reply, but try as she would she could not put words to her tongue. Not that it mattered. He seemed perfectly relaxed, but to her the time seemed to drag before the landlord reappeared to show them to their room. She fully expected Mitford to excuse himself at the door, but he followed her inside and cast a contemptuous glance around. "If you are harboring fears," he said, "calm them. I shan't be long, and Sawyer will be just downstairs."

She looked at him in some surprise, then shrugged to mask the consternation his words had brought. "As you wish," she said, turning away. Sending Sawyer about his business by the simple expedient of some ruse should present no problem.

Mitford strode to the door. "I am not so culpable as to expect Sawyer to resist your machinations," he said, reading her mind. "It is just that I would not leave you unprotected in such a place as this."

Damn the man! she thought. From the beginning she had suspected that he could read her mind when he chose, but why in the name of all that was holy must he choose this present? Then he was gone, and she sank into a chair to await the passage of time. A good fifteen minutes should see him well away, she determined. As for Sawyer, well, the good captain had a lot to learn about her if he thought to sell her short. Unable to sit still, she jumped to her feet and began to pace about, fetching up at the window. When she attempted to raise the sash, it proved to be nailed shut and, since it overlooked a rabbit hutch at the rear of the inn, offered little in the way of diversion. Each minute that passed seemed interminable, but she remained resolute. By the time she deemed it safe to leave, she could not regard her flight with anything other than a feeling of profound depression.

After peeking around the door to ascertain that the way was clear, she crept out into the hall and down the stairs. After finding herself nervously listening for sounds from below and continually pausing at the first faint creak of a tread, she gave herself a mental shake. This will not do, she decided. She would go on much better to step boldly forth. A stealthy flight savored very much of fright.

Arrived at the floor below, she caught a glimpse of the common room and had an impulse to go back upstairs but checked it. Going forward soft-footed and every moment fearing to be apprehended, she therefore experienced no great surprise when Sawyer stepped from the taproom and took up a stance before her, blocking her way. "Cap'n said you aren't to go out," he muttered, very red of face.

She stayed still, weighing her chances. Always reasonable, she could appreciate Sawyer's dilemma. Left to his own devices, he would undoubtedly let her pass. Wondering with a kind of detached interest just what Mitford's orders had been, she assessed her quarry. "I merely seek a breath of air," she said imploringly. "The window of my room has been permanently fastened down."

"Cap'n said you're to stay upstairs," he replied, discomfited but standing firm. He had no idea what had prompted

120

His Lordship to order her locked in her room if she should attempt to leave. A cantankerous female was not a thing to fool with. They never realized the damage they could do. But if the cap'n wanted her at the inn, at the inn she would be. He knew when to fear His Lordship's rage.

Charlie found no difficulty at all in reading the emotions flitting across his face. If she had the courage she would scream and fight in an effort to break free. She shrank from the thought, visualizing the scene. The landlord might find it in his heart to side with her, but the rough-looking men in the taproom would only crowd into the hall, sniggering witnesses to it all. Turning on her heel, she flounced back upstairs, followed closely by Sawyer, his expression one of dogged determination. She heard his murmured apology and the click of the door as it shut behind her, but she was halfway across the room before the grate of a key turning in the lock reached her incredulous ears.

Trapped, she sank into a chair. She had been so sure that she would win the day that her vulnerability fretted her unbearably. She wished she could convince herself that some means would yet arise that would prevent her marriage to Mitford, but having by now acquired a very fair knowledge of his temperament, she could not be convinced. Feeling, however, that she would need her wits about her regardless of the outcome, she tried not to allow the natural anxiety she was experiencing to overset her composure.

It seemed an eternity had passed when she heard Mitford's footsteps on the stairs, followed almost immediately by the sound of the key turning in the lock. With a strangled sob she started to her feet, the color draining from her face. Backing away, she fetched up with her back against a wall just as the door opened and he walked into the room. "You would try," he remarked, dropping a parcel on the bed.

"If an opportunity to escape from you presents itself, you may be sure I will take advantage of it!" she replied heatedly, the color coming back into her face.

"Then I will be advised not to let you out of my sight," he said. "The time grows short, my dear. You'd best dress."

"You can't think that I will dress in front of you!" she gasped, blushing hotly.

"I have some little experience of a lady's toilet," he said, and chuckled, crossing to the window to stand with his back to her. "If I can be of service, you need only let me know."

She almost panicked. "Please, I beg of you," she cried, fighting down the hysteria. "I would die of shame!"

He turned his head and smiled at her. "I applaud your modesty," he began, his eyes sweeping her in a way that sent her heart into her throat, "but you lack the strength to oppose me, should I decide to dress you myself. Would it not serve you better to trust me not to peek?"

She gazed at him despairingly. "Then you wouldn't?" she choked. "Peek, I mean."

"Have I not said so?" he replied, once again turning his back to her.

Every fiber of her being rebelled. What cruel sport would he visit on her next? She was boxed in, toyed with as surely as a cat would toy with a mouse. And after they were married, what then? Did he expect her to submit? He would soon see an end to such nonsense.

But that was for the future. To be forced to dress in the company of a man, albeit his back toward her, was the worst fate that could befall any respectable female and must be gotten over quickly. Her first impetuous impulse to defy him having sensibly abated, she snatched the parcel from the bed and retreated to partial privacy behind a chair. In addition to a gown with a modest decolleté, he had included a pair of slippers and filmy undergarments. Her cheeks flaming at the intimate nature of the purchase, she draped her coat over the chair and warily removed her shirt. Tears stung her eyelids; she forced them back and cast a worried look Mitford's way to be sure that he kept his back to her. How could she have imagined—it seemed a long time ago now—that she could prevail. The very idea of marriage without love must be repugnant to her, but she had too much pride to beg. She would not give him the satisfaction. Her fingers shook, and she experienced difficulty with the buttons of the gown, but at last she contrived.

The rustle of silk as she moved from behind the chair brought his head around. Of palest rose and made up at the neckline with a double ruff of pointed lace, the bodice of the dress emphasized her rounded bosom with a narrow ribbon drawn through lace inset beneath her breasts. His eyes darkened as they ran over her and came to rest on her face. Suddenly she felt discomposed; her legs began to tremble and the breath caught in her throat. Long seconds dragged past. Mitford stood as if rooted to the spot, his gaze locked with hers. She could not seem to tear her eyes away. Then the hiss of a log expiring on the hearth among its fellows shattered the spell, and he strode across the room to offer her his arm. "It is time," he murmured gently, a softened expression on his face.

Desperately she fought for calm; weighing the implications of the glint smoldering in his eyes a moment since, she dared not respond to his first tenderness. Her color deepening, she tried to brush past him, but he caught her hand in his and placed it within the crook of his arm.

Turning toward the door, he led her from the room and down the stairs to a carriage waiting out front. It was luxuriously upholstered, and there was a fur rug lying on the seat. Mitford handed her in and spread it over her knees before taking his place beside her.

She had never before ridden in a chaise so well sprung. Even over the cobbled streets she was not conscious of any particular discomfort. The quivering alarm that had possessed her from the moment they left the inn began to subside, and she felt that she would be able to face the coming ceremony with tolerable composure. Despite shrinking from the very thought of marriage, she nevertheless could not help but feel a paradoxical relief when the carriage drew to a halt before a church. Better to face the future with her chin held high than to cavil at it, she thought, allowing Mitford to catch her around the waist and swing her lightly down. Annoyed to find that she enjoyed the momentary sensation of protected helplessness, she jerked away from his restraining hand and went inside, a trifle pale but composed.

To her utter surprise Lieutenant Brompton stood waiting just within the sanctuary. His eyes widening, he smiled and carried her fingers to his lips, somewhat overcome by the vision she presented. Hearing the door shut behind her with unnecessary force, she turned.

Mitford had cast down his hat and gloves and was observing the tableau, a black scowl upon his brow. "Very effecting, Charles," he growled, striding up to her and seizing her wrist in a painful grasp. "If you have quite finished, we will proceed with the ceremony."

But Lieutenant Brompton only laughed. "If you must wed a beauty," he said, "you'd best accept it. You can't blame a man for looking. It's seldom enough he chances upon a pretty sight."

Mitford was looking at Charlie with an oddly prideful smile lifting the corners of his mouth. "You'll forgive my temper," he said, his anger rapidly abating. "I suppose the truth is that we all feel a trifle strained."

Lieutenant Brompton, feeling that the situation called for action, clapped Mitford on the back. "Run along to your place beside the priest," he said with a grin, turning to pick up a nosegay of flowers from a table beside the door. "It is my privilege to escort Lady Anne down the aisle."

Charlie's hands were no longer quite steady, but she accepted the floral tribute with a smile and buried her face in the fragrant blossoms. Going forward on Brompton's arm, she was certain the poundings of her heart must be clearly audible in the hushed quiet of the church. The long length traversed and her mind in a whirl, she was only dimly aware of Mitford waiting with the vicar before an altar banked with flowers. Later she would recall the beauty of the scene and her heart would go out to him for his thoughtfulness, but for the present she could only kneel by Mitford's side to repeat her marriage vows.

The ceremony concluded, he assisted her to her feet and took her in his arms, his face swimming before her eyes an instant before he lightly pressed his lips to hers. Releasing her, he caught her hands in his and held them a moment, his gaze on the plain gold band encircling the third finger of her left hand. Her face delicately tinged with color, she responded prettily to the clergyman's rather effusive accolade, found herself laughing gaily at Lieutenant Brompton's blandishments and lifted shy eyes to Mitford's face when he placed an arm about her waist. Then, at last, with the lieutenant's final plaudits ringing in her ears, she was alone with Mitford, breathing the sweet fragrance of the roses rioting gloriously beside the altar. She could not bring herself to look at him, but she knew that his eyes never wavered from her face. He made no movement to take her in his arms or to recapture her hands, but she somehow divined that he was perilously close to doing so.

The next move was up to her, she knew. "Thank you for a lovely wedding," she said softly, moving up the aisle.

"It was not what I would wish for you," he replied, placing a hand beneath her elbow to escort her from the church. "I will send you to my father in London. When I return from this voyage, we will have a proper ceremony attended by all society."

She gazed down at her wedding band, struck by a sudden thought. "Are you saying that we aren't really married?" she murmured huskily.

"Of course we're married," he replied, a look of amusement creeping into his eyes. "I obtained a special license immediately I left you at the inn."

"But how could we wed a second time?" she asked, alarmed. "What would people say?"

"They could be told that our love is such that we wish to share it with the world," he suggested in a caressing tone that sent a quiver down her spine.

And so it has begun, she thought. "Since ours is a marriage of—of convenience, our—emotions cannot be said to enter into it," she managed to say.

He did not reply until he had handed her into the carriage and resumed his seat beside her. "You no doubt speak of your own emotions," he said then, leaning back in his corner. "Mine lie along somewhat different lines."

She gasped. "You have no right to—to assume—" Appalled, she ground to a halt.

She thought his lips seemed to sneer. "My dear," he drawled, "you have provided me with whatever rights I choose to claim."

She became very still, not so much folding her hands in her lap as gripping them together tightly. There he lounged, completely at ease, his long legs stretched out before him, while she sat bolt upright, her back erect and stiff, a decidedly uncomfortable posture. It was enough to make one's blood boil. "You are talking wildly," she said coldly. "I know you despise the thought of marriage—"

"Why do I despise the thought?" he interrupted lazily.

"Oh!" she stormed, the strain fanning the flame of her passion. "Must you hold me in disdain?"

A strange expression crossed his face, but he regarded her passively and for the remainder of the return trip to the inn sat silent and pensive. When they drew to a halt before the door, she expected him to step down; but he turned in the seat facing her. "We will sheathe our swords," he said after a moment. "I will guard my tongue, and you will not act as if I have the plague. Neither of us is experienced of matrimony, but we should contrive to deal well enough together if we try. Agreed?"

Nodding mutely, she picked up her bouquet from the seat opposite and prepared to descend. No, she thought, staying the slight movement. Silence would never do. She was sketching him a remarkably poor notion of her character. For a breathless moment before the altar, when he had placed his arm about her waist, she had had a brief glimpse of what a strong man's love could mean. Shocked, she realized that her ill-considered remarks were due to the lack of it, a conceit in itself in view of the fact that she neither wished for, nor sought, affection. There was nothing for it. She must beg his pardon. "I find little to admire in my conduct," she said, the utterance sticking in her throat. "Indeed, sir, I am sorry."

"Don't apologize," he replied. Then as if, in his turn, the words were dragged from him with great difficulty, he added, "I am equally at fault. In future we will behave toward one another in a more civilized manner."

"I know of no reason we should not," she agreed, if a little stiffly. "But as for sending me to your father, I much prefer my own father's home."

"No doubt you do," he said. "I must inform you, however, I have not the least intention of permitting you to go there yet awhile."

"I don't understand why you should take that tack," she said, put out. Just when she had been in a fair way to acknowledging herself warming toward him, why must he anger her again? "For some reason I cannot fathom, you seem reluctant to quit yourself of the responsibility of me. In the circumstances, I wish to know what the reason is."

"At the moment," he replied suavely, "I much fear that I cannot call it to mind."

CHAPTER 9

A burst of raucous laughter greeted them as Mitford opened
the door of the inn and stepped back for Charlie to precede
him. The knowledge that they had returned to find a bawdy
revelry in progress could scarcely afford him gratification,
but from having spent the greater part of his adult life at sea
and from having witnessed the return of drunken seamen
following a leave ashore, he ruefully accepted the sailors'
desire to take their pleasure where they found it. As for
Charlie, he had rather have had her otherwhere. Waterfront
harlots could only disgust her, and although there would be
no question of her being witness to the spectacle, from
Sawyer having positioned himself in the open threshold to
help block the scene from view, he must expect at least a
part of the ribald humor to penetrate upstairs. She might not
be expected to understand all she overheard, but some of it
must be intelligible. It was an awkward business, and while
it might be singular that he should so expose her sensibili-

ties, at this present there really was nothing he could do about it. A respectable establishment would be certain to harbor acquaintances, the very thing he wished to avoid. She knew nothing of the fashionable world and had no one other than himself to present her to the *ton*. There was no considering sending her to London. A period of seclusion on his father's estate should see her hair grown long; only then, and suitably gowned as befitted her station, would she make her bow to society. There was nothing to do but place his hand beneath her elbow and lead her to the stairs, her body shielded from sight by his.

Relieved to have traversed the hall unnoticed by any curious roisterer, she ascended to the floor above very well pleased with Mitford. He had a protective air; the thoughtfulness he had shown in arranging their nuptial tie, the delicacy with which he had screened her from sight of the common room, all combined to impress her in his favor. She would in some measure be sorry to see the last of him. He had proven to be a rather decent person. She owed herself much beholden to him and would have been glad to have made his acquaintance under more fortunate circumstances, but was more immediately concerned with the means of quitting his vicinity.

She had no idea why he had remained below, nor what the orders were to which Sawyer had listened so attentively; should he not return immediately to his ship, she would be at a disadvantage and would have to find a way around it. Transport must be her first concern. A private conveyance was out of the question; to walk, unthinkable. Passage money for the stage must somehow be found. She would dine at once in her room, an unfashionable hour to be sure, but the food should sustain her on the journey north. It was now close upon five o'clock. At dusk she would slip away, dressed in her boy's clothing, only one more urchin among the many. Selling one's wedding dress was not a thing one cared to contemplate, but there was no coming by the stagecoach fare in any other way.

She was aroused from these musings by Mitford's unceremonious entry into the room. "Sawyer has gone to fetch those members of the crew not occupied in repairing the damage to the *Minotaur*," he said, casting down his hat and gloves on a table standing in a corner. "I have sent for a coach to bear you to Afton Hall, but it cannot possibly arrive before tomorrow noon. My men will be below to protect you, but I would prefer that you not leave the room."

"Afton Hall?" she murmured, startled.

"My father's estate near Bath. You will bide there until my return from sea. Fortunately my father has a sister who will undertake the dressing of you."

A vision of a straitlaced grande dame most forcibly struck her mind's eye. Clearly Mitford was a gentleman to be reckoned with. Thinking it of little moment since she would be residing far from Afton Hall, she nodded with a meek acceptance that concealed her inward glee.

"To ensure that you not find yourself ostracized by the *ton,* you will allow your hair to grow. My aunt has the undoubted entrée to the world I wish you to figure in and will be charmed to advise you when the time comes for you to take your place beside me. You will put yourself unreservedly in her hands. She may strike you as somewhat foolish, but for all that she fairly reeks of worldly wisdom."

"You are extremely obliging," she said, goaded, "but I prefer to see to my own affairs."

"Certainly," he said suavely, then added with the glimmer of a smile, "I will instruct my man of business that you choose to remain sequestered on the estate. No doubt you enjoy the solitary life."

She bit her lip but replied with dignity, "You are become a tyrant, sir."

He lowered his steel—or so it seemed to her. "There is one other matter," he said, his smile gleaming again. "You are far too lovely in skirts to put them aside for breeches."

"I didn't mean—you know very well—" She choked and ground to a halt, unaccountably flustered. It was evident that their conversation was fruitless and was leading nowhere. She suspected that further protests could well bring Mitford to the conclusion that the wedding ceremony had not altered her decision to flee one whit. If that were so, she would be advised to quell her tongue.

"There is no need for us to go downstairs," he remarked, staring at her meditatively. "In fact, it would be most unwise. We will dine here in our room."

In spite of her resolve an unladylike expression was wrenched from her. "Are you saying that you expect to remain here?" she demanded before she thought.

He fished his snuffbox from a pocket and took a pinch between thumb and finger. Over it his eyes held hers. "Surely you anticipated that I would," he said softly.

She glared and said bitterly, "I can readily believe that you think to—to—"

"—exercise my conjugal rights? Do rid yourself of the notion that I am in any way different from the usual husband."

She flushed to the roots of her hair and said, "You must

correct your own thinking! I would rather be anything in the world than your wife!"

"Possibly," he said, unmoved. "But the distressing fact remains that you are my wife."

She had been standing beside a chair, and now sat down hard. "I will fight you," she murmured, shaken.

"Certainly," he replied. "You will do just as you please."

Her fierce green eyes met his cool gray ones in a look that spoke volumes. "In my extremity I may have gone through a marriage ceremony with you, but you are my husband in name only, sir, and that is all!"

"You cannot have been attending the vicar, my dear," he replied imperturbably. "You did promise to obey me."

She rose in one swift, graceful movement. "I am most eager to come to an agreement with you," she said, a note of entreaty creeping into her voice.

"By all means," he agreed. "You will not find me at all unheeding."

"I don't know how to put it more plainly," she said, eyeing him nervously.

"Do allow me to assist you," he offered smoothly. "It is not my intention to make myself obnoxious by insisting upon spending my wedding night with my bride."

"Then you will return to your ship?" she breathed, almost afraid to believe it.

"You cannot be accused of flattery," he remarked somewhat dryly. "The lowliest of men are entitled to the warmth of home and family, but it would appear that it is up to me to secure that which others take for granted."

"What has that to say to the point?" she inquired stiffly.

"I was speaking of love, but if you are harboring thoughts of leaving me, I will advise you that I keep what is mine. Sawyer will spend the night in the hall just outside your door. I will order your meals brought upstairs, but beyond that I refuse to go."

She caught her breath and said, an edge in her voice, "Pray, sir, when do you plan to leave?"

"At once," he replied, his brows raised in an expression of faint hauteur. "If I had had the presence of mind I would have done so before now. I am persuaded that repairs to my ship are of a good deal more importance than dalliance with an unwilling spouse." He seemed to have no more to say to her, for he picked up his hat and gloves and went from the room without another word.

For some reason she could not fathom, Charlie felt oddly dejected. It was apparent that His Lordship ranked her several degrees below his precious *Minotaur*. By his own utterance he had intimated that the navy was of the first importance, which was tantamount to saying, she reflected, that a mere wife could not hope to hold a candle to a boat. Ship! she corrected herself, while putting from her mind the possibility that her rejection of him could be at the root of it.

She wondered why it had not occurred to her from the beginning that her foolish escapade might well end in disaster. She thought herself the most stupid ninnyhammer alive. Why had she not realized from the instant of setting eyes on Mitford at that horrid little inn that he was destined to play more than a passing role in her life? She had refused to look beyond the moment, had assumed that he would look upon her as a child. No, that was not quite true, she admitted, her conscience twitting her. She had exercised great care in concealing her rounded curves, not at all the action of a babe. She had pitchforked herself into her present scrape strictly on her own. She could not but admit to herself that she had by no means been enough eager to avoid a marriage she should have deplored, his offhand mention of the word *love* notwithstanding. She had failed to put forward sufficient objections, had allowed herself to be persuaded. It didn't make sense, she thought, only vaguely aware that the landlord approached her door with her dinner on a tray.

She passed a restless night, tossing and turning and rousing with each striking of a distant steeple clock, first shivering with the cold from having kicked the covers aside, next drenched in perspiration from having bunched the blankets about her head. The hours dragged on and on until it seemed that dawn would never break, but finally the first faint light streaked the eastern sky and she was able to leave her bed.

She spent a considerable part of the time before Sawyer brought her breakfast in considering how she could slip away without the sailors on guard below knowing anything about it. From what she had gathered of their shipboard routine, the ablutions with which they were prone to start the day were nothing if not sketchy. Unless she much mistook the matter, they were more than likely to be found quaffing ale in the common room, regardless of the earliness of the hour. There was, moreover, a reasonable hope that Sawyer would not be of their number. She had not so far seen him indulge in so much as a sip of wine. And certainly he was the only one among the crew who knew that the cabin boy was not the captain's nephew but was in reality His Lordship's wife. With Sawyer safely out of the way on some errand, there would be no one to penetrate her disguise.

The coach would pass through Tavistock, she felt sure, and she made up her mind to book passage on it or, if it was not due to run that day, to buy a seat on the first stage available. The more she pondered it, the more certain she became that the only wisdom she had thus far displayed was in not informing Mitford of the exact location of her home. All he had to go on was her father's name. With this thought she was confronted with a fresh alarm; that Mitford, upon discovering her flight, would send someone, probably Sawyer, in pursuit. She at once perceived that to proceed by a direct route would be an act of supreme folly. He would scour the surrounding countryside, and she would be undone. There was also her guardian to be reckoned with. Experiencing an inward disquiet, her spirits rose only after it occurred to her that she could cover her tracks by changing coaches, and thereby her seeming destination, several times during the course of her journey.

Having made her plans, she donned her wedding gown and nearly burst into tears at the necessity of having to sell it. Once dressed, she opened the door and smiled angelically upon Sawyer. His eyes burned with fatigue from having spent the night on the floor with his back propped against the wall, but he gave no indication of being tired. He did evince a certain skepticism of her glib explanation of the need for scissors, a comb, an assortment of embroidery threads and, to ensure his lengthy absence, a yard of jaconet muslin in an unusual shade of silver-gray. "His Lordship has informed me that his coach will not arrive before noon, so you have plenty of time," she continued. "I will be perfectly safe until you return. The members of the crew downstairs will protect me."

Sawyer was surprised at the request and shuffled his feet

in momentary indecision, but the fact that she was now Lady Mitford weighed heavily with him. So, upon her assuring him mendaciously that His Lordship was aware of the projected shopping expedition, he pulled his forelock respectfully and took himself off to do as he was bid.

She hadn't a moment to spare, she reasoned. Mitford's tendency to read her mind was pronounced enough to be discernible to the veriest nodcock. It would be just like him to take the plaguey notion into his head to return to the inn when least expected. The thought sent her flying to the window to peer into the street out front. She caught a glimpse of Sawyer's back as he hurried around the corner, but to her relief there was no sign of Mitford. Wondering with a kind of detached interest whether she was destined to spend the next months dodging shadows, she quickly changed into her breeches and wrapped the dress in her shawl.

Ready at last, she hurried to the door and stepped out into the hall. To her chagrin, two members of the crew lounged at ease upon the stairs. The other sailors, though she fancied she could hear them conversing in the common room, had not yet come into the hall. She supposed the time of reckoning had arrived and waited, outwardly calm, for them to refuse to let her pass. They did look surprised, but, when she took a few tentative steps forward, seemed disinclined to block the way. "I didna see ye coom in, laddie," the taller of the two remarked, moving back to make room for her. "Did Her Ladyship send fer ye?"

She had a momentary sensation of helpless panic, but, upon grasping the significance of his words, quelled it. "I arrived some time ago," she assured him, hurrying down the stairs. "Lady Anne has some errands for me to run. I'd best not tarry."

The second sailor eyed her with suspicion, but he was a hesitant individual who seldom questioned orders, a habit acquired during a childhood spent under the stern eye of a critical grandfather, so he too allowed her to pass without comment. Through the open door of the common room she caught sight of the remaining seamen, but since none of them glanced her way, she was able to cross the hall unseen.

The front door had been left standing ajar. Through it she surprised the innkeeper in conversation with a gentleman in a beaver hat and greatcoat who was standing with his back to her. The landlord ran an appraising eye over her and asked what she was about. There'd be no pilfering in his inn or he'd have the law on her. Swallowing a tart reply, she had just opened her mouth to explain politely her mission when the visitor turned his head, providing her with a clear view of his profile.

Good God! she thought, appalled. Her guardian, Lord Wroxly! In a flash she whirled on her heel and fled back down the hall, escape her only object. A door at the end of the passage caught her eye. She had no idea where it led but she pushed it open and darted inside into what appeared to be a pantry of sorts. Reasoning that it must lead to the kitchens, she hurried forward in the ill-lit space, spurred on by the sound of the landlord's running feet. She stumbled against a table in her haste and with calm forethought possessed herself of a loaf of bread lying on it. It was too large to stuff into a pocket, so she tucked it under her arm and stepped into the kitchen. A stout, dour-faced woman looked up from stirring a bubbling caldron of thin potato soup, and a scullery maid who had had her eyes glued to the task of scraping carrots started to her feet, but Charlie spared them not a glance as she ran across the room and out the back door.

The alley was cobbled and scarcely wide enough to permit the passage of a dray. She heard the landlord shout to the cook and wasted no time in looking back. She flew along the narrow way as fast as her legs would carry her and turned the corner into a side street just as the innkeeper erupted from the inn with several of the sailors hot on his heels. A woman with a basket over her arm stopped in the middle of the walk to stare, and the driver of a trap turned to gawk, but neither made a move to stop her. By the time she reached a broad thoroughfare the size of the hue and cry had grown, swelled by the addition of a delivery boy and a number of urchins drawn by the noise. There was only one way to shake off the pursuit.

Weaving in and out of the pedestrians thronging the walks, she set up a cry of *"Stop, thief!"* as she ran and pointed ahead as if in pursuit of the thief herself. Within moments others took up the cry, and she shortly found herself one of a mindless throng chasing after they knew not what. Seizing the opportunity, she dashed across the street and ducked behind a beer wagon piled high with kegs, effectively obscuring herself from view. The attention of passersby had been attracted and curious glances were cast her way, but it didn't trouble her in the least. The sound of the chase dying away in the distance was music to her ears.

To remain in the neighborhood would be foolhardy, she knew. Accordingly she set off back down the street, walking leisurely in what she trusted was a nonchalant manner. After traversing a number of blocks she turned

down an avenue leading to a district lined with shops.
Within a very few minutes she was wandering from window
to window, enthralled with the variety of goods enticingly
displayed with an eye to luring potential customers inside.
After gazing entranced at a high-crowned poke bonnet
fashioned of black and white striped satin, she turned away,
intending to view the offering of a cobbler's shop, and
received her second shock of the day.

A carriage had drawn to a halt farther along the street to
deposit Sir Randolph Ashmore before the door of a small
but select hostelry catering to the Quality. She didn't
suppose that he could do anything to detain her, but the
presence in town of both His Lordship and her guardian
smacked of collusion. She could not think it a coincidence.
They had traced her to Plymouth; perhaps even the police
had been alerted to be on the watch for her. Since she did
not wish to press her luck, she went into the millinery shop
and pretended to be searching for a gift for her mother. The
proprietress eyed the loaf of bread with suspicion but kept
her counsel. Business was business. Charlie could not help
giving a slight start upon being informed of the price of the
bonnet, and she avoided the woman's eye when she
murmured that she would look around and perhaps come
back later. The proprietress watched her leave the shop, not
at all surprised to see her glance guiltily up and down the
street before setting off toward the meaner section of town,
then shrugged. Waterfront brats were no concern of hers.

Charlie soon found herself in a rundown neighborhood,
but it did not bother her overmuch. In fact, she was glad.
Since she was unlikely to run across His Lordship in such
unsavory surroundings, it must be regarded as a plus, and
since she lacked the sense of direction that would tell her

whether she was walking northward or southward, there was no need to mark her route. She would be bound eventually to arrive at the edge of town. Once she was clear of the city, perhaps some farmer would take her up in his wagon. She could always book passage on the stage at the first village she came to. Anything must be considered preferable to skulking about Plymouth in search of the stagecoach office while endeavoring to avoid discovery by her guardian and Sir Randolph.

It did not seem as if she would ever find her way out of the labyrinth of narrow alleys that served as streets to the inhabitants of the tumbledown dwellings built flush with the gutters on either side. After detouring around several piles of refuse that had been forgotten and left to molder where they lay, she ventured to inquire the direction to the waterfront of a slattern whiling away the day in lounging on her doorstep. The quayside offered its own brand of terror in the person of Mitford, but at least she would be able to orient herself. The harpy looked her over in a speculative fashion, her eyes moving from the loaf of bread to her bundle, and Charlie knew herself adrift in a sea of thieves. By now frightened, she took to her heels and sped down the street with no idea of where she ran. Blindly rounding a corner, she bumped against a packing box and gasped in relief to discover the ocean a few welcome yards away. She stopped running and began to move along the quay rather breathlessly, in a direction she felt sure would soon see her beyond the warehouse area and to a business district of sorts that provided goods of interest to seamen.

The waterfront was rather empty at that hour of the day, a circumstance much to her liking. After walking for perhaps not more than five minutes, she came upon a store that had been converted from a storage shed and seemed to be in the business of dispensing, for a price, used clothing. Congratulating herself on her good fortune, she went inside and approached the only person present, an aging tar who appeared to be the proprietor. To her inquiry if he were interested in purchasing a secondhand dress that had been worn only once, he nodded laconically and gestured for her to spread it out upon the table. Complying, she smiled brightly and told him that it was her sister's, but it was now too tight for her. She had promised that she would get the best price for it that she could. He offered twenty bob, whereupon she countered with a suggestion of eighty, and they settled into the mutually enjoyable business of bargaining.

Unnoticed by Charlie, an officer of the law had been following her since she first arrived at the waterfront. In his book any young chub from the stews of town had to be a bad one. They were thieves and cutthroats every one and not fit to associate with decent folk. Yon rascal was a thoroughgoing imp of Satan, make no mistake about it, as witness the loaf of bread no doubt filched from some honest baker, not to mention the lady's dress stolen in a respectable part of town. Unless he much mistook the matter, it had set some poor bloke back a pretty penny. "Well, now, it's a right rare thief you be," he said, stepping forward to seize her by the arm. "You just come along with me, young hearty. Gaol's the place for you."

Charlie looked around and gasped in utter disbelief to find herself in the grip of the law. "I didn't steal the gown!" she cried, attempting to jerk free. "Why ever should you think I had?"

"You didn't, so you say," he remarked, his tone grim. "We'll let the magistrate be the judge of that."

"But I didn't!" she insisted, struck by the unthinkable possibility of being summarily hauled off to jail. "I wouldn't take anything that didn't belong to me, indeed I wouldn't. My sister knows I have her dress. As a matter of fact, she asked me to sell it."

"A likely tale," he grunted, looking at the proprietor in a philosophic way. "I never seen one of them as wouldn't swear to his innocence on his mother's grave. A regular cesspool is the stews. Well, this will be one the less what will rob honest men while they sleep."

"You must listen to me!" Charlie begged desperately. "I am telling you the truth. Just come home with me and I'll prove it!"

This gave the constable pause. But only for a moment. "And what of the loaf of bread?" he demanded, triumphant.

Charlie felt her cheeks grow warm and groaned inwardly. Why must she feel so guilty? If he was to relax his guard, she would need to be convincing. "The cook gave it to me," she explained, with no idea at all of how the allegation must sound to him. "I overslept, you see, and Virginia—that's my sister—was most anxious for the money. She has probably spent her allowance, I shouldn't wonder, and nothing will do but that she purchase a new reticule to carry to a ball. Since I'm a growing boy and need my food—"

"Tsh!" he remonstrated, with deep feeling. "So it's fancy clothes and gentry ways, is it? Burn me if ever I run across any chub to equal the likes of you. Mayhap you mistook me for a ruddy touch. Well, young hearty, if you're wishful to gammon me, you've took a very poor notion into your

143

head. Now, you just come along quiet like, and I'll soon have you locked up snug as you please."

Charlie began to realize that something other than protestations of innocence was sorely needed. Even the proprietor, no great paragon himself, she suspected, was looking shocked. Clearly there was no way she could escape other than by her wits. "I don't blame you for being suspicious," she said, changing tactics. "I would be myself if I were in your place. I will warn you, however, that if my father must appear in court to clear my name, it will be very much the worse for you. Why, I shouldn't wonder if he and the magistrate don't turn out to be friends."

The constable did not believe a word of it but was enough shaken by the assertion to wish to hedge his bets. He said more mildly, "If you've done nothing wrong, then you've no call to kick up a fuss. I'm only doing me duty."

"I didn't say you weren't," she replied evasively, a plan forming in her mind. "In fact, I suppose I have no objection to your taking the gown along for evidence. Oh, and don't forget the bread. We wouldn't want the judge to accuse you of negligence."

"You're mighty obliging of a sudden," he shot back while wondering where she had picked up her handy way with words. "Maybe you think to gammon His Honor, but it won't do you no good. No siree, young hearty, no good at all, make no mistake about that."

For a moment it appeared that he harbored a marked inclination to clap her in irons, and she gave herself up for lost. But it evidently occurred to him that resorting to restraint would make him appear unable to manhandle a mere stripling of a boy, for he shifted his grasp of her arm from his right hand to his left and reached for the gown and bread. Charlie saw her chance and seized it. Drawing back her foot, she kicked him in the shin with all the force she could put behind the blow, then tore herself free from his hold and vanished through the door while he hopped about in pain. The proprietor showed a marked disposition to laugh, but contented himself with the spectacle of a limping minion of the law unable to overtake his quarry.

Meanwhile Charlie flew like a deer toward the bales and boxes stacked in profusion about the warehouse area. She did not think the constable would look for her there. It would never occur to him that she would stop to hide. Still she must experience a certain trepidation, sure as she was that he would pass by. Crouched out of sight behind a particularly large crate, she made herself small and closed her eyes and felt more secure for it.

She hadn't long to wait. His muttered conversation with himself heralded his approach and left her with little doubt that she had escaped disaster by no more than a hair's breadth. He had the advantage, under normal circumstances, of knowing the town like the back of his hand, but in the instance of Charlie he was at a distinct disadvantage. Any self-respecting crook would seek to lose himself among the flotsam and jetsam crowding the slums of the city. Or so he reasoned. It was only after much fruitless searching that he saw his error.

Charlie had very little fear that he would return to effect a systematic search of the waterfront. He had most likely early in his career acquired the ingrained belief that wrongdoers were predictable in their behavior. Ideas of what to do next half-formed themselves in her brain and were rejected. The entire city had become fraught with danger. There were not only her guardian and Sir Randolph to contend with; there were now the police as well. Numerous ways out of her dilemma flickered through her mind, but no plan took shape. More and more Mitford's ship began to figure as a haven by comparison. His sentiments might have undergone a change. From finding her desirable, he might now elect to snub her. Her treatment of him had been nothing if not injudicious. She had rarely, during the nearly nineteen years of her existence, found herself at a loss, but now she discovered that she was totally incapable of molding fate.

Venturing forth from her hiding place, she gazed across the water in surprise at the *Minotaur* riding at anchor some distance from shore. She would have thought that the repairs would be under way by now. A short distance away a small, wiry man in a moleskin jacket and jean pantaloons provided her with her third shock of the day. To her query as to when the ship could be expected to be hauled in to dry dock, he replied with uncharacteristic brevity, "Already has been."

"Oh, dear," she murmured, looking dismayed. "Whatever am I to do?"

He paused in stowing a basket of lemons aboard his boat and said, "You the cabin boy?"

She nodded and explained to him glibly that she had encountered a friend in town and so was running late. "If I am missed, I shudder to think what the lieutenant will say. How could I have known the rudder would be replaced by now?"

"They been at it all night," he remarked unemotionally. "I'm goin' out there myself. You can come along if you want. You'll likely get aboard 'thout bein' seen."

She could not quite anticipate how this was to be

accomplished, but she accepted his offer gratefully. Finding a place to sit among the fruits and vegetables crowding every available space of the small craft, she gazed around with interest and said, "Do you usually provender naval vessels?"

"Only those which is not with a squadron," he replied, settling himself at the oars. "It's a livin', whatever any one may say, the missus not excepted, for a nicer lot than our boys in blue I never did see, and I've seen plenty of 'em in my time, though that's not to say aught against the army, and meanin' no offense."

"Of course," she murmured inanely, uncertain of a more suitable reply. "Mr.—?"

"Cripsholm. I'll drop you off to starboard and go on around to larboard," he continued, bending his back to the oars. "Think you can scramble aboard whilst the watch is in converse with me?"

"I am sure I can," she replied, certain that he possessed a most lively mind.

They fetched up unnoticed in the lee of the ship. Charlie grasped the rope ladder hanging over the side, her heart in her throat, then smiled over her shoulder at her benefactor when he guided her foot to the bottom rung. She knew she dared not look down and clung like a limpet as she slowly inched hand over hand upward. A grunt of approval so buoyed her courage that she ventured to waggle a foot in reply, then continued the climb. Cautiously raising her head, she peered over the rail, her eyes sweeping the deck.

Lieutenant Brompton and three members of the crew were standing with their backs to her, exchanging pleasantries with Mr. Cripsholm, but thankfully no one else was about. Slinging a leg over the rail, she dropped lightly to the planking and sped to a hatch leading to the depths of the ship. She did not think anyone had seen her dive down the steps and so was able to entertain a reasonable hope of reaching the orlop unchallenged.

In the feeble light of candles set in holders attached to the beams, she made her way down the narrow ladders to the murk of the cockpit and looked around for a place of refuge. The after magazine offered the likeliest spot. She had no idea of the routine aboard a warship but reasoned that in the absence of battle, the crew would have no cause to come below. The blankets piled atop the powder cases could serve her for a bed. The coming voyage would be a marvelous adventure, she thought, better by far than the stifling atmosphere of a ladylike existence passed at the Aftons' country home.

CHAPTER 10

Mitford looked up from the charts spread across his desk and frowned. "Are you certain?" he said in the tones of a man who foresees trouble and seeks to avoid it.

"I ascertained the truth of Cook's allegation before I bothered you with it," Lieutenant Brompton replied a trifle stiffly.

Mitford grinned and pushed forward a bottle of Madeira. "Relax and pour yourself a glass," he said. "On one point you may rest assured. It was not my intent to irritate you."

"Irritate me?" Lieutenant Brompton repeated, surprised.

"Perhaps *alarm* is the better word. Come, Charles, there is no need to look so grim. After all, how much food could be missing after only three days at sea? Cook probably filched it himself. God knows he's rotund enough."

"If that is so, I trust he will soon be a much wiser man," Brompton replied, picking up the bottle of wine. "I have been meaning to ask you, Richard. What became of your decanter?"

Mitford colored faintly and glanced across at him before his gaze returned to the charts. "By my calculations, Broke's squadron should be off Sandy Hook on the lookout for Rodgers. It's too bad that we have been forced to concentrate our ships to protect our convoys, but if Broke can find Rodgers and destroy him, our captains can still act independently in blocking America's ports."

Brompton had noted the flush in Mitford's cheeks and wondered at the cause, but respected his privacy. "I knew the *Africa* and the *Guerriere* were at Halifax, but I don't know if any other vessels are with the *Shannon.*"

"The *Belvidera* was damaged in a fight with the American *President* but has been repaired. I understand the *Aeolus* is also with Broke."

"That is all very interesting, Richard, but I am more intrigued by what you haven't said."

Mitford looked up with a sardonic smile. "Melville detached us from Allenwood's squadron shortly before we left Plymouth. We are posted as a single raider. I would have informed you sooner, but it was all very secret until we were well out at sea. Surely no captain ever received such damnable orders!"

Lieutenant Brompton stared with a good deal of astonishment in his eyes. "Indeed?" he said. "And what might that mean?"

"It seems that Melville has a plan," Mitford replied sarcastically. "Rodgers will know of Broke and will no doubt learn that a second squadron sailed from Plymouth for American waters. He might elect not to group his own ships

150

together if he thinks that we have detached raiders available to menace their ports and merchantmen."

"Good God!" Brompton ejaculated, stunned. "Melville must be the worst kind of fool!"

"You will have no doubt of it when you hear the rest. The capture of a single British ship is to convince Rodgers that we have raiders scattered all over the ocean. He will then send out his vessels one by one and provide our squadrons with easy pickings."

"And we're the single British ship!" Brompton exclaimed, grasping with commendable swiftness the gist of these remarks.

"We are ordered to sustain a convincing amount of damage before striking our colors. Melville is laboring under the delusion that Rodgers can be duped."

Brompton blinked and shook his head. "At least there is no disgrace in surrendering to a superior force," he said, his face brightening. "I presume it will be a superior force?"

Mitford, conjuring up a vision of his ship in tow of some blithering Yankee skipper, sprang to his feet and began to pace about the cabin. "If it hadn't been for that blasted rudder, we would have been beyond the reach of Melville," he growled, pausing in his perambulations to stare across the room at Brompton. "I must be cursed. Surely no worse fate ever befell a captain in any fleet!"

"I shouldn't inform the crew if I were you," Brompton ventured thoughtfully. "It will be time enough for them to know when we strike our colors."

"I shall no doubt make that decision after we have carefully considered the consequences. Perhaps tomorrow."

But Mitford was not destined to have the opportunity of talking the matter over with Brompton on the morrow. It

was shortly after noon of the following day when Lieutenant Spear, who commanded the first division of guns, came
on deck from the magazine dragging Charlie by the hand.
He had gone below on a routine check of the ship's
ammunition and had come upon her asleep among the
powder cases and racks of cannonballs. It had become her
habit to nap during the day and forage for food at night.

Mitford was standing on the quarterdeck when the
disturbance brought his head around. Seeing her, he was
betrayed into a start. His rather stern expression softened
for a moment, then hardened as he ordered her to his cabin
and dismissed Lieutenant Spear.

She had ample time for reflection before he came below.
Almost, but not quite, she began to regret the impetuous
impulse that had sent her scurrying back to him. It had
seemed then, and seemed now, infinitely preferable to being
thrust, a stranger, into the bosom of his family. She had
been presumptuous enough to think that he had been glad to
see her, but knowing him as she did, she felt certain that she
would need to exert all her influence to induce him to treat
her as if he was. I run so hot and cold, there must be
something wrong with me, she thought. One moment I
can't wait to see the last of him and the next I rush to fling
myself into his company.

She had no way of knowing how long she waited and had
begun to wonder whether he had forgotten her when the
door opened and he walked into the room. She had seen him
testy, she had seen him provoked, but never had she seen
him so blazingly irate. "I shall presently have a great deal to
say to you, but at the moment I do not trust myself to
speak," he said in a voice that froze her to the marrow.
"Your disregard of my authority passes all bounds. I had

thought that once you bore my name your conduct would become above reproach, but no, you seem bent on making yourself an object of disgust to any person of excellence and refinement. Your upbringing may have been grossly at fault, but your instincts should be such that it would be unnecessary for me to instruct you in the principles obtaining in the larger world."

Her eyes flashed. "For a person who does not trust himself to speak, you certainly have a lot to say!" she flung at him in high dudgeon.

"I need not remind you that you are aboard my ship, much as I deplore it, but I will give you fair warning, madam! You will be very ill advised to flaunt my authority, for if you do, I will not hesitate to warm your backside."

"Your threats, sir, are not as unnerving as you suppose," she shot back coldly. "I have no intention of remaining within reach of you!"

"And where, pray, do you intend going?"

Having no clear notion of where she could be other than in his cabin, and having no thought of gratifying him by admitting it, she felt it incumbent upon her to decamp. Before she could reach the door, however, he moved in front of her, blocking the way. "Do not think that I will permit you to make a spectacle of yourself before my men," he said, a slight sneer curling his lips.

"You are insufferable!" she breathed, her color mounting. "I cannot think what I have done to deserve being talked to in this manner!"

"In that case," he replied deliberately, "there is little point in continuing this conversation. I have no doubt that you will speedily make yourself at home. Perhaps in the coming weeks I will become flattered to earn your good opinion."

Her eyes fell before his at being put out of countenance, but within seconds her thoughts took another direction. "That is not very gallant of you, sir," she said, smiling pertly. "You should not assume that you lack my esteem. Rather, you should be sure that you have it."

His brows rose. "It won't fadge," he remarked, slight amusement creeping into his tone. "I trust you to my peril when you are being pleasant. I will have the truth, if you please. What scheme are you hatching now?"

"I wish you would not always suspect me of some ulterior motive," she said, giving an exaggerated sigh.

"Permit me to rephrase my question. What is on your mind?"

"Your mother's bed. It is no longer here."

There came a pause while Mitford gazed at her in a startled way. "Am I to gather from that that you have changed your mind?" he said finally, his meaning implicit in the slight lifting of his brows.

"Of course I haven't!" she gasped, flushing rosily. "I returned to you because—because there was nothing else I could do."

"Instinct tells me to allow that remark to pass, but my experience of you warns me against it. Explain yourself, if you please."

"I must confess it had not occurred to me at first to stow away, and I'm still a trifle doubtful, but there is no denying that the police were after me. I hadn't done anything wrong, except for one measly loaf of bread—but really, Richard, they could have put it on your tab. There was no need to go chasing after me as if I were a criminal. You do see that, don't you?"

"Your explanations," he said, "have seldom been edifying."

"Well, but I had just come across my guardian, so you can appreciate it that I had to get away. There was no time to lose. And then, between Sir Randolph and the constable, I was really in the suds."

"I can imagine that you were, but there is no need to employ vulgar language," he said crushingly.

"Then you do understand!" she declared, not in the least abashed.

"You are laboring under a misapprehension," he replied icily. "I don't. Of all the addle-pated vixens I have ever come across, I have never met your equal."

"I see it's no good expecting sympathy from you," she said, swallowing the lump in her throat.

"You may have been busily acquiring a most unsavory reputation in Plymouth, but I trust my credit with the world would have seen you through. What precise object had you in not coming to me?"

"You would have sent me to live among strangers. No, let me finish, please. Under the circumstances it was for me to determine my place of abode, but you did not so much as consult with me. And don't tell me that it is a husband's prerogative to decide where his wife will live."

"I am relieved to hear you say that you are aware of the customary way of doing things," he commented dryly.

"Well, yes, but no wife wishes to have her future arranged in a high-handed fashion," she said, her nose in the air.

"She no doubt prefers to disarrange her husband's," he

replied grimly. "When I learned of your flight from the inn, I naturally assumed that you would return to your former home. I would have charged Sawyer with the office of finding you, but the memory of society can be particularly retentive. It seemed safer not to draw the attention of the tattlemongers, but the indelicacy you have shown by the impropriety of your conduct may have damaged your reputation more than you imagine."

"I still don't see what the fuss is about," she persisted. "No one knows I'm a female but you and Lieutenant Brompton, and Sawyer, of course."

He sighed and began to pace about the room, the intent expression on his face speaking more clearly than words the extent of his concentration. Had he not glanced her way once or twice, she would have thought that he had forgotten her. She bore it as long as she could, then said, a slight accusation in her tone, "You believe that women should have no freedom of will."

He came to a halt before the window and stood with his back to her. "If you are wondering if I accept the doctrine of Pelagius, I'm not so sure that Eve did not eat that apple," he said, clasping his hands behind his back.

She was silenced and could only look across at him in a helpless way, mollified by the knowledge that her conceit had led her to suppose that she could run as she chose. At last she said, acknowledging that he held the reins, "I daresay I may have been at fault, but I assure you I had no thought of behaving in an odious way. Please accept my regrets."

He turned to face her, the anger dying out of his eyes. His whole posture relaxed, and his countenance took on a look of resignation. "If only it were that simple," he said. "I am

156

under orders and so not free to elect our destination. We must continue as before, with one exception. You will not find it necessary to erect a wall. Sawyer will install a bunk for you instead."

"I don't understand," she said, a merry twinkle in her eye. "Am I to have no partition behind which to dress?"

"I can conceive of nothing worse than having you forever occupying the bathroom," he replied. "You may have your wall."

She could not forbear to gloat. "Am I free to choose its location?" she gurgled, going off on a peal of laughter he could not help but think entrancing.

A muscle twitched in his cheek. "I sent my mother's bed to London lest it fall into enemy hands," he said, enjoying his own slight triumph. "I should hope that the memories it calls up are not difficult to entertain. Generations of Aftons have been born in it. I shouldn't like my own offspring to be denied the privilege."

"Oh!" she gasped. "You are abominable, sir. Abominable, I say!"

"Perhaps you will know not to fence with me in future," he replied with perfect aplomb.

She seemed to experience difficulty in finding words but rallied swiftly. "Only a total lack of delicacy on your part could prompt you to taunt me with an incident that put me to shame," she said, annoyed that the light from the window behind him cast his face in shadow, making it hard to read.

"Admittedly it was ill conceived of me," he offered by way of apology. "I appear to have developed a choleric disposition."

"Of the two of us, Richard," she said with commendable insight, "I fear it is you who is the most agreeable. I can

157

scarcely look upon myself with approval. What are you thinking?"

"So I'm to gratify your vanity by telling you," he remarked, crossing to her side.

"I don't understand why you must respond to a simple question by putting me in the wrong," she said with spirit. "What has my vanity to do with it?"

He caught her in his arms, his face swimming before her eyes an instant before his lips found hers in a kiss that left her gasping. "Satisfied?" he murmured, releasing his hold of her.

"If you imagine that I was angling for your embrace, you much mistake the matter!" she said hotly.

"Oh?" he said. "That is precisely how I understood it."

"Your amazing impertinence leads you to suppose that all females find your kisses acceptable," she shot back. "Well, they are not acceptable to me, sir, but are disgusting beyond all bearing."

"I must have been mistaken," he remarked, moving to the threshold. "For a moment there I would have sworn that you responded."

She watched the door close behind him and could not help but reflect that she seemed destined to appear forever foolish. Just why this was so suddenly occurred to her. She was by no means averse to his kisses, her protests to the contrary notwithstanding. For a few breathless moments she had forgotten that he did not care a snap of his fingers for her. It was how ladies were led astray. They put their faith in a man, only later to discover that their love was very much one-sided.

Crossing to his desk, she sat down and propped her chin in her hands. Considering it, she could find no reason

Mitford should look twice at her. It was not that she was ill favored. Her eyes were generally thought to be fine, and her profile with its straight nose and rounded chin had been called lovely. But while these attributes were all to the good, still, in a man's view, she had grave shortcomings. Her independent nature could not fail to disturb the male ego, and what gentleman would not prefer the company of a flighty blonde to that of a down-to-earth brunette. Then, too, by dint of an outstanding education, she was definitely a bluestocking, the worst of all possible drawbacks. No, there was no reason to believe that Mitford could have fallen in love with her. If he seemed to have developed a tendre for her, she was sure it was no more than a passing fancy. Certainly he wanted her, but should she welcome him to her bed, he would cease to desire her soon enough. Constancy? The very notion was absurd. She was no match for the sophisticated women with whom, she made no doubt, he dallied while ashore. Well, she mused, seething inside at the thought, if he thinks to treat me as a light o' love, he will learn something of decent women from the encounter.

Had he been consulted, he could have told her that she outshone all others in his eyes. For all her capricious ways, she had made no push to insinuate herself in his affections. So she would dissimulate, would she? Lord, but one could not help but admire her spirit. Clearly his motives had been brought into question. Humming softly to himself, he beat a strategic retreat to the quarterdeck, a slight curve lifting the corners of his mouth.

Although it was not Lieutenant Brompton's watch, Mitford found him leaning against the rail, his gaze on the far horizon. "Why so glum?" Mitford asked, strolling forward.

Brompton straightened. "What the devil do you mean by that?" he demanded, startled out of his reverie.

Mitford chuckled. "How long have you known me, Charles?" he said.

The question was purely rhetorical, but Brompton replied, "All my life. Why?"

"Only that experience should have taught you not to fret."

"Now you've brought up the subject, I'll tell you plain; you're for it, if you take my meaning."

"I take it," Mitford replied promptly.

"Then I've a piece of advice for you. Dress your lady in skirts, and the devil take the hindmost."

Mitford leaned against the rail and thrust his hands deep into his pockets. "I never listen to advice," he said. "It seldom turns out to be worth the trouble."

Brompton shook his head. "I'm glad I don't stand in your shoes," he admitted frankly. "I can't think what you'll do when we strike our colors. I'm not saying you won't contrive, but it could be a ticklish business."

Mitford shrugged. "Don't underestimate the effect of my title on the Americans," he said. "They will swallow whatever I choose to tell them. Charlie is and will remain my nephew."

"That's as may be, but I don't mind telling you, every day she looks less a boy."

A glint came into Mitford's eyes. "I know I need not remind you," he said, "that Charlie has the honor to be my wife."

"Don't take offense," Brompton adjured him swiftly. "I'm only concerned that someone will get wind of it."

"Do you expect me to panic and do something foolish? Of course it's a ticklish business, but most of our troubles have owed their existence to a female. I trust I can handle it."

Brompton grinned. "Don't let Charlie hear you say that," he advised. "That experience you place such store by might be put to the test."

Mitford cocked an eyebrow. "If you are going to chortle over my plight," he said, "I will remind you of a yellow-haired chit whom you called Angel Pie. You were far gone on her, as I recall."

"Lord, don't speak of it," Brompton groaned in mock dismay. "She'd have marched me to the anvil if it hadn't been for you. Did I remember to thank you?"

"You didn't, but I'm not repining."

"There's that damned supercilious tone again," Brompton remarked. "You've no need to grouse, even if I do interest myself in your affairs. I have a high regard for Charlie and want to see her happy."

Mitford glanced at him rather enigmatically. "I will strive not to make her unhappy," he said.

"I meant—well, you know what I meant. She is entitled to take her place by your side. As Lady Mitford."

"She will, when there is no longer cause for scandal. I'm damned if some Yankee skipper will look down his nose at her."

Brompton gave a little start. "I think—but I cannot be sure—that you have fallen in love with her," he said, surprised.

161

Mitford surveyed him blandly. "You are a fount of wisdom today," he remarked.

"Then you *are* in love with her," Brompton grinned. "For once in your life you show good sense where a female is concerned. I cannot conceive that you could be around Charlie for any length of time and not realize her worth."

"Far from it. I do. But if it is all the same to you, I will tell her so in my own good time. Meanwhile—if you have ceased being so profound—I have a favor to ask of you."

"In over your head?" Brompton inquired solicitously.

"Quite," Mitford admitted. "I don't mind telling you that Charlie has no conception of the mess we're in. She will need guidance, and I cannot be with her every minute."

"You're not to worry," Brompton assured him cheerfully. "I shan't let her out of my sight."

"I trust you will not put yourself to unnecessary trouble," Mitford remarked somewhat dryly. "I hadn't intended that you make a career of it. Just remain alert when others are about. Do not hesitate to interrupt if she seems on the verge of saying something indiscreet."

"I will teach her to tie knots," Brompton declared, very well pleased with the notion.

"Will you now," Mitford mused, looking aghast. "By Jove, I didn't know you had it in you. It will keep her out of mischief."

"Don't be too hard on her, Richard. She may have made a few mistakes—haven't we all—but you can depend on her discretion."

Mitford pushed away from the rail. "Moralizing ill becomes you, dear boy," he said, then walked away before Brompton could think of a suitable retort.

For the remainder of the afternoon he found it necessary

to invent excuses to avoid returning to his cabin. Visiting every space of the *Minotaur*, he went through the motions of inspecting the ship, conversed pleasantly with the crew and joined a group of awed junior officers for tea. By five o'clock even the midshipmen were glancing askance at him. By the time he made his way to his quarters, he could not regard the coming minutes with anything but feelings of profound misgivings. It would be more consonant with his dignity, he thought, if he could place dependency on being greeted with some show of respect.

He was doomed to disappointment. Charlie looked up from a book she had unearthed from his sea chest and said, "If you will arrange for my transfer to a ship bound for home, I daresay I would survive being separated from you."

He crossed to the wardrobe and carefully laid his hat on the shelf. "I fear there is no doing that," he said politely.

"But why ever not?" she protested. "I have quite decided that I prefer to go home."

"One does not hitch a ride on a warship, my dear," he explained. "It just isn't done."

She was thoughtful for a moment, then said with composure, "In that case, I must make the best of it, I suppose. Really, Richard, this is very bad of you. You could at least feed me, I should think."

"Dinner will arrive shortly. We keep early hours on a ship. If you wish to freshen up, you may have first use of the bathroom."

Charlie flushed scarlet, felt herself quite unable to meet his look of amused condescension, and fled to the relative privacy of the bath, her dignity in shreds.

Five minutes later Sawyer scratched on the cabin door, and upon being bidden to enter, busied himself in arranging the ham and potatoes on their plates. Mitford watched him add a helping of peas and swore softly under his breath. "Why Cook must needs exhibit a lack of imagination is beyond my comprehension," he said, "but that you should concur passes all bounds."

"Her Ladyship used to seem partial to peas," Sawyer explained, uncertain whether or not to remove them.

"You appear to expend a good deal of your time in ignoring my preferences," Mitford said. "Permit me to inform you that I am heartily sick of them."

"I'll remember, Cap'n," Sawyer promised solemnly.

"You will also, I believe, contrive to forget that Her Ladyship is aboard this vessel."

"Aye, I will that, Cap'n."

"You will further, I'm sure, remember to address Her Ladyship as Master Charlie."

"Master Charlie," Sawyer repeated dutifully. "Aye, Cap'n, I won't forget."

"Good. I am sure you won't. Well, what is it now?"

"Will Her Ladyship be wishful of tea or coffee?" Sawyer said, adding that, to be certain, he had brought both.

"Oh, go to the devil!" Mitford snapped, exasperated.

Charlie, overhearing, choked off the hysterical giggle rising in her throat, waited until the door closed behind Sawyer and then went back into the room. "I am famished," she remarked, taking her place at the table. "Oh, peas! How nice. I am particularly partial to them."

Mitford shot her a suspicious glance but elected not to provide her with an opening. The expression on her face was too angelic by far. He embarked instead upon an itinerary for the coming days that would largely confine her to the cabin. His further remarks on the dangers of consorting with his officers were well founded but elicited no reply. She continued to eat her dinner, nodding pleasantly from time to time but in no way indicating any real intention of complying. He thought it best to press her. "You do not seem to be taking the situation very seriously," he said, entreaty creeping into his tone.

She calmly laid down her knife and fork and touched her napkin to her lips. "I should think that the thought of a female having the vapors all over your ship would be unnerving," she remarked, the dimple peeping in her cheek.

"It is," he agreed with conviction.

"Then you should be glad that I am not given to missish ways," she said. "It would only put you out of temper." She paused, then added roguishly, "On the other hand, I do need my exercise."

Mitford slammed his fist down upon the table with a force that made the glasses jump. "You will drive me to distraction," he said. "Why do you do it?"

"Because you have upon several occasions expressed a lack of confidence in me. Moreover, you have yourself thus far displayed an extraordinary degree of impropriety."

He glared. "Pray do not keep your tongue between your teeth on my account," he said with irony.

She favored him with a sweet smile. "I would have kept my opinions to myself, but since you invite me to speak, I will tell you that I have found you to be demanding, easily annoyed and shockingly overbearing. It must be the result of your upbringing."

"Which, I mistake not, failed to approach the high level of your own."

She affected surprise. "I would hesitate to put it quite so badly as that," she said.

"On the contrary," he replied, "you would not hesitate. Tell me, my dear, have you found anything about me worthy of remark?"

She seemed to ponder. "Well . . ." she mused.

He pushed back his chair and got to his feet. "It will be best if you retire first," he said, his mouth twisted into a caricature of a smile. "I will send Sawyer to remove the covers immediately I go on deck. You may have thirty minutes—no longer. And that reminds me. After today I am well aware of how I must appear to my men. You must know that I cannot drastically alter my usual routine without occasioning talk, so in future I will not avoid my quarters. Starting tomorrow you will see much more of me. I am as a rule to be found at my desk of mornings, but my duties allow latitude in the afternoon. I will have time for you then."

"Indeed?" she said, stung, but hiding it behind an indifferent demeanor. "I certainly would not wish to disturb you. Not for the world."

He looked sharply at her. "I am becoming hourly more adept in anticipating you," he remarked.

Charlie digested this. "That was not very handsome of you, was it?" she said.

"No, not very," he agreed. "Shall we say that I am a trifle —crude?"

"I am sorry if I have wounded your feelings, but I always say what I think. Your sensibilities should not be so touchy. I know that I don't behave as a delicately nurtured female should, but—"

"You are not a delicately nurtured female," he interrupted, crossing to the door.

166

"I'm as much a lady as you are a gentleman," she said, thrusting out her lower lip.

"Ah, but I am disagreeable and—I believe you said shockingly overbearing?"

"If you ever decide to be civil," she returned, "it will be on your own behalf and not on mine."

The twinkle in his eyes belied the calm expression on his face. "The result of my deplorable upbringing, I infer," he said and, having bowed with practiced grace, went out into the companionway and closed the door behind him.

CHAPTER 11

It was fortunate for Charlie that, by reason of the quilts strung between the quarterdeck beams, she was spared coming face to face with Mitford immediately upon awakening the following morning. She felt the need to marshal her courage and sat up in her bunk, her chin cupped in her hands. She could not forbear the thought that nothing could have been more harmful to her chance for happiness than being pitchforked into marriage with a man who felt obliged to wed her. While she could not have anticipated that he would consider her compromised or that he would so engage his honor, there was no blinking the fact that the present situation was little short of onerous. If he was to come to love her, she would need to paint a better picture of herself than she had done up to now.

He had come in long after she retired, treading with caution, but she had not missed his state of mind. An alarming quiet had settled over the room that made the slight sounds of his disrobing more audible than they otherwise would have been, and even when he lay down, she knew that it was long before he slept. Were there two sides to his character? She thought not. He might view with amusement the peccadilloes of the *ton*, but he would be a stickler where his wife was concerned.

She had not expected to enjoy the first minutes of confronting him, but they turned out to be worse than she was prepared for. To begin with, she felt foolish when she poked her head through her wall of quilts. In the second place, Mitford's attitude offered little in the way of encouragement. He was seated at his desk, the quill in his hand moving back and forth across a sheet of what appeared to be the ship's log, but although she cleared her throat in an effort to attract his attention, he neither looked up nor betrayed by the smallest sign that he was aware of her presence. Watching him, her eyes began to dance when he put up a hand to tug at his cravat as though it were too tight, an action that belied the maddening deliberation with which he read through the entry in the log. Apparently satisfied, he closed the book and turned the full force of his gaze on her.

From dreading what he might find to say, Charlie found herself wishing that it were possible to stare him down. Failing this, she said, "I am sure you will not mind if I bathe before I dress. If you will hand me your robe, I will not spurn it."

Mitford's brows rose in faint surprise. After a moment's uncomfortable silence, he said, "I envy you your lightheartedness. You astonish me."

Putting in play her determination to improve her image, she said, "I was used to be very much indulged. Of course that was made inevitable, to a large degree, by my father's having possessed a title. I expect you will say that I was given my own way beyond what was wise."

"I will?" he said appreciatively.

"I should think so. Prudence has seldom been a virtue with me. Do I get the robe?"

He made no answer to this but merely took it from its peg and tossed it to her before returning to the papers on his desk. "The turtles in southern waters grow to an extraordinary size," he remarked as she withdrew her head behind the quilts. "Do remind me to show them to you."

Her vow not to retort coming to her mind, she wrapped herself in the robe and crossed to the bath, aware that his eyes were upon her all the while. She would have enjoyed bathing in the tub but eschewed mentioning it. Pouring water into the bowl, she scrubbed herself until her body tingled, then cast a rueful glance at her crumpled shift. She considered laundering it but decided against doing so. The sight of feminine undergarments hung up to dry might irritate him beyond all bearing.

By the time she was dressed, she had determined that nonchalance was the best course for her to follow. Accordingly she went back into the room and set about tidying it as if the ritual was, on this morning, in no way unique. Having smoothed the covers on her own bunk, she marched to his and picked up a shirt lying on it.

She had begun to fold it when he said, "It is for you. I would send for Sawyer to alter its size in your stead, but he might not be free at the moment, you know. I presume you sew, so I should not think it necessary. However, if you prefer—"

"It is very good of you to think of it, but I am sure that

171

Sawyer has a good many duties to attend to. I have wasted too much of his time already."

There was no missing the conciliatory tone in her voice. Mitford's lips twitched but he replied gravely, "You will treat my servants as your own," before turning back to his work, and the room became quiet again.

It was perhaps a half hour later when Lieutenant Brompton rapped on the door and, upon being bidden by Mitford to enter, found Charlie busily altering the shirt to fit herself. "Upon my word, Richard does accord you Turkish treatment," he said and chuckled. "Do allow me to offer you my most humble apologies for having given you to him in holy wedlock. It was presumptuous of me, but I did not dream he would turn you into his tailor."

She laughed back at him. "On the contrary, he would never trust me with his wardrobe. It is for me."

"I wouldn't phrase it quite like that," Mitford smilingly defended himself, a softened expression in his eyes, before turning his attention to Lieutenant Brompton. "Are the midshipmen ready for small-arms drill?"

"They are waiting at the main armament," Brompton replied, grinning. "I must say that turning it into a contest has each man eager to prove his mettle."

"What is an arms drill?" Charlie asked, laying aside her sewing and looking to Mitford for an answer.

"It is a procedure instituted by Broke in which I heartily concur. Not only do the men drill with both the large and small guns, they also practice aloft with the sails."

"Who is Broke?"

"He is captain of HMS *Shannon*. I'm told he can reef topsails in ninety seconds, and that on one memorable occasion he reefed all three topsails in one minute flat."

172

"Did you hear that he once sent up the lower yards and topmasts and crossed topgallant yards in four minutes forty-five seconds?" Brompton interjected. "If his officers are to be believed, their royal yards go across in never more than five minutes, and they once struck lower yards and topmasts in ten."

Charlie sniffed. "That all sounds very—very seaworthy," she said, "but I don't know what it means."

"It means," explained Mitford, "that with lower yards and topmasts down, the *Shannon* can make all plain sail in under five minutes."

"I had no idea it could be done so fast," she admired, though she still had no notion of what they were talking about.

Gratified, but suspicious, Mitford said he saw no reason the *Minotaur* should not soon equal the record, at which Brompton smiled and said, "None at all, but we will never persuade Charlie of the importance of shot if we continue to praise the importance of sail."

This was true, and since the *Minotaur* was first and foremost a gunnery ship, Mitford excused himself to supervise the arms drill, pleased and surprised that she put forth no suggestion of accompanying him.

"How on earth," demanded Brompton, walking beside him to the magazine, "did you contrive to turn Charlie up sweet?"

"Did you think I couldn't?" Mitford inquired, casting him a quizzical glance.

Brompton met the look with a twinkle in his eye. "Frankly, Richard," he said, "I had my doubts."

"Don't underestimate my talents. Having stormed her defenses by gifting her with a shirt—and one of my best ones, mind—I got next to her good graces by means of devilish cunning. What woman could resist being told that a garment became her far more than it had its previous owner? She was so pleased with me I was tempted to present her with another."

"You will end up presenting her with the ship, I shouldn't wonder."

Mitford gave one of his sudden shouts of laughter. "You are mistaken," he said. "She has already purloined it."

During the coming days he was to discover that he spoke more truthfully than he supposed. By subtle means known only to the female mind, she gradually broadened her scope until she literally had the run of the ship. She was always accompanied by Mitford, it was true, but few spaces of the *Minotaur* remained off limits to her, and to those that did she had no desire to go. Had she in any way shown him a smug front, it would have occurred to him that he was being manipulated, but she did not. She pleased him by taking an interest in the operation of the ship, found favor with the crew by the simple expedient of listening with a sympathetic ear to their reminisces of home and won the respect of the officers by the intelligence she displayed in grasping the finer points of the pecking order obtaining aboard any naval vessel of the day. But if she received the plaudits of the men (who had fully expected the captain's nephew to prove a lad of little bottom and less wit—not through disrespect but from an abiding belief that all modern young gentlemen were overly indulged), one at least among their number remained aloof. Sawyer could not approve. Had the Almighty intended females to shoot guns, he would have created them with a pistol in their hands. As for women taking part in small-arms practice, His Lordship should put his foot down, instead of which he swelled with pride every time Her Ladyship managed to put a ball through the target.

There was no denying that success had gone to Charlie's head, and the attention she received could not help but flatter her. While she could not entirely believe that her position as the captain's nephew had little to do with it, still a heady fare of being congratulated and marveled at resulted in Mitford's being bombarded with a daily recital of who praised this and who complimented that. If he raised no objections it was due partly to his wish to see her happy and partly to the care with which she guarded the secret of her sex.

It was a pleasant interlude in their relationship, but by its very nature it could not last. Charlie wanted more and, having given the matter considerable thought, divined a ray of hope. Lieutenant Brompton might well prove the key to awakening a spark of jealousy in Mitford's unresponsive heart. It was worth a try. Brompton was, of course, perfectly willing to fall in with her schemes. Through a spirit of sheer mischief he proceeded to flirt outrageously with her, but only in Mitford's presence and then with a worldly tact that stopped short of compromising her.

For all his knowledge of women, Mitford misjudged her motives. He suffered in silence when he should have known that her determined flirting was really designed to show him how willing she was to oblige him. But he was deeply in love and under the impression that his suit was disagreeable to her, and so was constrained to mask his emotions. Where he should have thrown caution to the winds and taken her in his arms, he felt impelled to postpone his ardor until the signs seemed propitious. Charlie, plagued by inner doubts but not yet ready to entirely believe defeat, resolved to lure him with womanly wiles, but just how this was to be accomplished, given the absence of feminine fripperies, was not clear in her mind.

Meanwhile the days passed uneventfully. The seas remained smooth and the ship ran easily before steady winds. Mornings were taken up in practice with the guns, while the afternoons found the men aloft racing against the watch in their drills with the sails. Between polishing the ship's brass and scrubbing down the decks, they were busy and content. Most important to Mitford, they accepted the coming surrender of the *Minotaur* with a fatalism born of a lifetime spent in battling the caprices of nature.

Once he had made up his mind to take them into his confidence, he had wasted no time in mustering them aft to make known his orders. Their frustration found expression in a few muffled oaths, but beyond this they faced the certainty of imprisonment with admirable restraint. The accumulated back pay, once they were set free, would amount to a tidy sum. Excepting Mitford, Charlie was perhaps the only person aboard who could find nothing to applaud in the situation. The officers might anticipate an early exchange for their American counterparts, but, supposing the fiction of her relationship to Richard was accepted by their captors, protecting her reputation would remain his prime concern. The day when she could abandon her breeches for the more alluring appeal of skirts was seen more and more as a time somewhere in the distant future. In the meantime he would never permit his heart to rule his head.

Or so she reasoned.

They were three weeks out of Plymouth when he awoke one morning, his mind still filled with dreams of her warm

...gaze alighted
...g before the window with
...manhood rising up at thoughts of
...ams into reality, past resolutions became forgotten on a rising tide of passion.

The last shred of propriety prompted Charlie to at least a pretense of resistance. Not one word of tenderness had she had from him in all the days since their marriage. It was as if he anticipated compliance on her part as his just due. She regarded him with a smoldering eye, the thought causing her to jerk away when his hand fell upon her shoulder. "I am sensible to the debt I owe you," she began, the pulse throbbing in her throat, "but the service you have rendered me does not encompass—well, what you think. If you felt the least tenderness for me—"

"And what leads you to suppose I don't?" he demanded, taking her hands in his.

"Of course you don't! You haven't given me the least inkling—"

"It is very true," he interrupted again, sweeping her into his arms. "Foolish girl, I would have received a slap in the face for my pains. You weren't ready then. You are now."

While she could still think, it crossed her mind that she was entirely too transparent. He was kissing her with an ardor she could not now resist even had she wished to. But

of
a vision wit...
from him
she lay submissive
on her
the memory of
lingered to

voluptuous flesh, gathered at the touch of his fingers on her
betray him. Blinking sleep from his desire standing
on the object of his desire standing ... his
her back to him. His
eager hands, lingered to
the memory of

beneath him, gasping with desire, she lay submissive
between eyelids drooping with desire,
encircling arms and trembling thighs. Gazing at him from
her kisses swam before his eyes in a vision wit...
and willing in his embrace. Her face softened
from his kisses

now
urgency
need and take
her body in one long
arms and carried her to

CHAPTER 12

Charlie awoke on a long sigh and lay for a moment with her eyes still closed, savoring memories of the night just past. In the week since Richard had succumbed to her wiles, or stormed her defenses, depending upon one's point of view, they had been hard pressed to hide their altered relationship before the crew. It had become so difficult, in fact, that she seldom ventured from their cabin. His duty to the ship proved an unwelcome taskmaster throughout much of the daylight hours, but the nights belonged to them. Though she had no way of knowing it, he made love to her with her pleasure uppermost in his mind, a consideration he had not before bestowed on any woman. Manlike, he naturally assumed that, by his tenderness, she would realize the depth of his love, but, womanlike, when he failed to verbalize his affection, she assumed he was motivated by lust. In her ignorance she could not know that a gentleman of his stamp would never whisper "dearest" and "darling" into the ear of a lady who did not own his heart.

Now four weeks into the voyage, they were cruising off the coast of Virginia as ordered, playing the waiting game. Mitford ruefully felt that they had some hope of being sighted by an American vessel, if not that day then surely tomorrow or, failing that, the next. Meanwhile all went as usual with the disciplined, healthy crew. With the possible exception of Captain Broke's HMS *Shannon*, every man aboard the *Minotaur* felt confident that no frigate in His Majesty's Navy could boast of a more well ordered ship.

It was shortly before noon when the American sloop *Hornet* was sighted some five miles from shore and reaching out to sea. A barked order brought the lookout shinning down from the crow's nest to wrap his legs around the back stays and slide to the deck below. Mitford strode to the quarterdeck railing and called down to him, "Is she one of a squadron, Briggs?"

"She appears to be alone, sir," the lookout replied. "There is no other sail in sight."

Mitford turned. "Give chase, Lieutenant Brompton," he said, unable to hide a grin. "Melville ordered us to sustain damage before striking our colors. He said nothing about returning the compliment. Our gunners are not to sink the *Hornet*, mind. We will much prefer her to return home to report. That should bring Rodgers's squadron out."

"I told you that you would never surrender to an inferior force," Brompton said with a chuckle as he hurried away to carry out his orders.

It was a cloudy day, with a strong wind blowing out of the northeast and a heavy sea building up. The *Minotaur* made haste to cut across her bow, but the *Hornet* sighted them before they had covered more than half the distance separating the two vessels and altered course toward a heading roughly south-sou'west. For nearly four hours the two ships tacked back and forth across the ocean, each attempting to make the most of the winds, but the breeze turned fickle, gusting and dying away at will and affording first one ship and then the other with the advantage she hoped for.

Mitford's intent was to remain just out of range until the wind was in his favor; with the *Hornet* becalmed, the *Minotaur* would dart in to rake the enemy before breaking off the attack. But the breeze first became light and then died down altogether, stranding both vessels just as nightfall was coming on. In the final light before darkness descended over the waters, the *Hornet* fired a broadside at extreme range with her main deck eighteen-pounders, but every shot fell short.

Mitford watched the light go, chagrined. The last thing a warship of any navy wished was to be becalmed in darkness with the enemy a scant three miles away. But when the wind returned, it did so only in spasmodic puffs and then fizzled out again. Wary lest the *Hornet* drift too close under cover of the darkness, Mitford lowered his boats to heave the *Minotaur* to a safer distance, the crew hauling the ponderous bulk along by sheer muscle power. Having done all that was possible for the time being, he ordered a double tot of rum for the men and went below to partake of a cold meal with Charlie.

She was seated at his desk, busily filling a sheet of paper with lines of writing in a very pretty script, but she smiled brightly at him and asked if he was hungry.

"Famished," he replied, bending over to plant a kiss on

her tender nape. "You are keeping busy, I see," he added, eyeing the stack of pages already written and neatly stacked at her elbow.

"I had the most fabulous notion," she explained, fairly bouncing in her chair with excitement. "I am compiling a diary of our adventures. It will be such fascinating reading for our grandchildren one day."

"Of all the harebrained—" He swore softly under his breath and appeared to clamp a lid on his temper. "I have been moving heaven and earth to keep your escapade a secret. Why you must needs advertise it to the world passes my comprehension."

"I cannot conceive why it should pass your comprehension," she shot back, bridling. "You told me to find something to occupy my time."

"I seem to spend the greater part of my waking days extricating you from some scrape," he replied just as bitterly. "I have informed you that we are to surrender to the Americans. Is it your purpose to lay our secret at their feet? You wouldn't have a shred of your reputation left."

She blinked back a tear and said around the lump in her throat, "I am sure they would recognize in me a person of impeccable virtue."

His remarks on the folly of trusting strangers with a titillating morsel for gossip were caustic and to the point but had little visible effect. "You have known from the start that I don't behave as you think I ought," she said, sitting much more erect. "If you had not forced me to the altar, it would have been the better for both of us."

"It would indeed," he agreed, goaded.

She hunted through her pockets for a handkerchief and blew her nose defiantly. Furthermore, she said with a sniff, no other lady of his acquaintance would have permitted herself to sniff. He was immediately contrite. "We are quarreling," he said. "Forgive me?"

"I am equally to blame," she replied, but with a challenging gleam in her eye. "If you insist, I will destroy my diary."

"I will see to that myself," he said, taking her hands in his and pulling her to her feet. "And you are not to begin another. I've no mind to have the Admiralty assume I smuggled you aboard to serve my baser needs."

"Are you concerned with saving your face or mine?" she demanded, putting her hands on his chest to hold him off.

He bent and swept her off her feet. "Both," he said, and grinned, carrying her to his bed. "Before you ask it, no, I'm not all that hungry, and yes, we have plenty of time."

"I understood the captain remained on deck when his ship was in peril," she murmured, leaning back against the pillows. "You, sir, are neglecting your duties."

"There are duties and duties," he remarked, sitting down beside her and pushing her robe aside to bare her breasts. "How did you know not to wear your breeches? Were you so hungry for me that you could not bear to waste precious time undressing?"

A startled exclamation broke from her lips. "Richard!" she gasped as his hands cupped her breasts and his thumbs brushed back and forth over her nipples.

"It's a shame we haven't had more time alone together," he murmured, burying his face in the hollow of her throat. "God knows how long it will be before we are free to love again. We won't have a chance to do so in a Yankee prison."

She ran her fingers through his hair, surprised at the

183

chagrin she felt. Clearly she had come thoroughly to enjoy his lovemaking. Ladies were not supposed to find pleasure in it. Or so she had been told. I must be wanton, she thought, then wondered if he considered her joyous response to him to be unladylike.

Something of her agitation must have communicated itself to him. He raised his head and gazed into her eyes. "What is troubling you, my darling," he murmured, lightly brushing her lips with his.

"Why should you think that something is troubling me?" she evaded, flushing slightly.

He chuckled and planted a kiss on the tip of her nose. "You have few secrets from me now, my pet," he said outrageously. "Come now, what is it?"

She looked doubtful for a moment. "I am afraid that you must think me—forward," she ventured in timid accents.

A startled expression crossed his face. "Are you saying that you find something reprehensible in the love act?" he said, staring intently into her eyes.

She glanced away and pressed a hand to her forehead. "I —really don't know what I'm saying," she sighed.

No fool, he recalled her tale of the elderly dame residing next door in the years of her growing up. The self-righteous old harpy had filled her head with pernicious nonsense, he made no doubt. There was nothing for it but to correct the damage done in the only way he knew. Murmuring sweet words of love, he skillfully stirred the fires within her with tender kisses and exploring, practiced hands until she trembled beneath him and abandoned herself to his passion. And in the supreme intimacy when he at last entered her, she luxuriated in the violence of her response to him and moved with him and found the ultimate release that awaited her. Her eyes widening in surprise at the sensations quivering through her thighs, she clutched his shoulders and buried her face in his neck, glorying in the closeness of the moment. He remained by her side, murmuring soothingly and smoothing the hair from her brow until she fell into a deep and dreamless sleep. Only then did he rise and go on deck.

At about four o'clock in the night watch just enough light streaked the early morning sky to reveal a sail off their starboard side. Signals blinking through the half light informed Mitford that other sail lay off his larboard quarter. With the night lamp he challenged the ship between the *Minotaur* and land but was unable to decide whether the return signal came from an American vessel. It seemed likely that it did, since the light was blurred. So far as he knew, Broke's squadron was cruising off the coast of Florida and Allenwood should be somewhere in the vicinity of Halifax. Coming to the conclusion that he had blundered into the midst of Rodgers's American squadron, he could not forgo to smile. The *Hornet* had turned the tables on Melville by becoming the lone raider dispatched to lure unsuspecting British ships into Rodgers's net.

Full dawn revealed the extent of the trap. Bearing down on the *Minotaur* were the big American frigates *President* and *United States*, the smaller frigate *Congress* and the brig *Argus*. Crowding on all sail, Mitford turned about to make a convincing run for it, but the wind again turned light and fickle, finally dying down altogether. When the breeze at last freshened, the American super-frigates felt the effects first and tacked to come within range of the *Minotaur* to fire their big guns. In danger of being blown out of the water, Mitford ordered wet sloshed on the sails to hold the first stirring of the breeze to reach them and began to zigzag across the water, presenting the Americans with an uncertain target.

The brig *Argus* came up on the *Minotaur*'s port quarter and delivered a ragged fire before the *United States* could maneuver to bring her big guns to bear. The damage was more spectacular than effective. The *Minotaur*'s mizzenmast crashed to the deck and the slings of her main yard were shot away, but although the loss of sail cut down her speed, the injury was far from fatal. Under ordinary circumstances Mitford would merely have ordered the debris thrown overboard and returned the enemy's fire. As it was, he ordered the ensign lowered in surrender, the most bitter act of his career.

Thirty minutes later the *Minotaur* was again under way, bound for Norfolk and manned by a partial complement of American sailors. Mitford and the other officers had been allowed the courtesy of their quarters, but the common seamen had been herded forward on the main deck under guard of a detachment of United States marines. Daylight was fast fading when the final voyage of the once-proud frigate came to an end and a gig was lowered to convey her former officers to shore. To a man the crew dared to risk the anger of their captors by drawing themselves up in rigid attention when Mitford appeared on deck. The rays of the setting sun drew flashes of light from the brass buttons and gold lace of his uniform when he turned at the gangway to salute them before descending to the waiting gig.

Charlie had been well coached. She trailed a respectful pace behind the other officers to the gangway, climbed down unassisted and found a seat at the rear of the gig.

The citizens of Norfolk had been gathering at the quay

since news of the capture of a British frigate had spread like wildfire throughout the town. The holiday atmosphere prevailing attested to their glee. The longed-for had occurred. A once-proud enemy man-of-war had been met and beaten. By the time the gig bumped against the wharf, every vantage point in town was filled. With much jostling and many catcalls, the people strained to observe the drama in the uncertain light of flambeaux illuminating the scene. So great was their excitement that when Mitford stepped ashore, they mistook his uniform for one of theirs and sent up a cheer.

In the absence of Commodore Farnsworth, responsibility for the prisoners fell squarely on the shoulders of his second in command. It quickly became apparent that he was woefully out of his depth. Having returned Mitford's salute, he presented the compliments of the commodore and then appeared not to know what else to say. Mitford took charge. He requested that his officers be adequately housed until such time as they were exchanged, demanded separate quarters for himself and Charlie and forestalled refusal by identifying her as his nephew and thus next in line to himself as heir to the earldom.

As expected, the Americans were impressed. Within the hour Lieutenant Brompton and the others were billeted in the homes of substantial citizens whose wives and daughters viewed the whole affair as an opportunity to hobnob with titled lords, albeit they happened to belong to the enemy aristocracy. Somewhat to their surprise Mitford and Charlie found themselves incarcerated in Commodore Farnsworth's quarters in a Georgian manor house situated at the edge of town. No one thought to require their word that they not attempt to escape, and no guards were posted at their door. After all, where could they go?

Mitford became frankly worried. He had never heard of the commodore and could glean no inkling of his character from the furnishings of his rooms. The very absence of memorabilia gave rise to apprehension. What kind of man found so little of moment in his personal life that he would wish no token displayed to remind him of it? His quarters were nothing short of monkish. Where his subordinates had swallowed what they were told concerning Charlie, the possibility that the commodore might prove less gullible teased Mitford more than he would have her know. Since he assumed that she did not know, he held his counsel on the assumption that few misgivings ruffled the serenity of her mind.

In this placid view he was very much mistaken. She took care to conceal the trepidation she felt, and while this did much to allay his uneasiness, it did nothing at all to soothe her own. It did no good to tell herself that he would do nothing foolish, such as effecting their escape; very likely he would not—though there could be no guessing what a desperate man might do—but surely he would first devise a plan before sallying forth into enemy territory.

In any event, their destiny was in the hands of fate. On the third day following their arrival Broke appeared off Norfolk in search of Rodgers's squadron. With the *Shannon* were the *Africa,* the *Belvidera,* and the *Aeolus.* By evening, as the light began to go, the *Guerriere* came up to report negative results in her search for Rodgers. In the gathering darkness and with no American ships in sight upon which to vent their spleen, the candlelight flickering in the town provided the gunners with a handy target. The *Guerriere* opened fire, its main-deck guns raining shot along the waterfront. Not to be outdone, the *Belvidera* and *Aeolus* touched off their eighteen-pounders, wreaking havoc in the residential district and sending the terrified populace streaming into the streets. By the time the battery of the *Africa* added its voice to the fray, total pandemonium reigned. Every man who owned a conveyance of any sort piled his family into it and sent his horses flying out of town as if all the demons of hell were after him, while those citizens lacking transport ran distractedly hither and yon, wringing their hands and bleating of utter destruction.

Mitford, by now convinced that the commodore would imprison Charlie with the crew, saw his opportunity and seized it. Grabbing her by the hand, he pulled her willy-nilly down Farnsworth's front steps and joined the stream of residents running for their lives in the direction of open country. In the darkness they were indistinguishable members of a mob. In the daylight they would stand out like a sore thumb.

Once across a field of wheat, he turned their footsteps away from the course of the hysterical throng and paused in the lee of a stand of corn. Satisfied that no others followed in their wake, he led her in among the stalks and paused while they caught their breath.

Mitford was familiar with the eastern seacoast of the United States but had no notion of what lay inward. From the reputed size of her cities he surmised the America north of Norfolk must be heavily populated, but since he understood her plantations to be located in the South, settlements in that direction would be few and far between. Contrary to popular belief, he did not think it safer to travel by night and hole up by day. Few people stirred abroad at night to stumble upon one while one slumbered. A change of clothing must be effected, and soon, but garments filched from some farmer's clothesline would serve the purpose.

He had too great a regard for the truth to assure Charlie that all would go well, but he did tell her that they stood a fair chance of escaping. So while she was trying to persuade herself that this was so, they set forth in a southerly direction, undisturbed by the knowledge that their flight had been discovered. Mitford's carefree summers spent in evading his tutor on his father's country estate now stood him in good stead. He eschewed open fields for the more indirect but safer route of the hedgerows, kept his distance from farmhouses with barking dogs and avoided all roads and traveled pathways. If once or twice the faint sound of distant pounding hooves reached his ears, he could not know that patrols were out searching for them.

The first pale hint of dawn found them crossing a flat countryside that offered nothing in the way of concealment. No stand of trees, no pile of brush, not so much as a haystack could be seen in any direction. Only the lone silhouette of a single farmhouse disturbed the unbroken line of the horizon. There was nothing for it but to hope that it was deserted, which was a possibility since the soil had become of poor quality and was unlikely to grow crops. This was soon seen as a forlorn hope. A fine wisp of smoke curling from the chimney carried on the early morning breeze and gave them pause.

Since Charlie's clothing seemed unlikely to attract attention, Mitford hugged the ground while she stole forward to reconnoiter. In not above ten minutes she was back, her expression, if not smug, then at least well pleased. There was a smokehouse out back where they could hide. No,

190

silly, she said, no one would have cause to enter it. Last year's meat had been consumed, and it was not yet time to butcher.

Mitford looked doubtful, but having no choice, he circled around with her to come upon the smokehouse from the back. Pausing only while he snatched up a sturdy stick of kindling, they slipped inside and quietly closed the door behind them.

It was not a situation conducive to slumber. Not only were they very hungry, they were afraid to both go to sleep at once. So they compromised, taking turns at napping. At midmorning the farmer's wife came out to hang her laundry on the line, but no one else left the house all day. Peeking through a crack in the door, Charlie had her eye on the rough work pants and shirts drying in the sun. One pair might not be missed, she thought; not for the present, at least. Before Mitford could stop her, she was through the door and across the yard, the laundry screening her from view of the house. It took only a moment to snatch the garments from the line and to slide others over to fill the gap. While Mitford watched in disbelief, the kindling ready in his hand, she darted back and slipped inside, out of breath but triumphant.

They weren't a bad fit as work clothes go. Fortunately the farmer was close to Mitford's size. The shoulders of the shirt were rather much too tight, but a ripped seam took care of that. It only left the boots. No farmer would own a pair of Hessians, not even badly mud-splattered Hessians. Seeing the gleam in Charlie's eye, he silently shook his head and moved to lean against the door. He wouldn't put it past her to try to steal a pair of shoes.

She thought he looked so much the lord playing at being

191

his tenant that she nearly laughed aloud. No country provincial's hair had ever been so expertly trimmed. A rusted knife stuck into a beam must serve for a pair of scissors. He was not very enthusiastic at the idea but knew it must be done. It took her a considerable time and caused him considerable pain, but she hacked away until the job was accomplished. It was a haircut to make a barber shudder. It did, in fact, make Mitford shudder when he ran a hand over his once-proud locks. To his credit he managed a smile before bending to gather the clippings from the floor.

While it was still light he tore his linen shirt into strips and used pieces of kindling to fashion a snare. Charlie wondered what kind of small animal could be lured with the grains of corn he fished from a pocket of his discarded pantaloons, but it didn't matter. She was hungry enough to eat anything. As it turned out, that was exactly what she was destined to do.

Watching her choke down the greasy meat, it struck him that no other lady of his acquaintance would be so brave. Not only had she endured a tramp of several miles without comment before he set the trap, she had settled down to wait with no snide remark falling from her tongue. Not even the appearance of the small creature he eventually snared elicited so much as a single word. It had a long sharp nose and black rings around its muzzle, but he had no idea what it was called. A full stomach, however, works wonders. Morning saw them refreshed by a good night's sleep and ready to push onward. After they had breakfasted on the remainder of the meat, he cut off his boots at the ankles with the rusted knife, then dug a hole, using the kindling for a

192

spade. Having buried the remnants of his uniform, along with any possessions by which they could be identified, he scattered the coals of their fire and assisted Charlie to her feet.

CHAPTER 13

Setting out on foot along a road meandering southward, they had covered somewhat less than three quarters of a mile when Charlie suggested blithely that they turn their footsteps in the direction of the sea. "Please, Mitford, do let us!" she begged, catching him by the hand. "It would be such fun."

"Fun!" he ejaculated, coming to a standstill in the middle of the road.

"We could walk barefoot through the sand. And now I come to think of it, we could look for seashells. Why, there is no telling what we might find. Our next-door neighbor, Mrs. Cogswell—remember I told you of her?"

"I do," he replied grimly.

"Well, Mrs. Cogswell had a piece of driftwood she brought back from a holiday at the seashore."

"I am not a beachcomber," he said dampingly. "Nor, I may add, are you."

"One needn't be to enjoy it, you know."

"No, I don't know," he said. "We are strangers in a foreign land. For all we know the coastline could be rocky."

"You needn't be cantankerous," she said. "After all, you are the one who brought us here. I had no desire to come to America."

"In that case," he said, "it seems perhaps a pity that you stowed away aboard my vessel. Come along now and save your breath. You will need it for walking. I have no idea how far it is to some place of habitation."

"I expect you mean a town," she said, tucking her hand in his arm. "What will we do there?"

"I will seek gainful employment to earn our daily bread. You, my dear, will contrive to remain inconspicuous."

"What work do you expect to find?"

"I am not prepared to say," he replied cautiously. "I promise you, however, that tonight we will sleep in a bed like Christians."

"Oh," she murmured, considering this. "You must regret having me on your hands."

"By no means. I have become entirely resigned."

"You must have hated sleeping on the ground."

"I hope with all my heart never again to spend a night in such discomfort," he replied, eyeing her with some severity. "The more I think of it the more convinced I become that I have been led astray."

She took it as a compliment. "I expect we have both become depraved," she said, giving a little skip in an excess of pure joy.

"You are a menace," he announced, a smile twitching at the corners of his mouth.

She looked gratified. "No, am I?" she said.

"Look what you have done to me."

"Yes, but I don't imagine that you were ever entirely respectable," she objected.

"I was once, but that was before I met you."

"I am well aware of the life you led before you met me."

"There was no occasion over which you should trouble your pretty head, believe me."

"By occasion I imagine you mean affair," she said, going off on a peal of laughter.

He looked down at her for an instant, then removed her hand from his arm. "You must not think me an incurable wet blanket, but if I am to extricate us from our present difficulty, you will at all times remember that you are a boy. No one must entertain any doubts of that."

Since they were on a deserted stretch of road it seemed safe to assume that there was no cause for worry. It was now considerably after ten o'clock. The sky had turned leaden while the air remained warm, a possible portent of rain. Mitford was in the act of scanning the surrounding countryside for a place of shelter when the squeal of wagon wheels coming up behind them reached their ears. Glancing back over his shoulder, he first moved aside, then stepped back to the center of the road, resolutely barring the way. "We will be obliged if you will take us up," he said to the farmer in what he hoped was a fair imitation of the speech obtaining in those parts. "We have been walking for days, and my young brother is about all in."

The farmer looked them over in a measuring way, then turned his head to spit a stream of tobacco juice at a stand of weeds flourishing beside the road. "Never coddled my young 'uns," he muttered around the chew bulging in his cheek. "Spoils 'em."

197

"I couldn't agree more," Mitford assured him with a perfectly straight face. "Charlie is a brat. I am tired myself, however, and would appreciate a ride."

"Mebbe so," the farmer drawled, a glint of suspicion in his eyes. "Seen some soldiers a few miles back."

Mitford's heart sank, but he managed an indifferent shrug. "We won't seek them out," he said. "If they are not drunk now, they soon will be. I won't have my young brother traveling in such company."

"Said as how they're out lookin' for some escaped prisoners o' war."

Mitford assumed an air of outraged hauteur. "Are you implying that I look like some damn sniveling Englishman?" he demanded.

The farmer was convinced. "Cain't say as how ye do," he said. "Howsomever, it don't make me no never mind. 'Tain't room for both of you'ns up here."

Mitford cast an eye over the household goods piled up behind and stepped back, resigned to the prospect of continuing the journey on foot. Not so, Charlie. Smiling brightly, she offered to sit on Mitford's lap, and at a surly nod from the farmer, she hopped up on the wagon. With nothing left for him to do but follow, Mitford settled himself and took her on his knee while mentally composing a speech destined for her sole edification.

Instinct kept Mitford silent, but Charlie volunteered the information that he was taking her to live with an aunt before enlisting in the navy. Turning his head, Mitford encountered the laconic gaze of the farmer and felt compelled to corroborate her fabrication. "I thought I would sign up while I still have the chance," he said, giving

Charlie an admonitory pinch. "I would hate to miss the action."

The farmer expertly sent another stream of tobacco juice streaking to the ground. "Be plenty o' fightin' to go 'round," he said, wiping his mouth on the back of his sleeve. "No need to get in a schivit."

Sheer devilry prompted Mitford. "Do you think we stand a chance against the might of England?" he said, a certain diffidence in the inquiring gaze he turned on the farmer's face.

His quarry unbent, as it was intended that he should. "We been through too much asettin' up this here country o' our'n to let a pack o' furreiners take it from us," he said, his opinion of Mitford soaring. "You young'uns just go out an' fight like yer grandpas fit, and we ain't got no cause to worrit."

"But their navy is larger than ours, you will admit," Charlie interjected, not to be outdone.

What passed for a smile stretched the farmer's lips. "Ever see a pack o' hounds tree a cat?" he asked.

Charlie blinked at him. "What happens to the cat?" she said curiously.

"Spits an' claws 'till the dogs take off with their tails 'twixt their legs. Cain't see no difference, m'self."

Mitford regarded him with dawning respect. "It has been my contention that we—that England," he amended, covering his slip, "has underrated us."

"Mebbe so," the farmer agreed. "Seems as how there's a pack o' fools over there, same as here. Never did see a politician as had a lick o' sense. Course they ain't the ones as has got to fight the wars," he added ruminatingly.

"Then you don't blame the British?"

"Don't do no good to lay the blame. Folks oughta try to git along. They got their way o' doin' things, and we got our'n. Live an' let live, is what I say."

Mitford, silenced, leaned back and gave himself over to the languor brought on by the steady clop of the horse's hooves. He had had good reason in the past to know that Charlie's tongue had a way of running away with itself. He had also been the recipient of her overly productive imagination, but she now proceeded to outdo herself.

In the entirely mendacious tale she poured into the farmer's ear, he was pictured as having tried his hand at numerous occupations, apparently with little success, while she had contributed her mite to the family coffers in any way she could. Since this last bit of embroidery was accompanied by heartrending sighs, the farmer found himself offering to share the contents of the hamper of food at his feet. Charlie, her mouth full of bread and cheese, directed a mischievous look at Mitford and graciously accepted a piece of chicken.

It was definitely time to part company with their benefactor. As the farmer plunged into a long and involved recital of his own wanderings, in which his present move loomed large, Charlie was looking entirely too solicitous. Alert lest the mention of some locale bring an untimely query to her tongue, Mitford scanned the road ahead for a crossroad that would provide an excuse to decamp. A mile farther on he found what he sought. After ascertaining that the farmer would continue on the road leading south, he disclosed that their destination lay to the west and asked to be put down.

The farmer drew the wagon to a halt and reached for the hamper of food. "Can't stand to see a young'un go hungry," he remarked, handing Charlie a generous portion of his bread and cheese.

"Thank you, sir," she said, jumping to the ground. "I will remember you in my prayers tonight."

The good man looked embarrassed. "See you behave yerself at your aunt's," he growled over his shoulder as he drove away.

Charlie turned from waving farewell and looked questioningly at Mitford. "I am sure I can walk anywhere you say, but I don't see the sense of it when we could ride."

"Nothing would have induced me to endure another minute of our erstwhile companion's afflictive company."

"I must own I was becoming a little bored myself," she admitted, stepping out by his side. "Why are we going in this direction?"

"The unexpected is often the best defense, my dear. The soldiers will expect our flight to follow a straight line. We will shortly retrace our steps and look for a road that more closely parallels the coast. Unless I am much mistaken, we have been angling away from it."

"What shall we do when we reach the ocean?"

"Look for a small craft of some sort."

"You mean steal one."

"Do you mind?"

"Not unless you expect me to do the rowing."

He smiled. "No, that would indeed be fatal. We will be wise to—er, select a sailboat. I'm sure you will agree it will be safer to sail down the coast out of sight of land."

She gave a ripple of sudden laughter. "Do you think you will be able to keep us afloat?"

"Thank you," he said.

They had not gone much farther when they were joined

by an overly friendly pup of doubtful ancestry. Amiable in the extreme, he first greeted them with hysterical yelps, then succumbed to an overwhelming desire to jump up at them. The first ecstasy of excitement out of the way, he further impeded their progress by gamboling around their feet and in general enacted the role of a dog long denied the pleasures of human companionship. They both knew better. Except for a few bits of bramble clinging to his flanks, he appeared to be groomed and fed. It came, therefore, as no surprise when he dashed off in the direction of a house some distance away and surrounded by a grove of trees.

A few hundred yards ahead a heavy farm gate provided access to a rutted lane leading off through a woods that had all the appearance of a wilderness. "The devil take it," Mitford muttered. "We must be coming upon a town. There is nothing for it. We must double back across country."

"But if there are only two houses—"

"I am afraid there could be more. Well, it is my fault for coming this way at all. Do you think you can keep up if we cut back through that woods?"

"I see I am more ramshackle than other females you have known. A few brambles hold no terrors for me."

Though this last was said with a twinkle in her eye, he was not looking at her but at a black cloud looming to the west. "We must find shelter before that storm comes down on us," he said, catching her by the hand and running with her to the gate.

They were no more than scarcely in among the trees when a troop of mounted cavalry came pounding down the road. Mitford immediately pushed her none too gently to the ground and flung himself down beside her, his head raised just enough that he might observe the riders. Fortunately their attention was so taken up in scanning the underbrush on either side while at the same time watching the thundercloud that their search was only cursory. Mitford fretted unbearably until the last of them was out of sight.

Pulling Charlie to her feet, he set off on a line roughly parallel to the road, with Charlie stumbling along behind him. Though the going was rough, an occasional wild flower reared its lovely head to lend a certain charm to the scene.

Coming at last upon a stream that wound its way through the woods, Mitford paused, debating the advisability of opting for the more direct route through the brambles as opposed to the easier going of the gentle declivity beside the water. A rustling in the undergrowth decided him. While he was not of a nervous disposition and would not as a rule find the sound in any way disturbing, nevertheless he had heard tales of a poisonous snake that gave off a rattling sound before it struck.

"You needn't stop on my account," Charlie gasped, coming to a halt beside him. "Where does this stream lead?"

"I haven't the slightest idea," he replied. "So long as it continues in an easterly direction, we will follow it. What have you there?"

"A stout stick, silly. I can see you have never wandered alone through a woods."

"Not an unkempt one, surely. And presently I shall have something to say to you on the subject of your having once done so."

She snorted. "What a poor-spirited creature you must think me," she said in disgusted accents.

"I suppose," he replied sardonically, "you would have me turn a blind eye to anything you do."

"You'be become tired, and worried," she announced promptly.

"So have you," he shot back, a dry note in his voice. "May I suggest that we continue this idiotic escapade of ours? Or perhaps you prefer to stand arguing in the rain."

"I did notice a drop or two a short while back. Do you know what I think, Richard?"

"Probably."

"Don't be snide. It is my belief that if we follow this stream we may come upon a mill. As I recall there was one much like it at home. Why else would the water seem deep enough to be coming from a spring?"

"Why indeed," he agreed. "I apprehend that there is a brain under all that beauty."

"Fustian," she said, falling into step beside him.

They experienced no difficulty with their footing and soon came to a pond formed by an earthen dam that had been thrown up across the stream. An old barn off to one side had once housed cattle but was now used as a storehouse for rusted tools and broken plows. The floor was strewn with wisps of straw that had sifted down from an open loft that covered half its length and was reached by means of a short ladder. If Mitford was a good deal taken aback by the obvious neglect, he contrived not to show alarm. While Charlie did not seem to be surprised, she did look a trifle worried. An abandoned structure could as well furnish criminals with a place to hide as it could provide them with a haven from the storm.

The gentle patter of raindrops striking the roof quickly turned into a drumming when the skies opened and the deluge came pouring down. Within minutes rivulets of water began to creep across the floor through the decaying foundation.

"Do you think the entire barn will come crashing down on us?" she inquired, casting an apprehensive glance around. "For if you think so, I'd as lief leave."

"No, we would be soaked to the skin in seconds." He spoke lightly yet with a hint of roughness in his voice as though he were not quite convinced himself. "Before we find ourselves standing in a river, we had best go into the loft."

"Well, if you think it is safe—"

"My dear, this structure has stood for years and will no doubt continue to do so. Up you go."

"Then you may take charge of our supper. That ladder looks none too steady, and I'd just as soon not have anything in my hands when I climb it."

He accepted the bread and cheese and smiled rather devilishly. "Shall I carry you as well?" he said.

She glanced at him with laughter in her eyes but replied, "No, odious wretch, you will not carry me. I have no wish to be dumped in the mud."

"At least permit me to steady the ladder," he said, grasping it in a firm hand.

"Do," she said, starting to climb.

He gave the ladder a slight shake. "You are jiggling it," he said with a chuckle.

"Horrible creature," she said, turning her head to smile down at him. "You are doing that yourself."

"No, not I. You must be putting on weight."

She tried to make her mouth prim but failed. "What an unhandsome thing to say," she said.

He reached out a hand and patted her rounded bottom.

"You have no idea how unlike a boy you appear from here," he grinned. "Those breeches are stretched very tight, believe me. Are you certain you haven't picked up a few pounds?"

"You just haven't before seen me upside down," she retorted, scrambling up the ladder. "Behave yourself, or I will forbid you the loft."

"Will you now," he murmured, going up hand over hand. "Nothing you can do will swerve me from my purpose."

"Be careful with our bread and cheese," she cautioned as he bounded from the top rung. "I'm famished."

"Must you think of food at a time like this?" he said, slipping an arm about her waist. "For shame."

"If you mean to make love before we eat, as I conclude you do, I wish you will say so."

"I am saying so."

"Heathen," she said, laughing up at him. "At least let me make the bed."

"The floor will be our bed," he replied, stripping off his trousers.

"No, I will rake the straw into a pile. Won't that be inviting?"

"It won't," he said, advancing on her.

"Ungrateful wretch," she said with a giggle, backing away. "I don't know why I work my fingers to the bone for you."

"You must like your reward," he said, and grinned, backing her into a corner. "Quit squirming. How do you expect me to unfasten the buttons on your breeches if you wriggle about."

"It is very becoming of you to pretend that you find me

enticing," she murmured, seeking reassurance. "I must look a fright."

He understood her need. "You have never before in your life been more entrancing," he said, sinking with her to the floor. "Darling girl, you are beautiful to me in any guise."

"I am?" she said, threshing about in an effort to more comfortably compose herself. "The straw is tickling me."

"Hold still," he admonished. "How am I to make love to you if you jump around."

"With finesse, sir," she gurgled, much pleased with her reply. "With finesse."

CHAPTER 14

"I have decided not to purchase the bonnet in Mrs. Crimmens's shop," Charlie remarked. "The price is nineteen shillings, mind. I shouldn't think anyone would pay so much." When Mitford failed to reply, she continued in a male sotto voce, "How is that, my dear? Nineteen shillings? You may purchase anything your little heart desires."

His attention caught, he turned his head and glanced at her, his brows raised in startled inquiry. "Were you speaking to me?" he said.

"How nice of you to notice," she remarked. "One feels so at ease when one finds oneself talking to oneself."

"I was abstracted. Forgive me."

"You have permitted the conversation to lapse, in addition to which you have forgotten to feed me. I ought not to allow you at table."

Since they were seated at the edge of the loft with their feet dangling in space, this last remark elicited a chuckle from him. "Quite starving, are you?" he said, breaking off a bit of bread and cheese and putting it into her mouth.

"It was most unchivalrous of you," she complained, pouting prettily. "The least you could do would be to tell me your thoughts."

"You are a born flirt," he remarked, nibbling at her ear and sending shivers down her spine. "I was thinking of the war. If people made a push to understand one another, there would be no need to fight."

"It can't be the weather," she mused, cocking her head at him. "I have seldom seen a lovelier morning. Oh! I know what it is! Your Christian bed turned into a hayloft. We can only hope that Cinderella found her pumpkin less untidy."

"Certainly she did not awaken with straw sticking to her bare bottom. And that, little craven, is the set-down you deserve."

An impish smile curved her lips. "Are you trying to pick a quarrel with me?" she demanded.

"I am trying to put an end to your witticisms," he replied. "Since you asked for my thoughts, it is only fair that you listen. An understanding of current events is a hallmark of a well-informed mind, my dear."

She considered this. "Are society ladies interested in such things?" she asked.

"Alas, no."

"I have heard that the haut monde spends its time in routs and balls. Is this true?"

"For the most part, yes."

"It sounds like fun," she remarked, brushing the bread crumbs from her breeches.

"Far be it from me to return to the original trend of our

210

conversation," he said, "but I am determined to have my say."

She assumed an expression of rapt interest. "I am all attention," she said, peeping at him from under her lashes.

He decided to ignore the provocation. "You have been brave—I admit that," he said. "But if anyone were to ask me why I have not taken a stick to you, I could not tell him."

"My manners are atrocious, I know, but it's not because I mean to vex you."

"You amaze me," he said.

"Well, but no one cares to bare his soul," she replied, giving an exaggerated sigh.

"Careful, my dear, careful," he said with a chuckle. "You will end up surprising me."

"To put it plainly," she persisted, intending to do just that, "I feel so—unschooled in matters of the world."

"Your apology is becoming rather involved," he said.

"Ignorant, then," she amended. "I haven't the vaguest notion what this war is all about."

"You aren't alone," he said ruefully. "I am sure that no one in London could put forth an explanation that made the least sense. Just about every action the politicians have taken has been shortsighted and petty. Although none of them would admit it, we had no more right to seize America's vessels than Napoleon had the right to say she couldn't trade with us."

"Couldn't she trade with—well, with someone else?"

"Not very hopefully. Her seaboard states had built their livelihood on commerce with both our nations."

"Hah!" she snorted. "If women were running things, I can assure you we would never go to war over money."

211

He looked first startled, then amused. "If women were running things, there would be no money," he said.

She looked annoyed. "You were the one who wanted to talk about it," she retorted. "I didn't."

"Calm yourself, my dear," he said, controlling a quivering lip. "I was only jesting. As a matter of fact, there was more to it than that. We had—well, fallen into the habit of impressing American sailors into service aboard our vessels."

"I suppose it is useless to ask whom we have to blame for that?"

"Quite useless, my dear."

"Or what we hoped to gain by it?"

"No, I can answer that. Our own sailors had been deserting in such numbers that we were desperate for seamen—any seamen—to keep our ships afloat."

"Why were our sailors deserting?"

"Our Admiralty is top-heavy with stiff-necked old martinets who can't, or won't, comprehend the lot of the common seaman. Perhaps I can help remedy that."

"But what can you do about it?" she said, more confused than ever.

"I can convince my father to express my views in the House of Lords. Parliament must be made to see that no nation will turn a blind eye on hostile acts against its people. Haven't we English built our standing in the world by refusing to do so? And that goes for injustices for our people at home as well as for acts against our citizens abroad."

"Are you saying that America went to war to defend her reputation?"

"I am saying that she is willing to fight to defend the

212

principles she holds dear. Any nation willing to tolerate terrorism against its nationals cannot hope to endure."

"Then responsibility for the war can be laid at our door?"

"By no means."

"I thought not. It takes two to fight."

"Very aptly put, my dear. As a matter of fact, negotiations to resolve our differences were showing signs of progress when America declared war. Had her Congress waited a few more weeks, I doubt not that it could have been avoided."

She snuggled closer against his shoulder. "Are you taking me to London with you? While you are convincing your father, I mean."

"I shall place you under my aunt's wing until a discreet time has passed. I will then marry you with all the pomp and ceremony society will expect." He saw her eyes grow apprehensive and added, "Your wedding gown will be white, of course."

"But I would feel out of place with your aunt, Richard. I don't even know her."

"That is easily remedied."

"I am sure she wouldn't wish a stranger foisted off on her. I would much rather go to your home."

"I am sure you know you cannot live with me while all the world believes you to be single. No, let me speak. There is no way we could explain our marriage. Where would you say you have been all this time?"

"I could have been at home waiting for your return. People do marry secretly, you know."

"Usually with cause," he replied dryly. "Do you think I will have people speculating about you and counting the

213

months when you become pregnant? No, you will do as I say."

There came a pause. "Perhaps I am already with child," she murmured, stricken at the difficulties the thought conjured up.

"You aren't," he said, tightening his arm about her.

She rested against him, her curls tickling his chin. "You can't know for sure," she whispered, a catch coming into her voice.

"I do," he murmured, brushing his lips against her hair. "Trust me, dearest."

"But—"

"Please don't worry. Now be a good girl and listen to my plans. We will tell the world that we first met when you were a student of your vicar and I had occasion to call at your village church. We fell in love, of course, and became engaged, but only after I sought and received the blessings of your guardian."

"Now that," she said, "is coming it much too strong."

"Not at all. He will fall in line, believe me. By the time I am through with him, he will be charmed to give the bride away."

"I doubt it," she said.

"Don't interrupt. We will allow Papa the privilege of sending the announcement of our banns to the newspapers. Bless him, how he will enjoy twitting Auntie Meg."

"Of course," she murmured, bewildered and trying to hide it.

"There is nothing that gives either of them more pleasure than pulling the wool over the other's eyes. Knowing that she isn't in on our secret will add a certain spice for him."

"Then you plan to tell your father that we are married?"

"The instant I see him."

"It seems unfair to keep your aunt in the dark. After all, if she is to have the responsibility—"

"Indiscretions have a way of falling from her lips. We shan't risk it." When she said nothing further, he got to his feet. "There is no telling what will next befall us, but it would be unwise to remain overly long in one place. Wait until I see if the coast is clear before you come down."

There was a troubled note in his voice, but she failed to notice it. The knowledge that their return to England meant a separation, however brief, put all else from her mind. She sat for a time, disconsolate and lost in thought, before getting to her feet.

She saw no sign of Mitford when she began to descend the ladder, but by the time she reached the floor she heard his voice, raised in furious protest and coming from outside the barn. There was no way she could have missed the warning in his tone. Going stealthily forward, she paused well out of sight and cautiously peeped through a crack in the double doors that were sagging on their hinges and hopelessly askew. His back was toward her and he was retreating backward, his attention riveted on two grinning ruffians advancing on him, obviously on the assumption that they had come upon easy pickings. The taller of the two still wore the tattered remains of an army uniform and was slowly moving his hand back and forth in a swiping motion. This puzzled Charlie, unfamiliar with the ruder ways of combat, until the sun glinted on the blade of a knife. Horrified, she clamped a hand over her mouth to keep from crying out and looked about for something to serve Mitford for a weapon.

A pile of rusted tools in a nearby corner caught her eye.

In a matter of seconds she had made her selection and was back beside the door, a pitchfork in one hand and an ax in the other. Mitford, backing through the door, saw her out of the corner of his eye and reached for the pitchfork just as the ruffians dashed forward, intending to close in for the kill.

Charlie didn't stop to moralize. There wasn't time. She swung the ax at the nearest scoundrel, splitting his head wide open, at about the same moment that Mitford buried the pitchfork in the other brigand's chest. On the instant he swept her up in his arms and carried her outside, her face buried in his throat.

He was prepared for hysterics, and he was prepared for tears, but he was not prepared for the gurgle of laughter that issued from her throat. "They nearly had us, didn't they?" she said.

He stopped stock-still and stared down at her. "So it brought you glee, did it?" he said, put out.

"They would have killed us," she pointed out reasonably. "We just beat them to it is all."

"Adversity seems to produce a strange effect on you," he remarked. "May I inquire if you feel any remorse at all?"

"None," she said. "Do you?"

"To tell you the truth, no," he replied, a curious smile curving his lips. "I believe I have to thank you. I had no idea what I was to do once I had backed into the barn."

"You would have thought of something. You may put me down now. I am quite capable of walking."

"It gives me pleasure to carry you," he demurred, striding off across a field.

"Did you always treat females in this high-handed fashion?" she said, raising her head to favor him with a look of sweet innocence.

216

He smiled. "I have only once in my life known one who deserved to be so treated," he said.

"Oh?" she gurgled. "And who was she?"

"An unprincipled brat who dressed in boy's clothing."

"She sounds enticing. Were you enticed?"

"You are a minx, my dear," he said, setting her on her feet.

Sudden tears welled in her eyes. "Do you think that I am bloodthirsty?" she said in a barely audible voice.

"What is this?" he demanded, wiping the teardrops from her cheeks. "My brave girl, crying? There is nothing more to frighten you."

"I just don't want you to think—"

"I think you are the grandest, most courageous woman in the world. You saved both our lives."

"I did, didn't I," she said, her buoyancy returning.

The big meadow separated the woods from the road and had a drainage ditch running through it that supported a thick undergrowth. It was just the cover Mitford preferred. Leading Charlie to it, he said, "Move carefully, sweet. We don't want it to appear as if a herd of elephants is passing through."

"Speak for yourself," she taunted, dancing away. "You can't catch me."

"Come back here!" he growled, making a grab for her.

"I shan't," she said with a giggle, fleeing down the ditch.

"Damn!" Mitford muttered, crashing through the underbrush in hot pursuit. "Stop making so much noise, you little fool!"

Throwing a saucy glance back over her shoulder, she chuckled upon finding him much nearer at hand than she had thought, then gasped when he tackled her to the ground.

The breath was momentarily knocked out of her, but she recovered quickly, her temper in shreds. "I will thank you to get off my back!" she said, wiping the chaff from her lips. "Of all the mean things to do!"

"Will you be quiet!" he hissed. "You will have the cavalry down on us!"

"You are heavy, let me tell you," she went on, heedless of the warning and beginning to struggle. "Will you please—"

Whatever she intended saying was forever lost when he clamped his hand over her mouth and breathed a soft "Shh!" in her ear.

She heard it then—the drumming of horses' hooves approaching from the north and rapidly coming nearer. Their situation was desperate, she knew. Soldiers seemed to pop up everywhere they turned. She did not see what they were to do once they had stolen a boat and were sailing down the coast, but she reasoned that Mitford must surely have some destination in mind. She felt cold inside, and her heart seemed to pound in rhythm with the galloping horses, but they swept by without breaking stride and vanished down the road.

Mitford waited until the last echo of sound faded in the distance, then picked himself up and reached down a hand to help her to her feet. "Saving us is becoming a habit with you," he remarked, carrying her fingers to his lips. "If you had not forced me to hurl you to the ground, we might have been seen."

"It is nice to be appreciated," she observed, rubbing an elbow. "Well, what next?"

"We have nothing to do now but to gain the cover of that woodland," he replied, jerking his head in the direction of the highway. "We need only cross the road and the open field beside it."

"I envy you your confidence," she confessed. "It would be dreadful to be arrested after all we have endured."

"I trust that will not come to pass," he said. "We need only remain alert against being taken unaware."

"I'm not afraid, you understand. It is just that I am —cautious."

"A good way to be, my dear. Are you coming?"

"Yes, but I wish you will tell me what I am to do if someone happens along."

"Enact your usual role of a scruffy schoolboy," he said and grinned. "Now, come along!"

She followed him out of the ditch and to the edge of the road. He appeared to have taken the close call to heart, for he looked carefully up and down before seizing her by the hand and darting across. The stubble of the cornfield made running difficult, and by the time they reached the shelter of the trees he was agreeable to her suggestion that they rest.

"I suppose you think me poor spirited," she murmured, dropping to the ground.

"Oh, I don't care about that," he said, grinning.

"You needn't tease. My feet are quite bruised, you know. Should you like to see them?"

"Immensely, but not at the moment."

"Perhaps I won't be able to take another step."

"I think you will. In fact, I am positive of it."

"If I can't, will you carry me?"

"No," he said, not mincing matters.

"That is what I feared," she said with a sigh, getting to her feet.

He led her in and out among the trees, through the

219

tangled undergrowth and along a small stream running in the direction of the sea, pausing often to listen intently before moving on and always keeping clear of a footpath that meandered through the woods, until they found themselves coming out into the open beside a rutted road that led to a farmhouse and, beyond that, a number of cottages clustered around a church spire.

"If there are other places of habitation in the neighborhood, access to them will lead off this lane," Mitford said, looking about. "The fields seem to be laid out in some pattern. If we follow the stone walls, I should think we won't be seen."

"Perhaps someone in the village would exchange a day's work for a decent meal," she suggested tentatively.

"It is too near the main thoroughfare. The cavalry has surely been this way by now. No, we will go farther before we trust to luck."

Expecting her to follow him, he forced his way through the hedge and set out along the edge of a field. Having been recently plowed, it made for easy walking; they were quickly across it and pushing into a marshy bog.

"I beg of you!" Charlie groaned, pausing ankle deep in brackish water. "We will catch our death!"

"Keep moving!" he growled, placing a hand beneath her elbow and urging her forward. "If you stop you will mire down. Try to step on those tufts of vegetation."

"It's a quagmire," she said, struggling to keep her shoes from parting company with her feet. "A demmed swamp!"

"My dear!" he ejaculated, startled. "That is an unladylike thing to say!"

"No lady would be caught dead sloshing around in here!"

she informed him, indignant but determinedly floundering onward through the mud.

"Be thankful for it," he soothed, his lips twitching. "Brackish water is found in marshes near the sea."

"Speak for yourself," she muttered half under her breath. "You'll pay for this, Richard. See if you don't."

"Watch out for those reeds," he cautioned, assisting her along. "They can cut like a knife."

"Cripes!" she yelped, jerking back an arm. "Now you tell me!"

Mitford stiffened. "I beg your pardon?" he said, incredulous.

"I said cripes," she repeated, cutting her eyes at him.

"I heard you," he shot back, his voice cold as ice. "It is a vulgarity. You will not use it again."

"You didn't say that *demmed* is vulgar."

"In future, you will refrain from all unseemly conversation."

Charlie wondered later how they endured the struggle to cross the marsh. It seemed to go on forever. Every step became a nightmare of swirling water and sucking mud. No sooner had one shoe been retrieved than the other became stuck in the slimy muck. Mitford would not hear of leaving them behind and going on unshod. There was no knowing what manner of life thrived in the spongy ground.

They paused often to rest and to scan the horizon from any hillock they came across, as fearful of what they might see as of being seen. They saw nothing at all. The reeds grew as tall as their heads and higher, screening the world from view.

It was coming on dusk when they at last broke through the outer fringe of the swamp and partially stumbled, partially crawled to higher ground. Charlie would have sunk down where she stood, but Mitford would not risk it. For the past hour brief glimpses of the heads of swimming serpents had had him half out of his mind with worry that they might be forced to spend the night in the bog. They must go on, he knew. Reptiles had been known to curl up on humans while they slept, drawn by the warmth of their bodies.

"I can't go any farther," Charlie groaned in weary protest. "Just let me lie down and die in peace."

"You said much the same thing aboard my ship, you will recall," Mitford chided her more cheerfully than he felt. "You lived then. You will now."

"If we could rest—perhaps an hour—"

"Trying to bargain with me, are you?" he said, guiding her staggering footsteps with an arm about her waist. "Remain my brave girl a short while longer."

"Are you disappointed in me?" she said, summoning a weak smile.

"Good!" he replied. "You are recovered enough to display an unseemly tendency to tease."

On this bracing note he led her toward the sound of the distant surf. After the problems encountered in wading through the swamp, walking through the sand was not at all difficult. It was another two miles, however, before the patches of gorse gave way to rolling dunes. Just as they were about to leave them to explore the beach, a voice drifted to them from across the water, and to Charlie's astonishment, Mitford clamped a hand over her mouth as though he feared that she would speak.

In the moonlight a fishing boat was clearly visible some distance from shore and moving in a northerly direction parallel to the shore. A slight pressure on her shoulder sent her down behind a dune. Mitford crouched beside her, peering over the crest of the sand until the craft was out of sight. By the time he too sank down, exhaustion had taken its toll, and she was sound asleep. Stretching out beside her, he cuddled her head on his shoulder, gently kissed her brow and gave himself up to slumber.

The sun rode high before Charlie stirred in Mitford's arms and opened her eyes, a little surprised to find her muscles stiff. Raising her head, she encountered his sleepy gaze and demanded, "Have we anything left for breakfast?"

"It's a pity that you must always think of food. Try to dwell on something else."

"What happened about the boat last night?" she asked, striving to take her mind off her stomach.

"I don't think anything of particular moment occurred."

"Then they didn't try to land?"

"No, nothing so exciting. They merely went on their way. We should now do the same."

Her good intention went for naught. "I hope you are not suggesting that we dispense with eating altogether," she said.

"What would you suggest?"

"Oh, I should think there would be a village nearby. Those fishermen we saw last night must live somewhere."

"Undoubtedly they must, but we are traveling south," he replied, getting to his feet. "When we come upon a house where the occupants are from home, I plan to enter it as —er, unobtrusively as possible."

"By a window, you mean. I'm sure I do not care whether you work for our food or steal it."

223

He threw back his head and laughed. "Neither do I," he said. "We are fast becoming a disreputable pair."

They had gone not more than two miles when they came upon a weatherbeaten inn situated in an isolated cove. It was reached by a narrow lane that wound its way among the dunes, and the ground around it was littered with a varied assortment of kegs and boxes. Mitford, running a knowing eye over the establishment, mentally wrote it down as a way station for smugglers and thieves. Circling to approach it from the rear, they discovered the landlord's wife in the act of stowing a basket of food under the seat of a trap.

"While I claim the good dame's attention, you will . . . well . . . filch the basket," Mitford whispered in Charlie's ear. "Do you think you can do so without being seen?"

Eyes dancing, she nodded, then stole forward to hide behind a large dune at the edge of the backyard. Satisfied, he retraced his steps to enter the front door and set up a shout that sent the woman bustling back inside. The door had scarcely closed behind her when Charlie darted forward, snatched up the basket and flew back out of sight.

Mitford, meanwhile, was favoring the landlady with a tale of hardship that would have done justice to one of Charlie's most outrageous flights of fancy. To hear him tell it, ill luck had dogged his footsteps from the day he was drummed out of the army for failing to display a seemly respect before his superior officers. Despite his blandishments, Madam remained unimpressed, as he had known she would. Strangers could hardly expect to be welcome in a veritable den of thieves. Still protesting his innocence, he backed out of the door and ambled off down the beach to the south, kicking at pebbles for all the world like a disgruntled wanderer.

Charlie crept from dune to dune, always hidden but keeping pace with him, until a bend in the coastline shut them off from sight of the inn. Whistling a jaunty tune, she danced forward to join him. "We did it!" she chortled, giving a little skip.

"We did," he agreed, smiling indulgently. "And now you may give me that basket before you drop it."

"I don't know if I should," she teased, gripping it firmly. "You might be one of those persons who needs must walk for miles before breakfast."

"You own an unseemly appetite, my dear," he remarked. "I had no notion you were such a glutton. Besides, if you continue jostling it about, you will have the contents spilled on the sand."

"You are just pretending that you aren't hungry," she gloated. "Admit it."

"I never pretend," he said, selecting a picnic site between two dunes.

To their delight, the basket contained two large packets of sandwiches, a container of fried chicken, a pie wrapped in a cloth and two bottles of a surprisingly palatable wine. Charlie, mindful of his remarks, accepted a sandwich but refused the chicken. Mitford did not insist. The viands might well prove their sole sustenance during the coming days.

Replete, they again set off down the beach, this time with a more purposeful stride. While that stretch of the coast seemed empty of human life, still the inn must boast of a patronage of sorts to camouflage its existence to the law.

At first Charlie found much to exclaim over. There was driftwood bobbing in the surf, and shells left behind by a receding tide, and even an occasional sea gull swooping and dipping over the waves. By early afternoon, however, everything that could be admired had been. There was no more to say. Charlie realized it and ceased darting here and there gathering seashells to walk sedately by Mitford's side. Beyond asking whether she expected him to carry her treasures all the way home, he raised no real objection when she added her souvenirs to the contents of the basket.

For all that he remained alert, he was unaware that their approach was being monitored by a man hidden behind a dune farther along the beach. He wore the baggy trousers of a common seaman, a circumstance that had nothing to do with the sailboat beside which he crouched. After squinting fixedly for some moments, his vision blurred by astigmatism, he suddenly came running forward, grinning from ear to ear.

"Ah, Sawyer," Mitford murmured, clapping him on the back. "We are well met, old friend."

"Aye, Cap'n," Sawyer gasped, almost overcome with relief. " 'Tis glad I am to see you. I figured I was a goner for sure."

"Why, what is this?" Mitford said in bracing accents. "How did you come to this place, and what are you running from?"

"Cap'n, you never seen nothing like the way them Americans acted when the shells started falling around the prison. I guess most of 'em were mighty young. Leastways they went running off, so we just climbed the wall. I told the others they'd best split up, but the last I seen of them, they'd stayed together. I expect they're caught by now."

"Let us hope not. What did you do next?"

"I didn't know what else to do, so I started walking. I don't know how I happened onto the coast, but there didn't seem to be many people about, so I just kept going. Then when I come upon a sailboat—"

"A what!" Mitford ejaculated, startled.

"A sailboat, Cap'n," Sawyer repeated, jerking a thumb over his shoulder. "I got it right over there."

"Why didn't you say so, man!" Mitford demanded, striding forward. "Hurry now! Let's get it in the water."

"Aye, sir!" Sawyer grinned, running to seize the prow in a firm grip. "Seems as how I been hauling it along forever."

"Where did you find it, by the way?" Mitford inquired, his gaze on the deep grooves in the sand made by its passing and leading off through the dunes.

"At some village on a stream back there. Why, Cap'n? Is something wrong?"

"You have left a track a blind man could follow," Mitford replied, putting a shoulder against the boat and shoving with all his strength. "When I push, you tug."

"What can I do to help?" Charlie asked.

"You can stay out of the way," Mitford snapped, straining to heave the small craft toward the sea. "How did you manage alone, Sawyer?"

" 'Twern't easy," Sawyer grunted, his muscles bulging.

Indeed it wasn't, even for two men. By the time they had dragged it into the water and climbed aboard, both were gasping for breath. Suddenly Charlie squealed. "The soldiers!" she cried, splashing toward them through the surf. "They're coming down the beach."

"Do strive for calm," Mitford said, reaching down a hand to her with never a glance behind him to see how close they were. "Don't scramble aboard like that! You will capsize us. Yes, that's the way. Now get down in the bottom of the boat, and for God's sake keep your head down!"

227

"They seen us!" Sawyer announced, making room on the seat beside him and grasping an oar. "Cap'n, are you sure—"

"I can row," Mitford growled, bending his back to it.

To Charlie, her head below the side, the next moments became an eternity as the men rowed desperately to escape the surf for the open sea. Each rolling breaker seemed possessed of a diabolic intent to hurl the small craft backward. Mitford and Sawyer, eyes narrowed against the spray, dug the oars in deep on the instant each wave expired in a crashing roar beneath them, spurred on by the sound of the cavalry horses thundering down the beach toward them. At last clear of the rolling breakers, they sent the boat racing forward to a safe distance from the shore, then collapsed over the oars, exhausted and triumphant.

Charlie ventured to raise her head. "Have we escaped?" she said, her eyes round.

"I wonder," Mitford murmured, the uncertainties ahead of them very much on his mind. "The soldiers need no longer distress you, my dear. Their frustration is understandable; we are beyond the range of their rifles."

Charlie watched bullets kicking up spouts of water far short and wide of the mark. "I could shoot better," she gloated, the dimple appearing in her cheek.

"We will leave your boyish capabilities out of this discussion," he said smoothly. "Raise sail, Sawyer, if you please."

"Aye, sir," Sawyer said with a grin. "'Tis a strong offshore breeze, Cap'n. It'll take us wherever we're going."

"That will be the waters off Florida. I trust you concur?"

"It's up to you, Cap'n."

"On the contrary, Sawyer, it is up to fate. With a slight assist from some ship on the Bermuda run, I infer."

Some thirty-six hours later they were to discover a good deal of truth in the old adage that fate moves in mysterious ways. The day dawned overcast, with a squall building in the west. By noon the sea was running high, and lightning slashed in jagged streaks across the darkening sky. As the day wore on the tempo of the wind increased, at first gusting and changeable, then with a fury that sent low flying clouds boiling and racing across the waters. When the sky turned an eerie translucent green, Mitford trimmed sail and prepared to ride out the storm. To Charlie the world quickly became a nightmare of howling wind and drenching spray, the sailboat a fragile haven cast adrift in a churning, crashing sea. Soaking wet and more terrified than she dared admit, she huddled in the bottom of the boat, fearful that the gale would continue throughout the night.

Just at dawn the force of the winds lessened and a gradual lightening announced the new day. Mitford made his way aft and knelt beside her to tell her that the storm was finally beginning to abate. "It will blow for some time yet, but the worst of it is over."

Charlie swallowed convulsively. "We should be thankful it didn't come out of the east," she said, summoning a smile. "I daresay we would find ourselves sailing across the Pacific Ocean."

"As it is we have been blown halfway across the Atlantic, I don't doubt. Well, no matter. We are that much closer to England. I shouldn't wonder if we aren't home for Christmas."

"If we are fortunate enough to be seen by some ship, you might add," she said.

"We will be," he assured her, his gaze on the blustery sky. "If it should turn out to be a naval vessel, and I imagine it will be, my family's history may be known to its captain."

"Am I to become Sawyer's nephew?" she inquired, intrigued.

"I am sorry to spoil your scenario, my dear, but the difference in your breeding is obvious. I am much afraid you must content yourself with the role of a mere cabin boy. Since you are the son of—I believe a vicar will do nicely—you are gently reared and thus entitled to special consideration. You will feel right at home behind a wall of quilts."

"As you once told me, walls can come tumbling down," she said, smiling pertly.

"No!" he snapped. "Until we are married before the world, I shan't touch you again. God knows it will be all but impossible; it won't help matters if you tempt me."

"I do believe you are serious," she said, aghast.

"I was never more so. You don't realize the—" He broke off suddenly. "Later there will be many decisions for us to make. For the present, have you something in your basket that is still fit to eat?"

"I pulled a tarpaulin over it to keep it dry," she replied happily.

"Very commendable," he remarked, accepting a sandwich. "Have you eaten?"

"It didn't occur to me," she admitted. "I have never spent a more miserable night."

"In retrospect, the hayloft wasn't all that bad, eh?" He grinned, then returned to the tiller before she could think of a suitable reply.

As the day wore on and the wind grudgingly died away to

a gentle breeze, Mitford and Sawyer held a conference well out of Charlie's hearing, with negative results. Lacking navigational instruments, neither could hazard a guess as to their location. Mitford could only hold to an easterly course and pray that they had been blown into the sea lane. It was nearly noon the next day, however, when Sawyer's exultant voice suddenly rang out. "Sail, ho, Cap'n! Off the larboard side."

"Where?" Charlie demanded, looking around excitedly. "Is it one of ours?"

Mitford heaved a great sigh of relief and altered course to cross the strange vessel's bow. "It cannot signify," he said. "The odds against our coming across any ship at all in waters as vast as the Atlantic must be astronomical."

Tense moments passed during which their small craft seemed to strain forward as Sawyer spread the last inch of sail to take full advantage of the freshening breeze. They were still too far away for Charlie to discern any identifying features of the ship when a smile wreathed Mitford's face. "You will spend Christmas at Afton Hall, my dear," he said, pulling her against his side with an arm about her shoulders. "She is one of ours."

CHAPTER 15

After so many exhilarating adventures, no rescue accomplished with efficiency and dispatch could offer much in the way of excitement. To begin with, the vessel turned out to be a merchantman, a far cry from a proud ship of the line. By comparison discipline was lax, the living quarters crowded, and the spit and polish Charlie had come to expect were completely lacking. Even so, no fault could be found with the seamanship. Three uneventful weeks later they sailed into the waters of The Solent and dropped anchor at Southampton.

Charlie had looked forward in high expectation to again setting foot on English soil. Mitford's description of Afton Hall had been couched in laudatory terms; since he obviously loved the place, she had a strong desire to see it. Then, too, the promise of a wardrobe hanging full of lovely gowns had brought her to a state of no common degree of anticipation. The only thing to mar her pleasure was his unswerving determination to house her temporarily with his aunt.

As they waited on deck for the gangplank to be put in place, Mitford ran an indifferent eye over the crowd that had gathered on the dock, then stiffened. There was no mistaking the owner of the flaxen curls peeping from beneath a high-crowned bonnet. "Good God!" he groaned, inwardly appalled. "Jennie Brodie!"

"I see news of your arrival has reached your friends," the captain of the merchantman remarked, his face wreathed in smiles. "Several days ago I signaled a fast inbound packet that Your Lordship was aboard."

Mitford's eyes narrowed, but he bowed politely before motioning Sawyer to one side. Charlie saw a bag of coins change hands and so was not surprised to learn that, in spite of all she had found to say, she was being sent ahead in Sawyer's care. She would have much preferred accompanying Mitford to London, but he was adamant. "You will pause at your former home only long enough to pack your belongings before continuing on to Afton Hall," he said when he rejoined her. "By the time you arrive, Aunt Meggie will have received a note from me."

"That should console her, no doubt," she remarked, her heart in her shoes.

"I think it will," he replied. "She will be in a pyrexia of curiosity; therefore you will remember that Charlie is dead, much as I hate to bury him."

"As do I," she murmured pensively. "What rigmarole will I spin?"

"None at all, my dear. Lady Anne Fitzhugh will be found to be of a shy and retiring disposition."

"She will?" she teased, dimpling.

"I trust so," he said, walking away.

As he descended the gangway, the pretty blonde separated herself from the throng and hurried forward to meet him. Charlie (née Lady Anne), noting the proprietory way she placed a hand on his arm, seethed inside, the color draining from her face. Then the others thronged around to greet him and she could only watch helplessly as they moved off through the crowd to a row of carriages drawn up along the quayside. In the last glimpse she had of him as they drove off, the blonde had appropriated a seat beside him and was snuggled intimately against his side. There was nothing left for her to do but follow Sawyer, willy-nilly, down the gangway to the quay.

Despite her arguments to the contrary, Sawyer nervously insisted that she bide her time at a nearby inn while he went to order a post chaise. While she could see no need for a closed carriage, still she could appreciate his dilemma. Much as he might desire to please her, he was under strict orders from Mitford. Contriving to smile, she sat down to wait, her fingers shaking slightly.

An hour later he returned. The chaise was luxuriously upholstered and a fur rug lay on the seat. Having pulled open the door, he let down the steps, then paused, cap in hand. "About that woman back there, my lady," he said, embarrassed but determined. "You've no cause to fret. His Lordship really never cared aught for the likes of her."

"Thank you, Sawyer," she managed to say, aware of the sympathy in his eyes. "I quite understand."

"Try to rest, my lady," he advised, handing her inside. "I figure we will be three days on the road. If you need something, I'll be up front with the driver."

"You will be more comfortable inside," she said. "There is plenty of room."

" 'Twouldn't be proper," he muttered, very red of face.

Her lively sense of humor got the better of her. "After our improprieties of these past weeks, such considerations now seem absurd," she said and chuckled, further disconcerting him.

"Aye, my lady," he said, hanging his head.

"You are quite right, I fear," she said with a sigh, drawing the fur rug over her knees. "I will step down for tea at the first change of horses. Do you have any idea when that will be?"

"In about three hours, my lady," Sawyer replied, very ready to close the door and mount to the box seat.

Always reasonable, she could appreciate his feelings. They were, in all truth, the same that others would harbor if they knew. Their adventure had been great fun, but that was all it was—an interlude snatched from life, a carefree, never-to-be-repeated episode free from the restrictions of the society to which they had been born, she and Richard. Henceforth their conduct must be exemplary; happily, their memories would linger on.

They reached the cottage she had called home too late in the day to continue onward. Anne, desirous of avoiding an argument, informed the couple who had reared her that she had been in the company of her guardian during the past weeks. She said further that he had dispatched her hence to collect her belongings, refused to explain her boy's clothing and went to her room to pack. Sawyer was waiting beside the chaise when she emerged early the following morning, but beyond casting an approving glance at her dimity gown, he seemed to find nothing to say. They broke the

236

journey that night at a village whose name she could not remember later, putting up at the best inn. Immediately following breakfast they were on their way again, but at a pace she soon found intolerably slow. Rolling down the window, she called to Sawyer to drive faster, then subsided in her corner when he informed her that to do so would put them at Afton Hall before Her Ladyship had come downstairs.

Anne's first sight of the place took her breath away. After they had passed through the main gate and had proceeded a short distance along the drive, they left the sheltering screen of a stand of old oak trees, and a magnificent view of the mansion burst upon them. It was huge. There was no other word to describe it. It was designed in the shape of a U, built of a whitish stone and three stories high. A colonnade of Corinthian columns decorated its front facade, and numerous finials and statues adorned its roofs. Anne learned later that its style of architecture was known as English baroque and that the house and its attendant buildings covered four and a half acres.

The chaise left the drive, circled the front court and came to a halt before the door. Anne thought the sheer size of the structure boggled the senses when seen at close quarters. The great hall proved equally awesome. It was eighty feet long and forty feet high and had a ceiling painted by Laguerre, of Aurora chasing away Diana from the sky. Anne followed in the butler's wake across the marble floor to the green withdrawing chamber, where Lady Margaret waited to receive her, and tried not to gape. At least the room appeared less frightening, she thought, crossing the threshold. The walls were upholstered in silk, and were hung with paintings by well-known Dutch masters. A fire blazing in the hearth added a cozy touch.

Now a widow of five years' standing, Lady Margaret had reached the age when life was beginning to seem monotonous. She was still a handsome woman in spite of a slight wrinkling about the eyes, had excellent taste in dress and enjoyed a jointure sufficiently ample to indulge her penchant to remain in the forefront of fashion. Since no person of note would be caught dead in London during the off season, she always retired to Afton Hall until society returned to town. She had never been one to appreciate the even tenor of country living and so struggled to support her spirit during the weeks of enforced solitude, with mixed results.

She was quite worn down by the time Mitford's letter arrived, but became restored by the hint of challenge in his words. She did not in the least understand the situation, but no matter. If ought were awry, it was up to Afton to gainsay his son. So it was, when the butler trod sedately to the withdrawing room to announce of the arrival of Lady Anne Fitzhugh, she rose from the settee where she had been dozing with a copy of the poems of Byron on the seat beside her, and went forward to greet Anne, a welcoming smile on her lips.

Her first glimpse of her benefactress stunned Anne and left her with her brain in a whirl. Never had she expected to be confronted by a sprightly dame modishly gowned in blue taffeta in the middle of the afternoon. More improbable still, her hair was lavishly crimped into curls about her face, and satin slippers were on her feet; both elements were most unsuitable for country living. Anne tried not to stare.

"How delightful," Lady Margaret exclaimed, clasping

her in a perfumed embrace. "Dearest Mitford apprised me of your coming. 'Tis prodigiously glad I am to see you. He did say you are betrothed?"

Anne disengaged herself and smiled. "Yes, ma'am, we are," she said, looking around rather helplessly.

"But how remiss of me," Lady Margaret cried, leading the way to the settee before the fire. "You must be exhausted from the journey, poor child. Just sit right here and tell me all about it. When and where did you meet Mitford? I declare, I've never seen you in town."

Anne shrank inside a little, then reasoned that a brief explanation would be best. "We first met some time ago when Richard had cause to call upon my vicar. Then, when other occasions brought him to the neighborhood, we became—attached to one another."

"How enchanting!" Lady Margaret murmured, her eyes dwelling on Anne's simple dimity gown. "Forgive me, dearest, but is all your wardrobe like the dress you have on? Yes, I see it is. Well, we will soon put that to rights. Let me warn you, child, you must never allow yourself to become behind the fashion. Nothing could more quickly bring about your social ruin; take my word for it. But there, you will wish to pass a quiet evening tonight in making yourself at home. Tomorrow will be plenty of time to send for Madame Rochiard."

"Madame Rochiard?" Anne repeated, flustered.

"The most divine dressmaker in town, my dear. She's French, you know, and most prodigiously clever. Mitford charged me with dressing you as befits your station. Poor boy, he did not yet know when he wrote that his brother had been slain. This horrid war! So many fine men lost! But there, I mustn't speak of sadness immediately after you arrive."

"His brother—killed?" Anne gasped, her eyes fluttering to Lady Margaret's face.

"Yes, Edward, poor dear. He was ever such a quiet boy, one cannot say that one knew him very well. Richard was the more outgoing of the two—quite wild, in fact. That is not to say that there is anything reprehensible in his addiction to the gaming tables; with his wealth it can't signify, and I am sure that everyone gambles at some time in his life. It is just that he always seemed more concerned with the cut of his coat and the pedigree of his horses than he was with women. I am sure Afton despaired that he would ever take a wife. Not that there was ever any harm in him, you understand."

Loyalty forced Anne to remonstrate. "He is a captain in His Majesty's Navy!" she said with some resentment.

"Yes, and a worthy accomplishment that is, I'm sure," Lady Margaret hastened to say. "However, it is neither here nor there. Afton will never permit his only remaining heir to expose himself to danger. Some position will be found for him that will keep him ashore; possibly something in the Admiralty. There is the succession to think of, you see. Oh, I suppose Mitford will continue to race his phaeton—he is a famous whip, you know—and I don't doubt that he is still taken with the horrid sport of fisticuffs—most gentlemen are —but marriage will force him to settle down. It is high time he took an interest in the earldom."

Anne did not seem to be unduly elated by this prosaic view of her relationship with Richard. She was stunned, moreover, by the intelligence that she would one day become a countess, and she could only guess at the shock the news would be to him. It must be terrible to lose a brother, she thought, glancing somewhat obliquely at Lady Margaret.

"Oh, my dear, that was ill considered of me, I'm sure," Lady Margaret admitted, her hands fluttering helplessly. "I should never have told you of dear Edward the instant you set foot in Afton. But I have known an age now—'pon rep, but it seems forever—and I haven't a tear left to shed."

Anne nodded vaguely, unable to know what to make of Richard's aunt. Of an amiable vapidity, she seemed more interested in the family's honors and social eminence than in discovering Anne's own antecedents. She must be very much in awe of her brother to accept his heir's betrothal with scarcely a query. Anne had not expected to be let off so easily. Clearly the earl was thought to have given his approval.

Lady Margaret suddenly jumped to her feet and crossed to the bell pull, her skirts rustling delightfully. "The excitement sent tea quite out of my head," she apologized, returning to her seat. "Cook will be so put out. He always kicks up a fuss when any of the household is late for meals. My dear, Afton is full to overflowing, I'm afraid. Andrew should be about somewhere—he's my son, you know —though he seldom puts in an appearance before the dinner hour. Then there is Cousin Bert, but he is on the distaff side, so you mustn't mind his temper. He is quite impossible to live with, but short of showing him the door, which I lack the authority to do, there is nothing to be done. You will find Miss Lillian much more agreeable, poor dear. She is some sort of distant relative, though I am not precisely certain of the relationship. I do know she disgraced herself by marrying beneath her station, but her husband is dead now, so we let bygones be bygones."

"I had no idea that you weren't alone," Anne remarked when she paused for breath.

"Oh, my gracious no!" Lady Margaret exclaimed, nodding to the butler bringing in the tea. "Just on this table here, Pelham, thank you. I do hope the scones meet with your approval," she added to Anne. "I wasn't sure just what to order."

Recalling her past meals with Richard, Anne was hard pressed to stifle the giggles. Caught up in her tale, however, Lady Margaret would not have noticed if she had laughed. "Now, let me see, where was I?" she mused to herself as she handed Anne her plate. "Oh, yes. Miss Lillian. Really, much as I hate to say it, I do not think her husband's kin should look upon Afton as a hotel. They are of rather common stock, you see, and so not of our milieu. Really, Anne—may I call you Anne—you must speak to Richard. The Lord knows Afton himself will do nothing about it. He has not set foot on the place since we buried his dearest Ernestine."

"But of course," Anne murmured equably, unable to picture Mitford hesitant to eject unwanted visitors from his ancestral home.

"Oh, dear!" Lady Margaret ejaculated as the sounds of a voice raised in inquiry drifted in through the open door. "It's Cousin Bert. Be very quiet, my dear. Perhaps he will go away."

Cousin Bert, however, was intent upon his stomach. Having ascertained from Pelham that the ladies were partaking of an early tea, he had come in search of them. "So, here you are," he muttered, appropriating a seat on the settee beside Anne. "I must say, this isn't much of a spread," he added, eyeing the tray with disfavor.

The dour comment embarrassed Anne, but apparently Lady Margaret was accustomed to such remarks. She said, with no inflection of surprise, "Cousin Bert, we are privileged to have dearest Mitford's fiancée come to stay with us."

He paused in the act of buttering a scone to glance at Anne. "That's you, eh?" he growled before returning to his task.

This boorish response dumbfounded Anne. Even sequestered in the country, people displayed a higher degree of social grace. "Yes," she murmured finally, inanely.

"Last I heard he was like to marry some yellow-haired wench called Jennie. What happened to her?"

"Really, Cousin Bert!" Lady Margaret interjected, appalled. "I'm sure Richard has never been tempted to wed anyone but Anne."

"You would think that, you being a female," he said with a chuckle, his gaze swinging back to Anne. "Where you from, girl?"

Suddenly Anne had had enough. "I will inform you that my name is Lady Anne Fitzhugh, but where I am from is none of your business," she said. "Please excuse me for being rude."

Rather than being put down, he seemed pleased. "Spunky, are you?" he said with a grin, spooning a generous dollop of marmalade onto his scone. "Well, it's high time new blood came into this family. What with Lady Margaret and all, it's been running rather thin."

The truth occurred to Anne. He delighted in distressing Lady Margaret. "You are expending your energy needlessly," she said with a faint smile. "Neither Lady Margaret nor myself is shocked."

His scone was halfway to his mouth. Pausing with it suspended in midair, his gaze locked with hers. "That other chit—that Jennie—may be empty-headed, but she had it all over you," he said viciously. "She don't sass her elders, besides which, she's a sight prettier, too."

It was Anne's turn to feel distress. What did he hope to gain by continually introducing Miss Brodie's name into the conversation? Obviously they were acquainted. But how well? Had she been a guest at Afton? If so, how often, and at whose invitation? Mitford's? It seemed unlikely that Lady Margaret would invite her. Was there some reason she, Anne, should be concerned?

Just as she was searching her mind for an excuse to leave the room, a slight young man came hurrying in and crossed to bow over her hand. "You're Lady Anne," he said, a smile of seraphic beauty lighting up his face. "Pelham said you'd arrived. Forgive me for not being here to greet you, but my prize orchid was just coming into bloom. I raise orchids, you see."

"Perhaps you will show them to me sometime," Anne suggested pleasantly. "You're Andrew, I imagine."

"Don't give him an opening to prose on about his damn posies," Cousin Bert said with a frown. "He'll bore you to death for sure."

"If we continue in this manner, dearest Anne will think herself in Bedlam," Lady Margaret admonished, fixing him with a stern eye.

"As you so sapiently remark, my dear Meggie, she is in Bedlam," he shot back.

Anne found herself at a loss to decide whether Lady

Margaret was more chagrined by Bert's words or by his attitude. The remark had given him away, however. He was an educated man and not the semiliterate brute he would have them believe. She wondered about the reason for his masquerade. There was only one way to rescue the situation. "I do appreciate your kindness in ordering an early tea, Lady Margaret, but I am rather tired," she said, rising to her feet. "If someone will be kind enough to show me to my room—"

Lady Margaret strove to mask her relief at her own opportunity to escape and failed. "You must be exhausted, poor dear," she said, losing no time in shepherding Anne to the door. "Your bedchamber is just down the hall from mine. We are in the west wing, of course. The east wing has always housed the immediate family of the earl. That's not to say the rooms are off limits," she hastened to add. "It's just that—"

"I quite understand," Anne murmured, her astonished gaze coming to rest on an erotic sculpture of Cupid seducing Psyche. It stood in a prominent niche at the top of the broad staircase and was life-size. Every anatomical detail was minutely portrayed. Embarrassingly so.

"Disgraceful, isn't it," Lady Margaret remarked. "I've grown so accustomed to the heathenish thing that I no longer notice it. Afton should have it removed to some less conspicuous place, but he would never do so. Just look the other way and pretend you don't see it."

Wide, vaulted corridors leading to the east and west wings branched off from the upper landing. Lady Margaret turned down the one to the right. Anne was gazing around curiously at the rows of family portraits lining the walls and wondering which were Mitford's parents when she became entangled with a group of cats and almost lost her balance.

"Naughty, naughty," admonished a newcomer rushing toward them down the hall. "I told you not to rub up against our visitor's legs. She's Lady Anne, you know."

Anne seemed to sigh. What next?

"Really, Miss Lillian!" Lady Margaret's tone was frigid. "You know you aren't allowed to keep livestock in the house. Remove those beasts at once."

Miss Lillian blushed and wrung her hands and dropped a curtsy. "Lady Anne doesn't mind," she said in a voice that was barely audible.

"Of course she does," Lady Margaret exclaimed before Anne could voice reassurances. "After this I am sure she longs for privacy."

In this Lady Margaret was correct. It seemed an interminable time to Anne before the last pleasantries had been exchanged and the door to her room closed behind her. Afton, it appeared, housed a menagerie.

Anne had been alone for the better part of her life, but she had never before been so alone. One day was much like another. She visited most of the rooms in the house, other than those in the east wing, and spent countless hours strolling in the gardens. While she could recognize the worth of the decorative arts displayed at Afton, she knew that years of study would be necessary to comprehend the artistic merit of each individual item. Gradually she began to spend more and more time out of doors. Between Lady Margaret and Cousin Bert's constant bickering and Miss Lillian's piteous attempts to please, they were growing tiresome to her. It was so blessedly peaceful in the gardens.

She was particularly fond of the grotto. Actually it was a manmade cave created by Isaac de Coux and tucked in beside Inigo Jones's artificial waterfall. Many thousands of seashells had been pressed into the wet mortar of its walls and ceiling to form a pattern of loops and scrolls. Stucco figures of Neptune rose majestically from a sea of scrolls where smiling dolphins frolicked. Originally it had served as an outdoor sitting room but of recent years had been used for an occasional picnic in the summer. Anne was enchanted when she chanced upon it and soon took it for her own.

Not to anyone's surprise, Lady Margaret took Mitford's instructions seriously. Within the week Madame Rochiard and her three assistants were established in a third-floor tower room, where they were surrounded by reels of frilly lace, colorful bolts of silk and satin and cards of fancy ribbon. Sewing a wardrobe suitable for the wife of a viscount was not to be taken lightly. Madame quickly became the bane of Anne's existence. The flurry of dressmaking seemed to go forward only as the result of continual fittings. When Anne suggested that they work from measurement instead, the idea was politely ignored.

On a day two weeks after her arrival she had made good her escape to enjoy the solitude of the grotto. Evening was fast approaching when a shadow separated itself from the gathering gloom and fell across her book. Startled, she looked up and found herself staring into the face of an older version of Richard.

"Forgive the intrusion, my dear," he said, "but I felt that we should meet."

"You are Richard's father," she said and smiled, holding out her hand. "He closely resembles you."

"Then I am to be congratulated," he remarked, carrying her fingers to his lips. "Lord Melville informs me he distinguished himself when under the most onerous of orders. A desk is waiting for him at the Admiralty."

"I doubt he will be relieved to hear that, sir," she said frankly. "He would much rather be in the thick of things, I'm sure."

"So am I, but it won't come to that," he replied, placing a hand beneath her elbow to lead her back outdoors. "Shall we stroll in the gardens? The grotto holds unpleasant memories for me."

"We appear to share a love of nature," she remarked, feeling the subject put them on safer ground. The grotto must remind him of his wife. "Before I came to Afton Hall I hadn't dreamed that any place on earth could be so lovely. The instant Richard arrives I will have its history."

"I understand that felicitations are in order. May I wish you joy?"

"Then you don't mind?" she said, throwing him a grateful look. "I was afraid you might take exception to our marriage."

"Not at all," he murmured, indicating a garden seat nestled in a niche formed by towering boxwood. "Will you be seated? It is a favored spot with me."

"Thank you for sharing it with me," she replied, enchanted by the old-world courtliness he displayed toward her. "You are very kind, sir. In the circumstances you have a perfect right to fear that I cast out lures to trap your son."

He smiled. "Your concern is commendable, my dear, but it is quite needless, believe me. Few ladies have been known to resist Mitford's charm."

She bristled. "He would never force his attention on an unwilling female," she snapped.

"I beg your pardon," he said gravely. "Your indignation is warranted, I agree. Doubtless you have developed a tendre for Richard?"

A slight smile curved her lips. "How could I not, sir?" she said.

"Then I apprehend that my son is to be congratulated, little though he deserves it. In my day gentlemen did not force reluctant females to the altar."

She flushed and averted her face. "Then you know all?" she breathed almost inaudibly.

"It was to be expected," he replied gently. "Richard was never one to dissemble. In that respect he is very like his mother."

"You need not tell me from whom he inherited his charm," she said, her spirits reviving. "He will have assumed full responsibility, but actually, sir, I was more at fault. I need not tell you that it was reprehensible of me to dress in boy's clothing, but I found it necessary. You perhaps have the acquaintance of Sir Randolph Ashmore?"

"I am known to any number of rogues, my dear."

"Then you will understand why I acted as I did."

"I do. Still, my sympathy must remain with Richard."

"He deserves it, sir. There were times when I thought that he would throttle me." A tender expression crept into her eyes. "I expect you are shocked, but I enjoy outwitting him. It would have been a great deal too bad if we had lost our lives on a foreign shore. The American calvary tried their best to shoot us, you know."

She had at last succeeded in startling him. "It would have

been an untidy ending, I agree," he said. "I trust no further incidents of a drastic nature occurred?"

She gave her throaty gurgle of laughter. "One might say that our entire association has consisted of an unbroken string of unlikely events," she remarked.

A quiet fell. Conscious that she had said more than she intended, she glanced at him, unaware that his thoughts had cast back to the happy years before a tragic accident snuffed out the life of his beloved, leaving a void that many a disappointed lady had unsuccessfully tried to fill.

She misread his silence. "You regret that I married Richard," she said in a constrained voice. "I did resist, but superficially, no more. I see that now."

"There is no reason your marriage should not meet with my approval," he said placidly. "Unlike many of my contemporaries, I had the good fortune to espouse the lady of my choice. I rejoice that Richard has had the good fortune to find a woman who can love him for himself. It is not always thus for the heir to an earldom."

A look of compassion came into her eyes. "I have been told of the loss of your eldest son," she said in a subdued voice. "Please accept my condolences."

"Thank you, my dear. One does not recover from such a wound, but in time one does come to accept it."

There did not seem to be anything more to say. She searched her mind for something. "Richard may have told you of his plan to satisfy society with a second wedding," she said at last. "With the family in mourning, it is now out of the question, of course."

"The ceremony will take place at Afton House in London immediately your trousseau is assembled," he said, effectively putting a period to any objections she might put forth.

"The presence of the Prince Regent will circumvent any talk of haste. In all truth, Richard has endured enough already without being forced to wait."

Anne could find no heart to argue with her future father-in-law. It would surprise her very much, she thought, if their affairs did not soon become the property of every tattlemonger in town.

She was correct in this assessment. London did begin to talk, at first in whispers, and then more openly, those persons fortunate enough to receive the coveted wedding invitation extolling the virtues of a love match, those who did not hinting at scandal and bemoaning the freedom of modern youth. The question that all society longed to ask and yet did not dare concerned Jennie Brodie. Mitford's pursuit of the fair damsel had lasted for months and was well known. Of its success few harbored any doubts. Many wondered at the truth of a secret liaison between him and his betrothed. Most believed it impossible for a gentleman of his stature to be able to carry on a courtship unbeknownst to anyone other than a country vicar, let alone his being able to return to the neighborhood on numerous occasions without being recognized. While few believed the tale, no one could find a way to dispute it. It was a riddle and added spice to the doldrums that set in between seasons.

The wedding took place one month after the publishing of the banns and passed off without a hitch, somewhat to the disappointment of those dwelling on the fringes of society, who were forced to make do with a secondhand description of the proceedings. Miss Brodie was not in attendance to call attention to herself, nor was Sir Randolph Ashmore present to mar the solemnity of the moment by voicing an objection to the ceremony taking place, a disturbance not entirely ruled out by the hopeful. The groom was strikingly handsome in full dress uniform, and the bride was achingly lovely to look upon. If there were those among the guests who considered her hair a trifle short, there were others who thought it likely to become the vogue.

At Anne's suggestion they postponed their honeymoon until some unspecified future date. Due to the war, there was nowhere they could go other than the country, of which she already had had a surfeit. London offered much in the way of diversion. There were historical sites to be visited, and the start of the social season was at hand. Where they lingered mattered not at all to Mitford. Acting the role of expectant bridegroom had sorely tried his patience. Feeling that he had acquitted himself nobly, he was now prepared to spend the coming days in bed.

He had drawn the line, however, at moving into his father's town house on St. James's Square. A gentleman set up an establishment of his own when he married. Since suitable houses were difficult to come by with all society in town, he instructed his man of business to close with the owner when he located a very respectable residence on Curzon Street. Although it was small, it would prove sufficiently commodious to satisfy their needs, at least for the present.

Due to the preparations that had kept her occupied in the days prior to the ceremony, Anne had no opportunity to see the house until they made good their escape following the wedding reception and their carriage deposited them before the door. Even then she had time only to glance at it in approval before Mitford escorted her up the steps and through the door with, in her opinion, unseemly haste.

"The servants will arrive tomorrow," he said, depositing

his hat and gloves on the console table that stood in the hall. "I assumed we could dispense with their services for tonight."

"I imagine we will survive," she said and smiled, her thoughts casting back to their trek through America.

"Are you hungry?" he asked, gesturing toward an open door. "A cold collation has been laid in the dining room."

Anne, on her way across the hall, looked at him over her shoulder and said, "You must know that I will first change out of my wedding gown. I shan't be long."

"It is the destiny of husbands to wait," he replied, and then stood watching as she ascended the stairs.

Ten minutes later he walked into her room moments after she had stepped out of her chemise. "Oh!" she squealed, startled.

He stopped dead in his tracks, his eyes sweeping over her body, caressing the soft curves. His breath catching in his throat, he put down the tray of food he carried and swept her into his arms. "Anne, Anne," he groaned against her lips. "It's been so long. I've wanted you so."

"I know, darling," she murmured, her fingers in his hair. "It's been a long time for me, too. Afton was so lonely without you."

"I didn't dare visit you, though God knows I wanted to," he said, gently laying her on the bed. "It would have spoiled everything."

"How could it? No one would have guessed our secret."

"No, just about everyone would have known," he replied, stripping away his clothing. "I would never have been able to keep my hands off you."

Anne had never before had more than just a glimpse of him. When they had made love, it had been at night, in the dark. Now for the first time, in the blaze of candlelight, she saw him in all his naked splendor. Fascinated, she frankly stared.

"Don't be shy," he urged, stretching out beside her. "Touch me, darling. Take me in your hand."

"Oh!" she breathed, startled by the rampant heat of him. "I didn't dream—"

"I want you to know my body as well as you know your own," he murmured, his lips seeking out the hollow at the base of her throat. "I intend to learn all there is to know about yours."

"I thought you already had," she said with a twinkle.

"I've only begun," he said with a grin, his hands moving over her with a thoroughness that sent a stab of desire darting through her loins.

She gasped. "Then do," she said. "Begin, I mean."

"Like this?" he murmured, moving up to bend over her, his manhood brushing teasingly against her thighs.

"I daresay eventually you will get the hang of it," she purred, eyes gleaming. "Until you do, I guess I just needs must settle for whatever I can get."

"Will this do?" he chuckled, moving into her with decision, at first slowly, and then more rapidly. His nostrils flared. A look of rapture came upon his face. Anne, caught up in the urgency of his loving, knew their souls were joined, made one, by the strength of their love.

Afterward, as she lay half-dozing within the circle of his arms, her head resting on his shoulder, he said teasingly, "I should never have agreed to forgo the country, my sweet. You will admit we had developed a certain empathy with the ground."

A giggle bubbled from her throat. "This is the first time

we have made love in a real bed," she said, snuggling closer. "Did you like it?"

"At the risk of trampling upon your maidenly reserve," he said, laughing softly, "I will advise you that you are about to spend the coming weeks between the sheets."

"Weeks?" she gurgled, raising her face for his kiss.

"Oh, at the least," he replied, obliging her.

Anne had other plans, but she waited until their third morning together before launching her own schemes. Emerging from her boudoir, she sat down on the settee in their sitting room, arranged the skirts of her negligee and cast a shrewd look at Mitford. He was busy glancing through the morning papers, and since no frown creased his brow, she thought it likely that there was nothing in the news to disturb him. "A note from Lady Jersey has been brought around," she remarked, feeling the moment propitious. "She is giving a drum on Thursday next and hopes we will attend. Who is Lady Jersey?"

"A patroness of Almack's and a great, good friend of mine."

"That is very well, but nothing to the point. Do we go?"

"If you wish to, my dear."

She shook her head. "You are to decide. It makes no difference to me, you understand, but you will recollect that you spent a fortune on my trousseau."

The corners of his lips twitched. "I will allow that to be true," he said.

"It would be a shame for it to go to waste," she prompted.

"That certainly must be considered," he agreed affably.

"Well, it would," she insisted, a frown creasing her brow.

"I know," he said, relenting. "I understand perfectly that

255

parameter

I cannot keep you to myself indefinitely. You long for feminine companionship."

"Oh, dear," she murmured, contrite. "I am sorry to have given that impression."

"I rather hoped you might be," he remarked, rising to take a seat beside her.

"You wonder why I am eager to go into society without delay," she said, looking at him hopefully.

"My inquisitive disposition," he murmured, smiling down at her.

"I used to dream of visiting Almack's," she explained. "Do you think I will receive my vouchers?"

"There is nothing for it," he said, taking her in his arms. "I must kiss you."

"Why?" she said, readily returning his embrace. "Have I said something foolish?"

"Very foolish," he replied, amused by her naiveté. "The patronesses of Almack's will most assuredly send you vouchers, but you must not imagine that the club is in any way out of the common. It isn't."

He was right. She saw nothing remarkable about it when they attended that evening. From its reputation one would expect the rooms to be splendid; instead they proved to be spacious but in no way outstanding. The refreshments were unimaginative, high stakes were disallowed in the card room and the permission of the patronesses was required before any unattached young lady might dance the waltz. It was a wonder that anyone attended.

The evening was not a total disappointment, however. The Prince Regent, arriving shortly before the doors closed precisely on the stroke of eleven, found Mitford discoursing amicably with a dowager, apologized for being unable to attend the wedding and asked to meet the bride. It could not be better. Half the town bore witness to the ease with which Anne enthralled the prince. If it needed royal approval to launch her in the world of fashion, which in fact it did not, her success was now assured.

Other diversions of society proved more stimulating, however much they might bore Mitford. In the weeks following there were teas and soirees, the opera and balls. They attended them all, but Anne informed Richard, upon the duke and duchess of Northumberland having extended an invitation to a musicale at Syon House, that he need not accompany her unless he wished. She had recently learned that fashionable couples seldom did things together.

"Of course I will accompany you," he said, miffed. "I did not marry only to catch an occasional glimpse of my wife as she is coming in or going out."

"To tell the truth, I'm glad you will," she replied, dimpling. "I will need someone to explain what I see at Syon House."

"Zion," he corrected.

"I beg your pardon?"

"Zion House. It's pronounced with a *z*."

"Oh," she said, digesting this. "I wonder why."

"I have no idea."

"What else can you tell me about it?"

"Very little, I'm afraid," he admitted. "I do know that some time during the 1760s Robert Adam redecorated a part of it in the classical style. I think you will find the anteroom particularly splendid."

"Really, Richard!" she said, exasperated. "Is that the best you can do?"

"As I remember it—and I haven't seen it for some years,

may I add—the entire effect is decidedly Roman. I'm sure you will recognize Adam's penchant for antiquity in the columns and statuary scattered throughout the house."

"Is it all classical?" she demanded, startled.

"No, only the Adam rooms. The rest is Jacobean."

Anne would bite off her tongue before she would admit that her knowledge of architecture was little more than rudimentary. Clearly a visit to a vendor of books was indicated. Accordingly, the following afternoon found her descending from her carriage before a book shop in Piccadilly just opposite an entrance to Green Park. She went inside and spent an exhausting time before the proprietor obligingly unearthed a thick volume at the bottom of a stack of equally heavy tomes. He was overcome. Few females of the fashionable world honored his humble establishment with their patronage. Nothing would do but that he escort her from the premises, to the accompaniment of much wringing of his hands and numerous deep bows. Anne felt like a fool. Mortified, she could only hope that no person among the throng passing by was acquainted with her.

As luck would have it, Mitford was the first person she saw upon returning home. "I've been looking for you," he said, crossing the hall to ascend the stairs by her side. "You've been shopping, I see."

"I bought a book," she admitted, flushing slightly. "On architecture."

He looked at her in surprise. "Syon House?" he said. "Very commendable. I'm confident your visit will benefit from your reading."

"I just hope it lives up to expectations," she remarked,

pausing before their sitting-room door. "Should I wear my yellow lace, do you think?"

He laughed. "You'll look lovely," he said, tilting her face up for his kiss. "I'm having my mother's pearls restrung. We must make the other ladies sick with envy, mustn't we."

"It only needs you in your full dress uniform to do that," she replied, not to be outdone.

They both came closer to the truth than they knew.

Anne's first glimpse of Syon House failed to live up to expectations. The exterior facade resembled a fortresslike structure of heavy walls terminating in square towers. It was only when they went inside that the anticipated elegance came into view.

Anne knew from her reading that the entrance hall resembled the atria of Pompeii. A half-dome inspired by the Pantheon stretched across one end of the room and sheltered a statue of the Apollo Belvedere. At the other end a life-size reclining bronze depicting the dying Gaul occupied the center of a Doric screen. Four additional full-scale statues stood atop pedestals spaced along the opposite walls, two on each side. Anne strolled around the black-and-white marble floor, intrigued by the quantity of busts displayed.

Her enjoyment was short-lived. Unhappily Lord Adam Wroxly was soon discovered among the distinguished guests. "Most impressive," he said, stepping in front of her before she could slip away. "Your fortune will not last long if you continue at this rate. I do not mistake when I say that gown set you back a prodigious sum."

Her lips tightened. However much he might despise her independence, it was none of his business who paid her bills. "You presume, sir," she said, looking around for Mitford.

He raised his quizzing glass. "I can only term your jewelry an extravagant excess," he said, eyeing the pearls with distaste. "As your guardian, I will remind you that I hold the purse strings. Don't expect me to increase your allowance, since it is unlikely that I would do so."

"You cannot have much understanding of the law," she replied. "You ceased to be my guardian the instant I married. My husband, Viscount George, has my affairs well in hand. He would never dream of letting me pay for my excesses."

He lowered his quizzing glass, much chagrined. Though he had no way of knowing, it was the first time she had referred to Mitford by his new title. It would take some getting used to and was the reason for her slip. Under ordinary circumstances she would never reveal the origin of her pearls. As for his guardianship, he was forced to admit to himself that she spoke the melancholy truth. She was free of his control, and he was aware that she knew it.

Across the room Mitford had been listening politely, though with little interest, to the prosing of Lord Amperbly's rather supercilious eldest daughter. Glancing up, he read the entreaty in Anne's eyes and immediately went to her. Remarking on the beauty of the house, he took her away with him to inspect its splendors, leaving Lord Wroxly alone with his thoughts. Clearly the viscount had gifted his wife with the set of pearls. An extravagant gesture, it could, if oft repeated, lead him into dun territory. However unlikely a circumstance, should it occur, he might seek an accounting of his wife's estate. It never occurred to Wroxly that Mitford planned to do so anyway.

Anne, meanwhile, passed with Mitford from the hall into the magnificent anteroom. "It must be Adam's most splendid work," she murmured, gazing around with a feeling akin to awe. Twelve columns of mottled green marble (she learned later they had been dredged from the bed of the Tiber River) terminated in Ionic capitals and supported an entablature on which stood twelve gilt statues of various gods and goddesses. The walls were pale green, a blue and gold frieze ran around the room and the floor was brilliantly executed scagliola work in blue and white and rose.

"Rather than classical antiquity, it's Rome of the high Renaissance," Mitford murmured in her ear.

"I'm impressed," was all she could find to say.

"Here is the statue of Hector," he continued, pausing before an alcove built to display the bronze. "Or perhaps you'd prefer Achilles?"

"I want to see them both. I cannot believe this is used only as a waiting room for servants."

"To say that Syon House is fit for king or pauper may not be wholly unjustified. Adam was allowed to complete only five staterooms in all. The rest of the house lacks inspiration, I'm afraid."

"Well, I'm sure the family will manage to scrape along some way," she said placidly.

Across the room Sir Randolph Ashmore watched Mitford turn away to greet a dowager and remarked acidly to Lord Wroxly standing beside him, "You were a fool to let Lady Anne out of your sight. Where else could we have laid our hands on sixty thousand pounds?"

"You mistake," Wroxly said, a hardened expression in his eyes. "Her Ladyship's inheritance is hers to do with as she will, pending Mitford's approval. I but manage her affairs."

Ashmore's lip curled. "You sing a different tune now that

our new viscount is come upon the scene," he said, mincing forward toward Anne.

She saw him coming, but short of creating a scene, there was nothing she could do but return his greeting with hard-to-conceal reluctance. She would have despised him in any circumstances, but the absurdities of jeweled heels and a spangled coat were difficult to sustain.

"How fortunate I am to have an opportunity for converse with you," he purred, waving away a young gentleman who had had the audacity to join her. "You perceive me quite atwitter with delight."

"You are too generous," she murmured, horrified to find herself alone with him and glancing around in hopes of discovering an escape.

"I had heard you always have a happy turn of phrase," he said, delicately touching a lace-edged handkerchief to his perspiring upper lip. "The gossips are in error. I see nothing scintillating in your remark."

She frowned, puzzled. "Apparently courtesy is not an attribute of yours," she said, turning away.

He laid a hand on her arm to detain her. "You should have chosen me, m'dear," he said, the unctuous smile on his lips not quite reaching his eyes. "Where the viscount elects to roam, I would have remained by your side. I need not identify *la Brodie* to you, I'm sure."

She looked a little surprised. From his tone she knew she was expected to become covered with mortification, but she was merely baffled. "But think how boring to dance attendance on a wife," she remarked, a gleam coming into her eye.

"Ah, but to have converse with a mistress—jaded spirits must become revived," he replied. "Do forgive me, m'dear, but I'd keep an eye on him if I were you. Even now a smile is all it takes from his paramour to fetch him to her side."

Startled, she glanced across the room. Mitford had just escaped from the dowager and was making his way toward Miss Brodie. "I doubt he would carry on a clandestine affair before all the world," she said, hiding her amusement at his blundering attempt at mischief.

"You will need your wits about you," he continued in a tone intended to sound bantering. Instead he came off as only querulous. "If I were not a gentleman I might tell you some shocking tales about the two of them."

Fortunately at that moment Lord Andrew, who was in the process of escorting Lady Margaret to the dining room for refreshments, caught sight of them and steered his mother in their direction. "Your very obedient, Cousin Anne," he said, nodding briefly to Sir Randolph. "You are just the person to join Mama for a glass of lemonade. You can't refuse, you know. I can't stand the stuff, and the duchess ain't likely to serve anything much stronger."

Lady Margaret playfully rapped his knuckles with her fan. "Naughty boy," she said indulgently. "Well, run along, dear. I am sure Sir Randolph will escort us in your place."

Anne linked her arm in Lady Margaret's, giving an admonitory pinch as she did so. "I am sure we must not impose on His Lordship's good nature," she said, sketching him the briefest of curtsies before leading Aunt Meg away.

"Really, child, that was very rude of you," Lady Margaret admonished the moment they were out of earshot. "What will Sir Randolph think?"

"I am sure I do not care," Anne declared. "He had the affrontery to accuse Richard of duplicity with Jennie Brodie."

Lady Margaret looked startled. "Really, Anne!" she said. "Ladies do not speak of—of—"

"Their husbands' former mistresses?" Anne finished for her. "Don't be a goose. Of course Richard had agreeable connections before we met. With any number of charmers, I shouldn't wonder."

This blunt reference to his bits of muslin, coupled as it was with Anne's throaty chuckle, intrigued Lady Margaret. Herself not one to subscribe to the convention that dutiful wives must turn a blind eye on husbandly peccadilloes, she saw no reason to pretend she did. "I have nothing to say of your relationship with Mitford and no right to meddle in your affairs," she said.

"Now that is a very different matter," Anne replied. "He may have had some high-flyer in keeping before we met, but to suppose that he should continue in that way of life now that we are married is a great piece of impertinence. If you don't know that, then you don't know him."

"Well, but I do know it," Lady Margaret replied soothingly. "I don't mean to set myself up against your better judgment, for naturally it is not my place to do so, but don't you think that we should avoid calling attention to ourselves by quarreling in public?"

Anne shook her head. "Avoid anything you like," she said, "but I intend to put a stop to scandal by calling attention to Richard's meeting with Jennie Brodie. Everyone knows all about his former pursuit of her. I don't intend for anyone to suppose there is more to this than his pausing to greet a friend."

She was gone on the words, leaving Lady Margaret at a loss to know what to make of it all. Mitford had been observing the exchange and had a fair idea of what had passed between them. While he was perfectly capable of extracting himself from Miss Brodie's clutches, he watched Anne approach with an expression very much akin to a smile twitching at the corners of his mouth.

"Ah, Miss Brodie," Anne said sweetly while extending her hand for the benefit of their audience. Every eye in the room was upon them, as she well knew. "How vastly kind it was of you to entertain Mitford while I was engaged."

Miss Brodie curtsied, then turned beet red at the gaffe. "I'm sure I don't take your meaning," she muttered, unstrung.

"Then I will make my meaning abundantly clear," Anne said crisply. "You desire to uphold your reputation as a femme fatale, but you shan't do so at my expense."

"And what do you mean by that?" Miss Brodie demanded.

"I imagine," Anne said dryly, "that you will not in the future see fit to opportune my husband. He will no longer have—shall we say?—a nodding acquaintance with the demimonde."

Mitford kept a straight face with difficulty. "Tut," he said, bowing to Miss Brodie before leading Anne away.

CHAPTER 16

During the coming weeks Miss Brodie came to accept the snub with tolerable equanimity. Had not subsequent events proved her own triumph? Mitford sought her company on numerous occasions. In her conceit she naturally assumed that she had been the fair bride's undoing. The happy couple had quarreled over her, and no wonder. They were an ill-assorted pair. Divorce was not unheard of. Probably he was considering it. No, he must be considering it. Why else had he lately shown her so much flattering attention under the very nose of his wife?

It suited Mitford very well to permit her to continue in this vein of thought. After all, she neither asked for quarter nor gave any. Her provocation at Syon House had been prompted by a desire to demonstrate her mastery over him before the world. Alas, poor Jennie, he thought. She could not know that he sought to pique the interest of his wife by pretending interest in another. While Anne had given him no cause to doubt her love, still she had had no opportunity to turn him down. He had an overwhelming desire to make certain that she would have married him under normal circumstances.

Nothing could have been more proper than Anne's whole bearing. Unable to disabuse her mind of Sir Randolph's insinuations, she found herself strangely reluctant to discuss them with Mitford. Somewhere in the recesses of her brain there still lurked doubts of the ability of a country-bred girl to fill the shoes of wife to a gentleman of distinction. Rather than chance bringing the whole thing out into the open, with possibly unpredictable results, for after all he had never precisely said that he loved her, she would engage not to interfere with Mitford. They were enjoying a life full of social engagements, and if he did not accompany her to all of them (what husband did?), at least she could count on his support when she most needed it. The more often she observed him tête-à-tête with Miss Brodie, the more determined she became. Half a loaf was preferable to no loaf at all. Somehow she would cope.

Lord Adam Wroxly watched and waited, very well pleased with the course of events. While Mitford had taken no hand in his wife's affairs, there was no knowing when he might take it into his head to do so. He was very much a man of wealth, accustomed to the vicissitudes of finance. There would be no putting him off with vague references and ponderous explanations. He would glance at the total of Her Ladyship's estate, a speculative gleam would come into his eyes, and he would take the whole into his own stewardship. Lord Wroxly considered himself very much a man of the world. Still he could not quell thoughts of the injustice of it all. While he had never desired the responsibilities of guardianship, he had carried on in the best tradition, nurturing the money entrusted to his care as carefully as he tended to his own. Gradually through the years he had come to look upon it as belonging as much to himself as to his ward.

It did not need marital bumbling to spur him on. A divorce, while unlikely, was not beyond the realm of possibility. Once free of her shackles, Lady Anne would turn to him with gratitude. She would look upon him as a pliable gentleman who knew to a nicety how to turn a blind eye on her excesses. He himself would appear not to have a hand in it; no one need know that the young gentleman whom he had in mind to replace Mitford had had a cuckold for father while he himself had actually sired the boy. Young Lord Wrothingham would do as he was told; when all was said and done, the fortune that he had husbanded with such care would remain under his jurisdiction.

Anne's first meeting with the gallant who fondly expected to replace Mitford in her affections occurred during a visit to the Pantheon. The evening began on a propitious note, Mitford being of the party. The building itself was breathtaking with its marble pillars, ornate plaster ceilings and soaring dome. The company sparkled with scintillating wit, a mild success in the card room had been enjoyed and Mitford was so assiduous in his attentions that she would have labeled her fears groundless had it not occurred to her that Miss Brodie's absence was the reason for his attentiveness. It was really most incensing, quite enough to make one's blood boil.

Lord Wrothingham, arriving midway through the evening, sought out Lord Andrew to obtain an introduction. Fearful lest Lady Anne turn out to be an antidote, he could scarce credit it that he was to court the vision in diaphanous jonquil cambric. She certainly was a beauty, which may have been the reason for his latent hesitation. Aware of his antecedents, he dared not cross the man he knew to be his sire. Where a title inherited from his mother's husband was well and good, no money had come with it. Still, no man married to a paragon such as Lady Anne would give her up without a struggle. He must, however, make the push. He frankly stood in need of the allowance promised by his father.

He found an opportunity for an introduction when he spied Lord Andrew at a ball at Almack's. "I cannot help but admire your cousin," he said, pausing by his side. "Do present me, dear boy."

Lord Andrew turned in surprise, momentarily at a loss to identify the gentleman. "I fear you have the advantage of me, sir," he said.

"Andy, you fool, it is I, Tom Wrothingham," the young man announced, thrusting out a hand. "We were at school together, remember?"

Lord Andrew looked sharply at him. "Why—Tom!" he gasped, wringing Lord Wrothingham's hand. "When did you come to town?"

"Recently," Wrothingham replied evasively. "I have been rusticating in the country and so am eager to know the current crop of beauties. I will start with your cousin, I believe."

Andrew looked doubtful. "She is married, you know," he said.

"Dear boy, I want to meet her, not elope with her," Wrothingham replied cheerfully. "Make me known to her, I beg you."

Anne had no desire at all to meet a gentleman who was possessed of very few more years than she. After Mitford, he seemed merely a callow youth. Spreading her skirts in a curtsy, she arose, extended her hand and said all that was civil. Wrothingham had dutifully practiced the graces before a mirror in preparation for the moment. It had not prepared him for reality. Clutching her fingers in an unnecessarily firm grip, he bent with a jerk, missed her hand and deposited a wet kiss in the general vicinity of her wrist. A flicker of interest tinged with amusement awoke in Anne's eyes. Clearly the boy was coached. But by whom? And why?

Unaware of the figure he cut, he launched into a spate of phrases prepared for him by Lord Wroxly. "I am sure you are as bored as I to be indoors on such a night as this," he began, his voice firming with the realization that he recalled his lines. It was too bad that they were intended for another occasion. "Perhaps we could stroll together in the gardens?"

There were no gardens. She smiled. "My tastes have not yet become jaded, sir," she said, striving not to wipe her wrist. "I am enjoying myself immensely."

He searched his mind in vain for the correct reply in the event of a refusal. "Another time, then," he blurted, a painful flush spreading across his cheeks.

"I will look forward to it," she said kindly before turning away to greet Lady Wyndwood.

In his naiveté he believed that she would. Had he not acquitted himself in the fashion of a gentleman who had an air? Quizzed by Lord Wroxly the following day, he reported himself smack up to the mark on every count. While one can be blind to one's faults, still courage is not a thing that one acquires by boasting. Certainly he did not. He let their next several meetings pass without doing more than bestowing a self-conscious nod in her general direction. He did determine to approach her at Lady Sefton's drum, but by the time he arrived, she was winning against the bank at faro, and he knew enough not to interrupt.

Probably nothing would have come of it had not Mitford passed an injudicious remark to Anne. "What do you mean it is very bad *ton* on my part?" she demanded. "I am sure he avoids me when we meet."

"Ah, but that is because I am usually to be found lurking in the background," he pointed out.

"Your implication is only too plain," she said tartly. "Perhaps I am a dangerous person for a young man to know."

"Are you—you will forgive my asking—are you expecting me to make some remark?"

"You always do," she shot back, prepared for battle.

"I imagine that Wrothingham will come to little harm," he said, obliging her.

"I have given you no reason to take exception to anything I may choose to do," she argued with spirit. "Perhaps I ought not to say it, but you have shown no inclination to end your, well, your association with the Brodie wench."

"Would you reply, I wonder, if I were to inquire—quite neutrally, you understand—if envy prompts your anger?"

For a moment she did not say anything at all. Then she rose to her feet. "No!" she said, the word uttered with an unmistakably defiant ring. Nevertheless she could not quite meet his eyes and swept from the room feeling somewhat deflated.

So he thought to make her jealous, she mused, closing the door behind her with a definite snap. It would not be a difficult matter to turn the tables on him. Lord Wrothingham moved in the same circles. She need only claim his notice on those occasions when Mitford was around to witness her triumph.

It was a simple plan and one destined to bear fruit. Very strange fruit.

Quite apart from mere sympathy, which she had for Wrothingham, having herself been a country transplant and decidedly gauche, she felt it safe to involve him in her schemes. She had no intention of wounding him, but if his feelings became hurt just the least bit, it would do him a world of good.

She found it not at all difficult to put her plan into action. At Almack's Rooms in King Street a ball and supper were given each Friday for three months of the year. Unlike Almack's in Pall Mall, where the food was meager, it was favored by a cross section of society and so had come to be known as the Marriage Mart. Anne, reasoning that Wrothingham could be expected to turn up at a place where young ladies were to be seen, teased Mitford to escort her to a ball. Suspecting that she had more on her mind than a mere dance, he expressed himself unable to put in an appearance at an early hour and suggested that she petition Andrew in his stead. Andrew, trapped, and having first warned that he would probably desert her should Miss Washburn be in attendance, reluctantly agreed.

Happily for her, Mitford's curiosity got the better of him; he arrived shortly before ten o'clock, just in time to see her going down one of the country dances with Wrothingham. Observing the friendly, not to say intimate, glance she bestowed on her partner immediately she caught sight of him, he strolled across the room to take a seat beside Lady

273

Margaret. "Frowning will give you wrinkles," he remarked, leaning back at ease.

"Is that all you mean to say?" she murmured, keeping her voice low. "Dearest Anne should know not to twit the teases."

"Oh, I imagine she will emerge unscathed," he replied, amused by his wife's gyrations.

Lady Margaret attempted to catch the truant's eye, but Anne, acutely aware of Mitford, elected to appear engrossed in a little show of gay frivolity. "I cannot understand what has gotten into her," Lady Margaret said, genuinely worried. "I should not wish anyone to speak ill of our dear girl. Really, Richard, you should put your foot down."

"But think how fatiguing," he objected in his most languishing tones.

Lady Margaret was scandalized. "She seems bent on jeopardizing her reputation, while you do naught to keep her from making a spectacle of herself," she said, sniffing.

"You see," he explained, "she has merely picked up the gauntlet that I—er—tossed down."

"Mark my words, you will rue this day," she said, contriving to fix him with a stern and foreboding eye.

While Mitford chose to ignore this look, it had not escaped Sir Randolph, who was observing the scene from his seat a short distance away. A pleasurable feeling seized him. His luck, it seemed, had taken a turn for the better. Never one to neglect an opportunity, he returned to his lodgings on the Steyne and spent the remainder of the evening engrossed in the agreeable task of deciding how best to capitalize upon events, turning them to his advantage. No less than three possibilities were considered and discarded before the perfect answer was found. Amazed by his own acumen, he could not doubt that the signs denoting success were extremely propitious. He would soon be a very wealthy man.

Accordingly the following morning he called up a hackney and directed the driver to set him down at the viscount's residence. He hoped that Mitford would be at home; still, now that he was so near the fruition of his dreams, he owned to a slight feeling of trepidation. Curzon Street was soon reached, and it seemed no time at all before they were drawing up before a house of respectable size. Sir Randolph paid off the coachman and turned a jaundiced eye upon the pleasing facade. Money would not enter into it, he thought, mounting the front steps. Mitford had more than enough to pay for a broken heart. Everyone knew he was swimming in lard and had been since his grandmother's will was read. Ushered by the elderly butler into a small salon located on the ground floor, somehow his discomfort returned.

Mitford was not an inhospitable host, but he was closeted with the earl's man of business when a footman rapped and entered to tell him that Sir Randolph was below. He frowned and glanced at the tall case clock standing in a corner. The hands marked the time at a quarter after ten. "The devil!" he exclaimed, fixing the unhappy William with an outraged eye. "You know not to admit callers before the hour of eleven!"

"It was Pelham what did so, m'lord," William disclaimed, glad to shift the blame onto the butler's shoulders.

Mitford looked surprised. "Then you may present my compliments to Sir Randolph and inform him that I will be with him in due course," he said, turning back to the stacks of coins laid out in neat rows across his desk.

275

Mr. Watson shifted uneasily in his chair. "I could come back when you are free, My Lord," he said, making a movement to rise.

"I find the idea of entertaining Ashmore to be appalling at any time of the day," Mitford replied, waving aside the offer. "We will continue here until the hour for morning calls has arrived. I believe you said my brother collected Roman coins?"

"He did, sir," Mr. Watson averred, shuffling a stack of papers. "The checklist enumerates—"

Forty-five minutes later Mitford entered the small salon precisely on the stroke of eleven to find his unwanted guest pacing up and down the floor, a large pocket watch in his hand and a dark scowl upon his brow. "It pleases you to keep me waiting," Sir Randolph said, restoring his timepiece to a pocket. "Well, sir, you won't be so cheeky when I am done with you!"

"Oh, but I flatter myself on my promptitude," Mitford remarked with a nonchalance that set Sir Randolph's teeth on edge. "Time was when a certain carelessness marred my progress, but I have since learned that promptitude is everything. I imagine you agree?"

"I don't care tuppence for your prosing!" Sir Randolph shot back, nettled. "You are a laggard, sir, and rude into the bargain."

A faint smile curved Mitford's lips. "I will bow to the part about being rude—I often am—but I am damned if I'll admit to being sluggish."

"Don't take that tone with me!" Sir Randolph snapped, seemingly on the verge of apoplexy. "It amuses you to dawdle about upstairs while I kick my heels down here."

"Nonsense," Mitford said. "I was not dawdling about

upstairs; indeed, I was tending to my late brother's affairs. He was a numismatist, you know. Do you know anything about the science of numismatics, Sir Randolph?"

A vein throbbed in Sir Randolph's forehead. "No, I don't know, nor do I care! We will dispense with your brother's affairs!"

"Accept my apologies for bringing up the subject," Mitford replied calmly.

"Your apologies be damned!" Sir Randolph said through gritted teeth. "I don't want your apologies. I have come on quite another matter."

"I had not supposed that you were here to exchange pleasantries with me," Mitford remarked dryly. "How may I serve you?"

Sir Randolph took a deep breath. "You lured my fiancée away by stealth on the eve of our espousing," he began in what he hoped were positive tones. "I am here to appeal to you for justice to be done."

Mitford fished his snuffbox from a pocket. "If my wife refused to marry you—and who could blame her—I suggest that you forget it," he said, taking a pinch between thumb and finger. "Otherwise you will find that you must deal with me."

"With you?" Sir Randolph exploded. "By God, sir, but that's presumptive on your part. It is becoming clear to me that Wroxly is the man I want."

Mitford's gaze did not waiver from Ashmore's outraged countenance. "Having had so much experience of matrimony yourself, I am sure you know it is customary for the husband to handle his wife's affairs. You will appreciate that I feel a certain degree of curiosity."

Sir Randolph drew himself up to the extent of his rather

portly height. "Your concern, sir, is surprising, coming late in the day as it does," he said.

"It doesn't," Mitford said, "but we will let that pass for now."

"Damme, but there's something devilish queer about you!" Sir Randolph exclaimed. "It is my belief you're too lazy to bestir yourself. Your laxity, nay, your degree of indifference—"

"We will leave me out of this discussion, if you please!" Mitford shot back curtly.

"Upon my word, you are mighty cool," Sir Randolph declared. "For a man with no idea that his wife is worth sixty thousand pounds, you are curiously sure of yourself."

A muscle twitched in Mitford's cheek. "To carry this conversation further will only make us both appear ridiculous," he said, crossing to pull the bell cord. "It is a source of profound regret that I must excuse myself, but I am sure you will understand."

Sir Randolph had not come to be fobbed off so easily. "I'll not be given the runaround," he said with a fine show of determination. "I came to—"

"I know why you came," Mitford interrupted. "You will get not one sou from me. Ah, Pelham," he said to the butler answering his ring. "Escort Sir Randolph from the premises, if you please."

Sir Randolph was defeated and knew it. "You are insolent, sir," he proclaimed in an attempt to salvage what remained of his dignity. "I will not linger an instant longer than necessary under this roof."

Pelham looked impassively from one face to the other, then, having bowed Sir Randolph out, passed him on to a footman and went back into the salon. "Will that be all, my lord?" he inquired, his voice pregnant with suppressed expectation.

Mitford had crossed to stand with his shoulder resting against the mantel shelf, his gaze on the roaring fire. "Convey my compliments to Her Ladyship and ask her to join me here at her earliest convenience," he said without looking up.

"Her Ladyship is not upon the premises," Pelham replied, palpably interested and seeking to hide it.

Mitford straightened up and faced him. "Don't beat about the bush," he snapped, annoyed.

Pelham bowed. "As you wish, my lord," he said, loath to see the only excitement the staff had known for days slip through his fingers. "I have ascertained from Her Ladyship's personal maid that Her Ladyship is gone for the day."

"Gone where?" Mitford demanded, exasperated by the brevity of the reply.

"On a picnic, my lord," Pelham announced, savoring the mystery to the fullest.

Mitford heaved a sigh. "With whom has she gone?" he said.

"With Lord Wrothingham, my lord," Pelham replied, his voice heavy with the portent of impending doom.

Mitford's lips twitched. Clearly Anne thought to turn the tables on him by making him jealous of a suckling babe. "Thank you, Pelham, that will be all," he said, crossing to seat himself at the writing desk.

Pelham sought to prolong the moment. "Perhaps I should inform Your Lordship that Her Ladyship ordered a picnic lunch," he said. "Cook found the request posted on the board when he entered the kitchen this morning."

"I trust the staff will follow my wife's orders to the

letter," Mitford said, pulling forward a sheet of crested stationery.

All was suddenly right with Pelham's world. Bowing himself out, he took himself off to pass the good tidings along to the housekeeper. Since His Lordship saw nothing to remark in his wife's behavior, it was unbecoming of the household to question it. There was too much of the old earl in the son for His Lordship ever to do anything that was unbefitting his station. Take his word for it. The viscount was a reasonable gentleman, albeit newly come into the title.

CHAPTER 17

The reasonable gentleman, precisely at three o'clock on the afternoon of that same day, walked up the steps of No. 16 Norfolk Square and inquired for Lord Wroxly. Upon being informed that he was expected, he climbed the stairs in the wake of the porter (no other servant being in evidence) to the salon overlooking the street where His Lordship awaited him.

Lord Wroxly was standing with his back to the room, staring out the window, but he wheeled about when the visitor was announced. "I am pleased, though I will admit to some surprise," he said, coming forward. "I had not known it was your custom to pay calls."

"It isn't," Mitford said, laying his hat and cane on a chair, the porter having forgotten to relieve him of them. "You will permit me to remind you that I am here on a business matter. I believe my missive made that clear."

Wroxly reddened. "The account books dealing with your

wife's inheritance are open for your inspection at any time," he said, waving a hand toward a stack of ledgers. "Which aspect of her affairs are you interested in?"

"All of them," Mitford replied, putting up his quizzing glass. "The journal will do for a start."

Lord Wroxly recoiled a step. "The journal!" he sputtered, the blood draining from his face. "Pray, sir, what business is that of yours?"

Mitford let his glass fall. "The business of any husband," he said, a faintly sneering note in his voice. "What is all this wondering at my interest on everyone's part? I vow it is nothing to marvel at."

Wroxly bridled. "It makes no odds to you that for years I have been charged with caring for Her Ladyship. You cannot come bursting in here making demands of me!"

"I did not come bursting in, as you put it," Mitford replied coolly. "I agree, however, that I am here to make certain demands. I regret it extremely, but you must prepare yourself for the inevitable."

"You choose to make light of my efforts at guardianship, but—"

"You must forgive me for interrupting, my dear fellow, but I do not make light of your contribution. Rather, I applaud it."

"Be that as it may," Lord Wroxly said testily, "if you have come here to accuse me, you are wasting your time. The accounts are in order."

"I am sure you are an honest man," Mitford replied gently. "You will therefore not mind turning them over to me."

"To you!" Lord Wroxly gasped. "Whatever that chit has been telling you—"

He got no further. In one swift movement Mitford had seized him by his cravat, hauling him half off his feet, the fabric tightening around his throat until the breath was nearly choked out of him. "You abominable gallows bait!" Mitford gritted furiously in his ear. "You put your foul mouth around my wife's good name and I will see to it you hang!"

Wroxly's gasping moans filled the room but he could do no more than ineffectively wave his arms about in terror of his life until he was flung away from Mitford. Reeling back and wheezing to suck air into his starving lungs, he fetched up against a table, the roaring in his ears only gradually subsiding.

"You will live," Mitford remarked, a look of contempt such as Wroxly had never before witnessed staring from his eyes. "You made a deal with Sir Randolph Ashmore, I believe."

Lord Wroxly fairly goggled. He was sure a bruised throat would keep him abed for days, and his legs shook so that he could barely stand. Grasping the table edge to keep from crashing ignominiously to the floor, he croaked, "Ashmore?" in unbelieving accents. How much had that devil Mitford gotten wind of? he wondered, searching his mind for some way out of the trap in which he found himself.

"You realize, of course, that I am far from being a fool," Mitford said levelly. "I trust we may dispense with further protestations of innocence on your part. Between you and Ashmore, you partitioned my wife's inheritance as it suited your fancy, did you not? Were you to get the lion's share, or did you find Ashmore not so easy to diddle?"

"I don't know what—you are mistaken," Wroxly insisted desperately.

"I am not mistaken," Mitford replied. "Nor am I wrong in saying that for reasons of personal conceit you would have given an untouched maiden into the hands of a lecher. For that alone you deserve to hang."

"No, no, you have it all wrong. It would have provided her with a position in society which—"

"Spare me, I beg you. When our marriage put my wife's fortune—I presume Ashmore correct in declaring it a fortune?—beyond your reach, your cohort in crime could find nothing better to do than to call on me to demand recompense for a broken heart."

"I know nothing of that!" Wroxly disclaimed earnestly. "It is no wonder that you were ill pleased. I am sorry for it."

"You realize, I am sure, that you will be more sorry if you fail to produce the journals setting forth Her Ladyship's monetary worth. Do I make my meaning plain?"

"Yes. Yes, indeed, my lord," Wroxly muttered, the dismay he felt written all over his face. "I—I will be glad to explain her situation."

"I believe that I will be able to decipher the accounts," Mitford said placidly. "Kindly have your man carry the ledger books to my carriage, if you please."

"But surely you can't intend removing them from my care!" Wroxly protested in an attempt to gather the reins back into his own hands.

"I told you that conceit is at the root of your odd behavior. Of course I am removing them. You would retain control, not for nefarious personal gain but for the feeling of importance that has come to mean so much to you. That was most foolish."

"But I did not dream that you would think the less of me for it. I have not served you ill."

"I will send your porter to remove the ledgers, since you seem disinclined to do so," Mitford said, picking up his hat and cane and walking in a leisurely fashion to the door. "Be thankful that I am leaving here without having wrung your scrawny neck."

Meanwhile Anne had passed a miserable day, though no one of the picnic party could have suspected from her demeanor that she was wishing most unfashionably that her own husband were among the group. Sorry that she had come and determined to arrive home before Mitford's return, she commandeered Lord Wrothingham's coach, assigned him a seat in Lady Margaret's landaulet and drove off without a pang.

At not long after five o'clock she turned off Piccadilly into St. James's Street, the press of traffic forcing Lord Wrothingham's coachman to slow his horses almost to a standstill. Farther along the way Mitford was just coming out of White's, but before she could urge her driver forward to take him up, Miss Brodie's carriage pulled to a halt beside him.

Perfectly aware that Anne watched, Mitford doffed his beaver hat to Miss Brodie, bent his curly head to salute the hand she held out to him and entered her carriage to take the seat beside her.

Anne turned her head away and effected interest in a ravishing bonnet with several curling plumes displayed in a milliner's window on the opposite side of the road; she would have given all she possessed to be able to hide behind a parasol, but for all Lady Margaret's urging she had refused to carry one. Casting a fleeting glance at Miss

Brodie's carriage, she surprised a look of amusement on Mitford's face and wished that she did not blush so easily.

As luck would have it, by the time Lord Wrothingham's coachman wound his way among the carriages, curricles and phaetons crowding the road and turned into Curzon Street, Mitford had already entered the house. Miss Brodie had insisted upon depositing him on his own doorstep, though he had asked to be set down at the bottom of the street. Anne, upon learning that he was home before her, fled upstairs to the blessed privacy of her own rooms. The last thing she wanted was an inquisition about the pleasures of her day.

Probably all might have gone well had not Lord Wroxly chosen that very night to get even with Mitford. They had gone to the opera, of which Mitford was a patron, and Wroxly had gone there, too. As usual the house was packed; a few of those in attendance were there to enjoy the performance, but the majority of the fashionable throng wished only to be in the mode. The curtain falling on the first act signaled the real business of the evening—the start of the promenade. While the ladies held court from their seats in the boxes, the gentlemen strolled around to pay their respects to those who caught their fancy.

Lord Wroxly, scanning the house in search of congenial companionship, chanced to observe that while Anne was surrounded by a group of ardent swains, Mitford was making his way to visit Lord Wooton's party. Wroxly saw him start upon discovering Miss Brodie seated at the back of the box where the buxom form of Mrs. Twisdale had obscured her from view, and smiled. Thus simply did Anne become his quarry.

A few minutes later he entered her box and ousted from her side the young puppy sighing pretty nothings into her ear. "How humiliating for you to find yourself deserted," he murmured, helping himself to the seat just vacated. "My dear, Mitford is a philanderer. I would have for you a husband who came to you with a clean heart."

She stared unbelievingly at him. "I would not describe Sir Randolph in just that way," she said.

"I blame myself for not doing something to warn you against a disastrous marriage," he confided, ignoring her remark. "I could not have foreseen that any husband would desert you openly for a public assignation with his mistress."

The barb struck home, as he hoped it would. "He —hasn't," she asserted, visibly shaken.

A smile stretched his thin lips. "Oh, did you not see him enter Miss Brodie's box? No, I see you didn't. Forgive me. I should not have mentioned it."

"Why shouldn't he, if he wishes?" she demanded, recovering her poise. "There is nothing wrong in that!"

"Of course not," he murmured soothingly. "Since you wish it."

"What are you implying?" she snapped, refusing to become unstrung.

"I imply nothing," he said, smiling a secretive little smile. "I merely thought—but there, perhaps I am mistaken. We mustn't draw attention to them, now, must we? Frankly, my dear, people are staring."

Anne flattered herself she was well bred, but she turned her back on him and made herself force his insinuations from her mind. Whether they were true or not, there was precious little she could do about it. During the years of her growing up she had often heard the village wives say that men were perfectly capable of rising from the marital couch to seek the bed of some strumpet. Anne had no notion of joining the ranks of long-suffering and betrayed women. Mitford, returning to their box in time for the second act and observing her excessive frivolity, wondered what to expect next.

There could be no question that his strategy had taken root in fertile ground. In her heart she was jealous. Several times she came close to demanding that he explain his conduct, but each time she backed down. In public she was gay to the point of becoming the life and soul of the party. In private she was polite, and extremely elusive. Each time he attempted to take her in his arms, he found himself embracing empty air. Anne had danced away, a glib excuse on her tongue. It was too late, or she was tired. Mitford, afraid of alienation (she had never said precisely that she loved him), let matters slide. No one attending the same routs and drums could have suspected that anything was amiss.

It all came to a head two weeks later, when the family gathered in the drawing room following dinner, there being no entertainments planned for that evening. Declaring that she was worn out and glad of a quiet time at home, Lady Margaret picked up her embroidery frame and became absorbed in selecting one of the array of silk threads. Andrew, having paced about the room in a fair imitation of a caged lion, declared that a sedentary existence was not for him and took himself off in search of congenial companionship. Anne was bearing her part in a conversation with Cousin Lillian, who seemed to think herself much in the family's debt for providing her with a roof over her head, a belief that resulted in numerous and embarrassingly flattering complaisances, when Mitford sat down beside her on the sofa and fixed his enigmatic gaze on her profile, her face being turned away from him. Cousin Lillian, sensing the strain between them and not knowing the reason, assumed her own presence to be at fault. Eager to please, she professed an interest in Lady Margaret's stitchery and crossed the room to inspect it, leaving Mitford alone with Anne.

"A good night's rest will do us good," he remarked, the gleam in his eye making her suspect him strongly of harboring plans for the night.

She hesitated, then said, a slight flush spreading across her cheeks, "I am almost dead with fatigue. I plan to go to bed early and sleep the clock around."

He was amused. "You have come to understand me tolerably well," he remarked, stretching his long legs out before him. "I can't have you suffering from ennui."

She raised her brows. "I hope that I have not become so inured to the many pleasures London has to offer that I am unable to appreciate the things that bring enjoyment," she said, a hint of reproach creeping into her voice.

"Such as shopping?" he teased.

"No such thing," she said. "I have spent too much of your money as it is. I don't like doing so."

"That is probably because you do not know that you are wealthy in your own right," he replied, dumbfounding her. "You are worth sixty thousand pounds, my dear."

She laughed, then said with a rueful smile, "I only wish I were. You can't know how it feels to be a pauper amongst a set of affluent people. The melancholy truth is, I am sadly out of place."

"My dearest love, I would not proffer Spanish coin," he said. "Your father left you financially secure. I know. I have had the truth from Wroxly."

She found it almost impossible to believe. "He never allotted me more than a meager allowance," she said, trying to take it in.

"He was sparing with you, I know, but to give him credit, he pocketed none of your money for himself. I have had an audit of the books and am assured they are in order."

"Then I am financially independent?" she murmured almost inaudibly.

"Quite independent," he assured her, smiling.

She said no more. Indeed, for the remainder of the evening she seemed abstracted. Professing fatigue, she slipped away early and went to her room, a wan expression on her face. Mitford would probably leave the house in search of his paramour, she thought, surveying her reflection in the full-length mirror. It was a good deal too bad. The diaphanous gauze nightgown displayed her curves to advantage. Even a mistress would be hard pressed to do better.

Mitford, unceremoniously entering the room carrying a wine bottle and two glasses, was treated to a glimpse of flashing thighs as she whisked herself out of sight behind the dressing screen. So it's to be hard to get, is it? he mused. "Champagne?" he said when she reappeared swathed from head to foot in a brocade dressing gown.

"What are we celebrating?" she asked, accepting the glass he handed her.

"Our reunion," he replied. "May our nights be fruitful and our days divine."

She sipped her drink while eyeing him warily. Suddenly

the wine tasted sour. "I don't know what you expect from me," she said, putting down her glass carefully so the champagne would not spill.

"Can't you imagine how I've been wanting you for the past hour?" he said, advancing on her. "I thought you would never come upstairs."

"It's not that simple," she protested, retreating until the edge of the bed blocked her backward progress. "One has one's—whims, you know."

"Has one, now?" he chuckled. "Be quiet and kiss me. Ah, that's better. That's very nice."

Somewhat to her surprise she found herself responding with an intensity that was at once thrilling and mortifying. Held tight in his embrace, the breath nearly crushed out of her, she strained to press closer still, her body starved for his. As her passions soared, strove to match his, she was carried along on a glorious tide of lust.

"You're using me abominably," she gasped, shaken out of her usual poise.

"What?" he muttered, witless with emotion. "What did you say, Jennie?"

The echoing silence that fell upon the room seemed to go on and on. She was devastated, utterly dumbfounded. "Oh!" she stormed into the empty quiet. "I should have known better than to let you near me!"

"I'm sorry," he said, appalled. "I cannot think why I said that."

"I can!" she snapped. "If you think to come to me straight from that—that—"

"I haven't come to you straight from—I never kissed her like—Oh, hell! It was the word *abominably*. She employs it incessantly, and when I heard it, I just—"

"You just forgot whom you were kissing!"

He groaned. "Have you never been startled into saying something foolish?" he demanded, a pleading note creeping into his voice.

She was not to be won over so easily. "Nothing is to be gained by talking of it," she said. "And now, sir, I will appreciate it if you will leave my room."

It was not the moment to pursue the matter. He bowed and turned on his heel. "We will speak of this when you have had time to collect yourself," he said over his shoulder as he went through the door.

She sank down on the bed, her thoughts in chaos. Whether he spoke the truth, she could not know. She only knew that she must leave. Marriage did not suit him. He was accustomed to a happy-go-lucky, carefree existence. She had become a burden, an unwanted ball and chain. After all he had done for her, to leave was the least that she could do. Once rid of her hindering presence, he would be free to live the life he chose.

Rising to cross dejectedly to a window, she stood for a long time staring blindly out upon the moonlit street, deciding just where she should go. There was only one place possible. Finally, her decision made, she sat down to pen a farewell note to him. So sunk in misery did she become, it was all she could do to rouse herself to pack a valise before crawling into bed. When Mitford, intent upon a reconciliation, entered her room a short time later and stood gazing down at her, she pretended sleep, then sobbed into her pillow when he sighed and went away again.

He was not an early riser as a rule, but he had spent a restless night disturbed by dreams of Anne held fast within his arms and so had tossed from side to side while sleeping only in fits and starts. By the time the sound of Big Ben tolling the hour of six floated across the city, he was astride his favorite stallion galloping through Hyde Park in an effort to quell the desire bedeviling him. Upon his return to the house an hour later, his passions only partially subdued, he was met in the hall by Pelham. "Her Ladyship's maid found this when she entered Her Ladyship's chamber a short while ago," the butler said, presenting a silver salver bearing a sealed note on crested paper. "It is addressed to you, my lord."

Mitford strode forward. "Is Her Ladyship not in her room?" he demanded sharply.

"So far as I have been able to ascertain, Her Ladyship seems not to be in the house," Pelham replied gravely.

His lips tightening, Mitford broke the seal of the note, spread out the single sheet and read:

> Dear Richard,
>
> It is best that I leave before I make you more miserable. I regret that you were obliged to marry me when you loved another. You will want a divorce, I know. Your lawyers can get in touch with me through my vicar. Good-bye, and thank you for your many kindnesses.
>
> Anne

Mitford stared at the missive in disbelief, then folded it and put it in a pocket. "You will order my curricle brought around immediately," he said, crossing to the door to the dining room. "Her Ladyship's maid and my valet will pack our belongings and proceed to Afton Hall. They will await us there."

293

Pelham dared to say, "Her Ladyship, my lord? If I may presume to inquire."

"Quite safe, thank you, Pelham. Send in a fresh pot of coffee, if you please. I will breakfast before I go."

Reassured, Pelham bowed and went away to send the servants scurrying to carry out his orders; within minutes the house resembled nothing so much as an anthill that had somehow been disturbed. Twenty minutes later Mitford stepped out onto the front walk, pulling on his gloves. The bays were dancing with impatience to be away. Mounting to the box seat, he gathered up the reins, disappointed Sawyer by ordering him to remain at home and set the team in motion. Within seconds the curricle had rounded the corner and was bowling out of sight on its way to Agecroft, aided in its passing by the scarcity of traffic at that early hour of the morning.

The village amounted to little more than a row of cottages strung out along the highway and a town square flanked on the south side by the blacksmith's yard and a livery stable, on the west by a number of shops and an inn, on the north by the slightly larger homes of the more affluent and on the east by a gray stone church with its vicarage alongside. Mitford pulled up his team before the residence of the vicar, hitched up his reins and jumped lightly down to the ground. Other than the trill of birdsong, there was nothing to disturb the quiet as he strolled up the walk to the front door.

The Reverend Robert Atkins remained relatively vigorous for a widower approaching his sixty-fourth year. He was tall, slightly stooped, with expressive blue eyes and a fringe of white hair below a shining bald pate. He was seated at the desk in his study working on his Sunday sermon when Mitford was ushered into the room. "Viscount

George?" he queried, rising. "Forgive me, but you have the advantage of me, sir."

"I have but recently come into the title," Mitford explained, bowing respectfully. "Habit dies hard. You may have heard me referred to as Lord Mitford."

"Ah, yes. Lady Anne's husband," the vicar replied, putting forward a chair. "How may I serve you?"

"Am I correct in thinking she has come to you?" Mitford said, sitting down.

The vicar's eyes dwelt searchingly upon his face. "Before I consent to answer that, I will need to know your intentions."

"I intend to take her home."

"And if she does not wish to go?"

"I have come to assure her of the depth of my regard. When she has heard me out, I trust she will want nothing better than to come away with me."

The vicar smiled. "You will find her in the garden, my lord," he said, indicating a passageway leading outside. "I would suggest that you seek her out before she makes a shambles of the roses. She has been in a high state of agitation since her arrival."

The good reverend was incorrect in thinking she might damage the flowers. She was on her knees cultivating a rose bed with meticulous care when Mitford came up behind her. Since she had been blinking back tears, she was not aware of his presence until he spoke.

"So I am to include horticulture among your accomplishments," he said teasingly.

Gasping, she jumped to her feet and whirled to face him. "Oh!" she uttered inanely. "Richard."

"Just so," he said, smiling.

"You startled me," she said unnecessarily. Looking around a trifle doubtfully, she added, "Where is Reverend Atkins?"

"In his study, where he had the good sense to remain. My dear, common civility should prompt you to grant me a warmer reception than I have thus far received."

"Well, but it was very unhandsome of you to come popping in on me with no warning. And you needn't get in a huff that I didn't expect you. After all, you had a mistress to visit, not to mention any number of other antidotes."

He threw back his head and laughed. "So I'm to be taxed with being a rogue, am I?" he demanded, his eyes brimful with amusement. "If I were the nodcock you seem to think me, I can assure you I would not bestow my attention on an antidote. Were you afraid I might?"

"No, and you needn't talk to me as if I were one of your bits of muslin. And while we are on the subject, just why have you come?"

"To take you home."

The pleading in his voice caught her unawares. Tears stung her eyelids. "You can't know what you're saying," she said, trying for a flippant tone. "Just think how tiresome to be stuck with me when all the wide world beckons."

"I don't want all the world," he said, slipping an arm about her waist. "I want only you."

She gave an uncertain laugh, her composure set aside. "You can't expect me to believe that," she said. "I know you were bored with me. Not that I blame you," she hastened to interject when he would have interrupted. "You were obliged to marry me, and Miss Brodie is most attractive."

"I suppose one would find her attractive if one were

296

partial to vapid blondes," he replied, tightening his arm about her waist. "As you know, my taste runs to surrogates."

"Oh!" she gasped, making a halfhearted attempt to thrust him off. "You have been pursuing her for weeks."

"But only to make you jealous," he said, fiercely kissing her. "I had to do something to prove to myself that you still loved me."

"Then you love me?" she breathed, subsiding limply against his chest. "You really do love me?"

"Of course I do, you silly goose. What a damnable thing to ask me. I have loved you almost from the moment of first setting eyes on you. You may rest easy on that score."

This made her lift her head from his shoulder. "Easy!" She chuckled, going off on a peal of laughter. "Since we contracted it, our marriage has had nothing to do with freedom from worry—or from trouble."

"What a wretched time you had of it," he said, kissing her again. "I can't tell you that I am perfectly sure that things will be different now, but I can promise to do all within my power to make it so."

"Then you won't coerce me, or order me about? You won't act the tyrant, or impose on my good nature?"

He gazed at her softly parted lips and slid his hand down her arm to clasp her fingers. "Come," he said.

She fell into step beside him. "Are we going home?" she asked, giving a little skip.

"You can't suppose that I intend taking you here among the good vicar's roses," he said outrageously.

297

"I shouldn't be surprised if you did," she replied, her eyes full of tender affection.

He chuckled. "Look at me like that and I will!" he threatened, grinning.

"Odious man!" she said. "Abominable reprobate."

A woman's place—the parlor, not the concert stage! But radiant Diana Ballantyne, pianist extraordinaire, had one year before she would bow to her father's wishes, return to England and marry. She had given her word, yet the moment she met the brilliant Maestro, Baron Lukas von Korda, her fate was sealed. He touched her soul with music, kissed her lips with fire, filled her with unnameable desire. One minute warm and passionate, the next aloof, he mystified her, tantalized her. She longed for artistic triumph, ached for surrender, her passions ignited by Vienna dreams.

A DELL BOOK   19530-6 $3.50

Vienna Dreams

by JANETTE RADCLIFFE

A cold-hearted bargain...
An all-consuming love...

THE TIGER'S WOMAN

by Celeste De Blasis
bestselling author of *The Proud Breed*

Mary Smith made a bargain with Jason
Drake, the man they called The Tiger: his
protection for her love, his strength to protect her secret. It was a bargain she swore
to keep...until she learned what it really
meant to be The Tiger's Woman.

A Dell Book $3.95   11820-4

**VOLUME I
IN THE EPIC
NEW SERIES**

*The Morland
Dynasty*

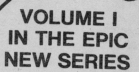

The Founding

by Cynthia Harrod-Eagles

THE FOUNDING, a panoramic saga rich with passion
and excitement, launches Dell's most ambitious series to date—THE MORLAND DYNASTY.

From the Wars of the Roses and Tudor England to
World War II, THE MORLAND DYNASTY traces the
lives, loves and fortunes of a great English family.

A DELL BOOK $3.50   #12677-0

SWEET WILD WIND

by Joyce Verrette

In the primeval forests of America, passion was born in the mystery of a stolen kiss.

A high-spirited beauty, daughter of the furrier to the French king, Aimee Dessaline had led a sheltered life. But on one fateful afternoon, her fate was sealed with a burning kiss. Vale's sun bronzed skin and buckskins proclaimed his Indian upbringing, but his words belied another heritage. Convinced that he was a spy, she vowed to forget him—this man they called Valjean d'Auvergne, Comte de la Tour.

But not even the glittering court at Versailles where Parisian royalty courted her favors, not even the perils of the war torn wilderness could still her impetuous heart.

A DELL BOOK   17634-4   ($3.95)